Off the Chain is pure escapism to small-town America with a ~~~~, heroine and a warm cast of characters in a warm-hearted community. You'll want to curl up in front of the fire with this humorous, face-paced mystery that offers intrigue, romance and of course, adorable puppies. Janice Thompson offers the perfect read to turn off the outside world.

- Kristin Billerbeck, author of *Room at the Top.*

Off the Chain is a delightful 'tail' of a young woman with big goals, a big heart, and a big penchant for trouble! Full of humor that leaves every dog-lover face-palming and saying "me too", this hilarious, relatable story of puppy love (of both the human and fur variety!) is an off the chain kind of read!

- Betsy St. Amant, award-winning author of *Tacos for Two.*

Janice Thompson does it again! This delightful book is another example of Janice's ability to pull readers into the story, making them feel as though they're right there with the characters on a lighthearted jaunt through life and love. Whether you're a dog-lover or simply appreciate a fun read, you'll thoroughly enjoy *Off the Chain!* I can't wait for the next book in this series!

- Debby Mayne, author of the Bucklin Family Reunion series and blogger at Southern Home Express

Marigold Evans is a vet tech with a heart of gold and a love for animals, especially dogs. Her passion is to rescue, and rehab lost or abandoned dogs and nurse them back to health. And when she's not working at the veterinary clinic, she's following up on dog sightings, scouting vacant lots and drainage pipes with her best friend Cassidy at her side. But there is more to Marigold's life than wayward pooches. There are handsome hunky guys, lots of pies, a mysterious burglary, and romances blossoming. I refused to *paws* through this fast-paced story. In fact, I couldn't stop wondering what was going to happen next! Love the characters, Corgis, chihuahuas, and all the other canines. Furry fun throughout! Warning…when you read Janice Thompson's, *Off the Chain* it is likely to start a chain reaction. You'll want to read all the books in the Gone to the Dogs series!

- Linda Kozar, author of *Sunshine For The Soul-Morning Devotions to Warm the Heart,* a 2021 First Place Selah Award winner and 2021 Nonfiction Book of the Year.

Janice Thompson writes a doggone good cozy mystery and lighthearted romance! She can make you laugh with her quirky characters and tug at your heartstrings with adorable furry sidekicks.

- Leanna Ellis, award-winning author of *Elvis Takes a Backseat*

GONE
to the
DOGS
Mysteries
BOOK 1

OFF the CHAIN

JANICE THOMPSON

BARBOUR
PUBLISHING

Off the Chain ©2022 by Janice Thompson

Print ISBN 978-1-63609-313-0

Adobe Digital Edition (.epub) 978-1-63609-315-4

Cover illustration by Victor McLindon.

Published by Barbour Publishing, Inc., 1810 Barbour Drive, Uhrichsville, Ohio 44683, www.barbourbooks.com

Our mission is to inspire the world with the life-changing message of the Bible.

 Member of the
Evangelical Christian
Publishers Association

Printed in the United States of America.

DEDICATION

To Jenny and Patti, two of the finest dog rescuers I've ever known. Thank you for all you do for those precious pups. Many lives have been changed because of your dedication and kindness.

Good people take care of their animals,
but even the kindest acts of the wicked are cruel.
PROVERBS 12:10 NCV

CHAPTER ONE

A shiver wriggled its way down my spine as I eased my way into the opening of the large metal drainage pipe. Off in the distance I heard the faint *drip, drip, drip* of water, and within seconds a trickle of foul-smelling liquid seeped into my tennis shoes. Gross. The shadows of night closed in around me, and I realized I would need the cap light to pull off this mission. With a trembling hand, I reached to snap it on and then squinted to make out the view in front of me. Narrow. Dark. Creepy.

And wet. I took note of the pool of murky water in the distance.

"You can do this, Mari."

My little pep talk didn't exactly instill confidence, but, hey. . . sometimes a girl just needed to hear someone cheering her on. Even if the voice was her own and happened to echo off a metal drainage pipe under the shadows of darkness.

I did my best to press back the lump in my throat as I stooped a little lower and then willed myself forward in an awkward spider-like crawl. The first couple of feet? Yeah, I managed those pretty well in a crouched position. After that, not so much. The passage tightened and I dropped to my hands and knees, ready to brave the water and the dark shadows ahead.

Even with the cap light casting its tiny beam, I could barely make out the area in front of me. Instead, I had no choice but to trust my instincts. And my nose. Ick. What *was* that?

"Here, puppy," I called out, my voice a trembling mess. "Make this easy on me, sweet puppy."

A kink in the pipe narrowed the passage even further, which forced me to slide down onto my belly. Well, terrific. The overspill from Brenham's largest drainage ditch trickled down the pipe's rough interior beneath me, the water slimy and ice-cold. A nervous shiver threatened to stall my efforts, but courage won out. Courage mixed with a healthy dose of fear, anyway. I'd always found fear to be a terrific motivator.

I wriggled my way along, and my gaze finally landed on the injured dog curled up a few yards away, just beyond my reach. Bingo. Even with the pup's matted fur, I could still make out the concern in his eyes. I also took note of the injured back leg and the gash above his right eye. This little guy would require a lot of effort to rehab, but my work as a vet tech had prepared me for that.

First, though? I had to win this sweet pup's trust and pull him from this makeshift home he'd created for himself in this pipe. Then the rest of the pieces would fall into place.

"It's okay, baby." I steadied my voice as best I could and nudged myself a couple of inches in the dog's direction. "I promise, I'm not here to hurt you. Just the opposite, in fact."

A low growl in the bottom of the pup's throat caught me off guard, but I did my best not to aggravate the situation by flinching—until something that looked like a snake slithered by. I let out a bloodcurdling scream and jerked with such a start that I slammed my head against the top of the ridged pipe, almost knocking myself senseless.

In that moment, the cap light on my hat flickered off, which left me in complete darkness. The sound of the dog's nails against the pipe clued me in to the fact that the terrified pup had taken to flight, moving deeper into the narrow pipe. I'd never catch up with him now. Foiled. On my very first mission, no less.

I fumbled to get the light back on and realized, as my eyes adjusted to the glare, that the dog had backed himself into a corner but was still within eyesight. Thank goodness.

"Marigold? You okay in there?" My best friend's concerned voice echoed from outside the pipe.

"Yeah, I—"

"I heard a scream. Are you hurt?"

"I'll be okay, Cassidy. I thought I saw a. . ." I shifted the light on my hat to get a better view of what had frightened me moments before. A stick, not a snake. I breathed a sigh of relief and focused once again on the mangy mutt.

"Saw a what, girl?" Cassidy's voice sounded closer than before. "You're going to have to speak up. There's a ton of noise out here from the highway. Cars and trucks going by like crazy. The dog didn't get away, did he?"

"No," I called out, my voice still echoing against the pipe. "He just moved farther upstream, that's all."

"Upstream?" Now Cassidy sounded genuinely worried. "Is it *wet* in there?"

"Yeah." I let the shiver slither down my spine before explaining. "Runoff from the drainage ditch."

"Oh man!" she called out. "You're gonna wish you'd changed out of those scrubs, girl."

Yeah, I was already regretting the decision to handle this rescue in work attire, but what choice did I have? When that call came in to the veterinary clinic an hour ago, I took it as a sign. Finally, a chance to rescue a pooch in distress. For weeks I'd thought about it—prayed about it. When the opportunity arrived, I jumped in with both feet. And my hands, knees, and belly, apparently. But, wasn't this what dog rescue was all about? I'd certainly watched enough videos to know what I was up against. Who cared if my scrubs got dirty? I'd wash them when I got home. But first, to catch this pooch. So far, he had eluded me.

From the opening of the pipe, Cassidy carried on, oblivious to my internal ponderings. "If we're gonna keep this up, we'll have to keep extra clothes in the back of your car. I'll never get the mud off these shoes. Ugh."

Oh well. This was our first mission. There was no shame in admitting we were on a learning curve. I paused to think through a plan of action. If I could rescue and rehab this sweet pup, perhaps others would follow. Before long I'd get that tax-free status for the organization and devote my life to rescuing Brenham's abandoned canines. Second Chance Ranch would be more than just a pipe dream.

Pipe dream. Ha.

The dripping continued, but I refused to be swayed. Determination swept over me and gave me the courage I needed to move forward with the task at hand.

"Cassidy, hand me the catch pole," I hollered. "I don't have any choice. Wet or not. Dirty or not. I'm going in. All the way."

Seconds later my friend pressed the pole into my outstretched hand and knelt down to have a look. "Have you got her in sight?" Cassidy's words echoed against the metal enclosure.

"Not sure if it's a her or a him..." I wriggled a couple of inches deeper into the pipe. "But the pup is definitely in sight."

And what a sight this poor pup was. Frantic eyes blinked against the light coming off my hat. The poor matted thing looked terrified. And frail. I couldn't tell the breed from here, but something of the medium-ish, hairy variety. Definitely a hot mess. Kind of like me right now.

"Hurry up in there, okay?" Cassidy sounded worried now. "My phone's going to die any second, and it's getting dark out here. I—" She groaned. "It just died."

"I'll hurry." I inched my way toward the dog, the pipe growing narrower with every move. I extended the pole in the direction of the pup's head and clucked my tongue, hoping to win his trust. It took a few tries, but I finally managed to get the loop over his neck. As I secured it, the poor little fellow let out a yelp and pulled away from me. He whimpered and lifted his back leg, the one with the gash.

"I promise," I said again. "I want to help you. I really do." And boy, did I. I'd wanted to rescue dogs for as long as I could remember. Hopefully tonight would be the first of many interventions, a divine appointment, as my Grandma Peach would probably call it. She used every excuse in the book to throw in a little Christianese.

The whimpering intensified and my heart twisted. This pup's pitiful cries nearly wrecked me. After a couple of moments, however, the frightened animal settled down a bit.

From above ground, the sound of voices caught my attention. I did my best to ignore them and keep going before fear got the better of me.

"C'mon, sweet puppy." I gave the pole a gentle tug and eased the dog in my direction. The terrified pooch fought me at every nudge but relented when I passed off a scrap of the fast-food cheeseburger I'd brought for this very situation. "See? It's going to be okay. I told you." I gave him another bite, now honing in on multiple voices from above. Sounded like Cassidy was talking to someone. What in the world? Who would turn up out here? At this time of night?

I managed to gain the pup's trust and reached to scratch him behind the ears. He relented, his stiffened body posture relaxing at once. Looked like the poor little guy needed some TLC. That, and a lot of medical care, judging from the condition of that leg.

"Marigold!" Cassidy's voice sounded from outside.

"Yeah?" I slipped my arm around the pup's midsection and he nuzzled against me, ready to give in.

"Um, Marigold, I think you'd better come out."

"I'm trying to do that right now." I adjusted my grip on the dog, feeling his ribs beneath my hand. "Poor baby." I shivered as more of the slimy water penetrated through my clothing.

"Marigold! Could you hurry, please?"

"I'm coming, I'm coming." I bumped my head once again, and this time my cap came off. Oh well. I would have to return for it when my arms weren't so full. For that matter, I'd have to get the catch pole later too. I'd somehow managed to drop it along the way.

I continued to ease my way backward until I reached the opening of the pipe. Filthy, wet, and smelling a bit like the dog I now cradled in my arms, I twisted around and attempted to stand, but an unexpected beam of light hit me squarely in the eyes. I blinked and tried to see past it.

"Stay right where you are until I can see you more clearly, ma'am."

The firm male voice stopped me in my tracks.

I peered up but couldn't make out much with his flashlight blinding me. "W–what?"

"Officer Dennison, Brenham PD. Don't move, ma'am, until I've assessed the situation."

I froze in place, but the dog didn't get the memo. He threatened to pull away from me, so I gripped him tighter than before. The light moved up and down, then to the right and the left. It finally shifted. Thank goodness. I blinked several times to get my vision back. Thanks to the halogen streetlamp that framed the entrance to the pipe, I could now make out a tall stranger in front of me. My heart went crazy, but I tried to sound calm, cool, and collected.

"W–what's the p–problem, Officer?"

"The *problem* is, you've chosen a nonresidential area to take up residence."

"*Residence?*" I didn't mean for the word to come out as a squeak, but it did.

"Exactly. The sewer might seem like a safe place to set up camp, but it's really not."

"Oh no! I didn't. I—"

"I heard you screaming. Is someone else down there attempting to hurt you?"

"Oh no, sir."

"I was patrolling the area and heard yelling, ma'am. I came running and saw this young woman here at the entrance to the pipe."

He flashed his light in Cassidy's direction and she offered a little wave, her red hair looking a little catawampus. "That's me," she said. "I'm the young woman at the entrance of the pipe."

He shifted the beam back at me. "Point is, I heard yelling and came right away. She told me someone was in the sewer line and that worried me, of course. I would hate to think of you spending the night in there."

"Oh, I don't plan to spend the night. And, sorry about the yelling! I thought I saw a snake, but it turned out to be a stick. My bad." I tried to stand, but he pointed his flashlight directly in my eyes once again and I flinched, almost losing my grip on the dog in the process. The pup whimpered, and I realized I must've bumped the cut on his leg. Poor pooch. But, man, did he stink!

"I asked you not to move until I could see you, ma'am." The officer's tone grew stern once more.

"But you've got this all wrong," I argued. "There's no problem, Officer. And I don't plan to stay here, that's for sure. I'm only here because—"

"There's a homeless shelter just a few miles from here. I'm going to give you and your friend here a ride. I'm pretty sure they'll put you up for the night. You can decide tomorrow what comes next." He gestured to the dog, which shivered in my arms. "But you can't take the mutt. They don't allow dogs."

I squared my shoulders. "I'm telling you, Officer, I'm not homeless. I live in a perfectly wonderful place."

"This is a sewer line, ma'am."

"Actually, it's not. This pipe isn't part of the sewer system at all. It's a drainage pipe that leads to that ditch over there. It provides runoff in case of flooding. I know this specifically because I have a good friend who works for the flood district. He's the one who called the vet clinic an hour ago to let me know about the dog. He was working in the area earlier and heard barking from inside the pipe."

"Mm-hmm."

"He tried to get the dog to come to him but couldn't win his trust, so he called me. I hate to brag, but folks call me the dog whisperer."

At this point, the pup began to wail. Well, perfect.

"I can see that, ma'am."

"I knew the drainage pipe would be more difficult to navigate in the dark, which is why I came prepared with a cap light, so that I could get him out unharmed."

"You're not wearing a cap light, ma'am."

I did my best not to groan aloud. "I know. It fell off when I saw the snake. I mean, the stick. Or maybe that was earlier. Anyway, you're worrying for nothing. Everything worked out perfectly."

"How so?"

"I got the dog! And I plan to take him to my apartment for the night."

"The address of the apartment, ma'am."

He would have to ask. "I've only been there a week, sir. I can't really remember the address. I'm terrible at remembering things sometimes. It's on Wilson. That much I know. The Landmark." I paused. "No, The Landing." I shot a pleading look at Cassidy. "That's it, right?"

"Land's End, silly. You really need to work on your memorization skills, Marigold. Are you taking those supplements your Grandma Peach gave you? They're supposed to help you focus. I think you need them, girl. Maybe double up for a few days?"

"No. No, I'm not taking them. I can't seem to remember."

Officer Dennison cleared his throat. "Ladies. . ."

I did my best to steady my voice and appear confident as I faced him. "I just sold my mom's house. She died very unexpectedly three months ago, and I just couldn't stay in the house after she passed. I'm sure you understand. It just felt weird without her there. So, I moved."

"I know that grief can do terrible things to a person, but that's no reason to—"

"I decided a new place was in order. I just moved in a week ago and I've been redecorating the living room. Brand-new sofa and everything." I wrinkled my nose as I thought it through. "Though, I don't think Mama would've like it much. It's kind of modern, and she was never into that. But it's very comfy."

"I'm not really keen on the color, though." Cassidy chimed in. "I mean, it's okay, but not exactly my taste. I'm not a fan of pea green."

"It's *mint* green." I shot a curious glance my friend's way. "But why didn't you tell me that when we were shopping? Your opinion means a lot to me, Cassidy."

"I dunno." My BFF shrugged. "You seemed to like it. And hey, I hold firmly to the belief that friends should let friends get whatever sofa they want."

I flashed the policeman a broad smile. "See? I have a great apartment, a so-so sofa, and a terrific best friend. What more could a girl ask for?"

"A reality check?" His gaze traveled to my hair and soggy scrubs, then clucked his tongue at the holes in my pants. "Look, I'm not saying I blame you for making up that big story about your beautiful apartment and your pea green sofa—"

"Mint green."

"Mint green sofa. But you deserve better than this." He gestured to the opening of the pipe.

"No, *he* deserves better than this." I pointed at the dog in my arms, who was starting to feel heavy. "This horrible place has been his—" A quick glance at the pup's underbelly confirmed my guess. "Yes, *his* humble abode, but no longer. I plan to take him straight to Lone Star Veterinary Clinic in the morning for a checkup. Then, hopefully, we'll find him a forever home. Did I tell you I'm starting a rescue for homeless—"

"Homelessness is a real issue. And everyone deserves a forever home." The officer patted me on the shoulder and then wiped his palm on the edge of his slacks. "Promise me you'll never give up on that dream."

"I won't give up on my dream, I promise. Once I start this new rescue, I'm sure donations will start pouring in."

"Folks from Brenham are very giving. I feel sure they will come to your rescue if you just have the courage to ask."

"Not *my* rescue. . .the *dog's* rescue. I've been thinking about asking my Aunt Trina to help. Do you know her? Trina Potter?"

"The country music star?"

"The one and only. She's my aunt. On my Mama's side."

"Of course she is."

"They were very close, and Trina's a dog lover too. But she's living in Nashville now." I turned my attention to Cassidy. "I'm going to try to talk her into moving back, though. Did I tell you?"

"Only ten or twelve times." Cassidy chuckled. "But then again, you do have a tendency to repeat yourself."

The officer reached for his radio. "Right. Your aunt is a country music star, which would explain why I found her niece living out here in these conditions."

"Oh no, sir. I'm telling you, I have a wonderful apartment."

"She does, Officer. She really, really does." Cassidy's tone changed. "Only, I'm not that keen on the breakfast table you picked out. It's cherrywood. I've never been a fan of cherrywood. That look went out in the 90s, right?"

"Hey, I thought you liked my table. And I got it for a song at the secondhand store." I eased the dog to a more comfortable position in my arms as I faced my friend head-on underneath the glow of the lamplight above. "Do you think I should paint it? What color? White? Cream? What's in right now?"

"Anything but pea green."

Cassidy doubled over in laughter and I joined in. When I finally came up for air, I turned to the police officer.

"Point is, sir, I live in an apartment with an ugly sofa and a secondhand breakfast table that apparently needs to be painted. That's the whole truth and nothing but the truth." I released a nervous laugh, wishing I was at home in that apartment right now, then shuffled the dog's position in my arms once more. Where was a leash when I needed one? Oh, right. . . in my car, where I'd left it.

The officer nodded, as if finally accepting my explanation. "If what you're saying is true, then I'm sure we can clear this up in a heartbeat. Just show me an ID with your address on it and I'll sleep better tonight knowing you're on your way to your 'forever home,' when we part ways, okay?"

"Of course." A wave of relief washed over me. "My wallet is in my car, right over. . . there. . ." I pointed to the side of the highway to the spot where I'd parked under the glow of a streetlamp, but was a bit bumfuzzled when I saw the empty space where my SUV had been.

"Um, Cassidy?" I managed, my erratic heartbeat now taking up residence in my ears. "What. Happened. To. The. Car?"

CHAPTER TWO

"I...I..." I stared off in the distance, bug-eyed, then shifted my attention to my friend. "I gave you one job."

"Hey, I was busy keeping an eye out in case the dog escaped! And then my phone died, so I couldn't see anything, anyway. And I told you it was loud out here! Do you hear that noise from the highway?"

I did. My gaze shifted back to where I had parked the car on the shoulder of the busy highway, as if I expected it to materialize. Was I having some sort of out-of-body experience? Maybe this was all a weird dream. I'd been having a lot of those since Mama died.

I turned to face my friend. "You still have the keys, though, right?" The shivering began in earnest now.

"Sure. They're right here in my—" Cassidy reached into her jacket pocket and came up empty. "Wait. I remember putting them on the dashboard while we loaded up our stuff, and then I, I..." She clamped a hand over her mouth. "Oh, Marigold."

"Ladies, I've heard enough." The officer put his hand up in the air. "There's no car. And I suspect there's no apartment. And don't even get me started on that whole country music star bit. Good try, though."

"Oh, but she *is* a country music star," I argued. "Ask anyone!"

"One of the best," Cassidy chimed in.

"Eleven songs at the top of the chart over the past six years," I added.

"And, honestly? 'Don't Mess with Mama' should've gone to number one but got nudged out by that weird Kenny Chesney song. So dumb."

"I love that Kenny Chesney song," Cassidy argued. "But I get your point. And we both know that Trina had the best fodder in the world for that 'Don't Mess with Mama' song. Your Grandma Peach is something else, girl."

"Tell me about it. And she was tickled pink to have a song dedicated to her."

"Look, I just want to make sure you're both safe before I clock out for the night," Dennison said. "So, please accept my offer of a ride to the shelter, okay? It might not be the Taj Mahal, but it's a big step up from this place, for sure. And warmer too." He pointed his light at Cassidy to give her a closer look. "Though, to be honest, if you show up dressed in those nice clothes they might wonder about you."

"You like my outfit? It's new. I paid a fortune for it at that new boutique on Main."

"Right."

"I work at the clinic too," she explained. "I'm a receptionist. Though, to be honest, I've always wanted to be office manager, so that's kind of my goal."

"Wait, you want to be an office manager?" This news totally caught me off guard. "How did I not know this?"

A pout followed on her end. "Hey, don't you think I'd make a good office manager?"

"The best! I mean, you're already subbing for Victoria, now that she's out with the new baby. And who knows? Maybe she'll decide not to come back?"

"I'm kind of picking up on that vibe, which is why I'm upping my game." Cassidy giggled. "I'm hoping to do such a great job that Tyler slides me into that position if Victoria decides to be a stay-at-home mom."

"You're the perfect candidate."

Officer Dennison lifted his hands. "Ladies, I've heard enough. I need you to come with me. This place isn't safe, you know."

"Tell me about it. My car was just stolen." I shifted my gaze to the road once again, still confused about the missing vehicle. My heart sank as I realized I'd also lost my wallet, complete with identification and credit cards. Great. Would I have to cancel all the cards? Again? I'd just gone down that road a couple of months ago after misplacing my purse while at the grocery store. Okay, so it wasn't really lost. . .I'd placed it in the wrong basket. But the point was, I'd recently canceled all my cards, *thinking* it was lost.

Maybe I was a lost cause—or maybe I needed those supplements to boost my memory—but no one could fault me tonight. My intentions were honorable. I was off to save the world. Or, the canine corner of it, anyway.

The rescued pup wriggled in my arms, begging to be put down. "What are we going to do about my car? Can I file a stolen vehicle report?"

"We can decide when we get to the patrol car," the officer said. "But I'll have to call the pound to pick up the pooch first."

"No!" I didn't mean to react so strongly, but how could I help it? I'd invested too much time in this abandoned dog to let him slip through my fingers now. "I just want to go home, sir. And I want to take the dog with me."

"I see the appeal. He is kind of cute." The officer reached to scratch the dog behind the ears. "I'll bet my son would love him. After a shower and a shave." He laughed. "The dog, not my son. My boy's only eight. But that dog needs a bath and a grooming."

"Tell me about it." I couldn't help but smile as I felt the pup's tail wagging. He was finally settling down in my embrace. "If I get this rescue up and running, we're going to need good foster homes and more pet adoptions, but this little guy needs medical intervention first. That's what I was doing here, saving his life. Giving him hope."

"Hope. Something we all need." The officer flashed his light in my face once again. "C'mon, ladies. It's getting late, and I want to get home to my family. Maybe I can talk some sense into you once you've warmed up."

I tagged along on his heels, the squirming pup still in my arms. All the way, I wrestled with my thoughts. With no proof of ID, no keys to get into my apartment, and no car to get me there, I'd have to call on someone for help.

Thank goodness, I had just the right "someone" in mind. Tyler Durham, head vet and owner of Lone Star Veterinary clinic. My boss, and the man who held my thoughts captive when I wasn't thinking about dogs.

Tall. Handsome. Kind. A lover of dogs.

Tyler.

I did my best not to swoon, right then and there. But still. This man was on my mind a lot these days. Maybe too much.

Officer Dennison opened the back door of his patrol car, and I settled into the back seat with the dog in my lap. To my left, Cassidy rambled on and on about our work at the clinic as the officer climbed into his spot behind the wheel. He picked up his radio and muttered something garbled to someone on the other end, but my thoughts were elsewhere.

I turned to face Cassidy as the reality of our situation settled over me. "What are we going to do?"

"I dunno." She groaned. "Without keys, we're both locked out of our apartments. We could always get a hotel, I guess."

"With no money?"

"Oh, right." My friend released an exaggerated sigh. "Hey, maybe we can get into your place after all. Don't you always keep a spare key hidden under the plant outside your front door?"

"That was at the old house. I . . ." I flinched as the reality hit. "Actually, I just remembered that I left it there when I moved. I should probably tell the new owner. But what about you? Don't you have a spare key to your apartment?"

"Yeah, hanging on a hook in my kitchen . . . inside of my locked apartment. Just three doors down from your locked apartment. We're doomed, girl."

I sighed.

So did Officer Dennison, who had apparently finished his conversation over the radio.

"You should totally call our boss," I suggested. "He'll clear this up in a hurry, I promise. And I'm sure he'll give us a place to stay for the night. Or..." An idea came to me. "I'll call the manager at our complex. He'll let us in. I know he will."

Dennison turned to face us, speaking through the barricade that separated us from the front seat. "You know your boss's number? Let's start there."

Did I ever. I'd had Tyler Durham's number memorized from day one. And I'd used it, any excuse I could find. Okay, so tonight's need was a little embarrassing, but once he heard I was rescuing a lost dog, he'd be happy to help out. I mean, the man already gave two hours a week to the local shelter. He was a giver. No doubt about it.

Officer Dennison punched in the number I gave him and made the call...but no one answered.

Really, Tyler? You're going to leave me hanging in the lurch when I need you most?

"Maybe he's already asleep?" Cassidy suggested.

"At nine o'clock?"

"Tomorrow morning is surgery day, remember? He always goes to bed early the night before."

"Oh, right." I usually did too, since I had to assist him. "I guess we could call Parker."

"You don't think he'll mind if we show up at his place with a dog smelling like this?" Cassidy asked.

"He's great with animals. He'll love this little guy. He'll probably even help us get him bathed and patched up."

"Okay." Cassidy didn't sound as sure as I felt.

I gave Dennison the number of Parker Jenson, good friend and fellow vet tech. A few seconds later Parker picked up.

"Mr. Jenson, this is Todd Dennison with Brenham PD," the officer explained. "I've picked up two women from the sewer line down off of Highway 36 at West Main."

"Sewer line?" I heard Parker's response from the other end of the line and was grateful the call was on speaker.

"A drainage pipe, Parker," I called out. "Not a sewer line."

"Ah. Marigold. Why am I not surprised? Who's with you?"

"Cassidy!" my friend hollered. "She made me, Parker. You know how persuasive she can be."

Really? I *made* her? I couldn't let that comment sit there, so I turned to face her, ready to deal with it. "I did not make you. You volunteered!"

"To get in a sewer line?" Parker groaned from the other end of the line. "Really?"

"Drainage pipe," I countered.

"Point is, I've got them in the back of my patrol car right now," Dennison said. "Just need to make sure they have a safe place to go. Can I bring them to you?"

"Bring them to me?" Parker sounded understandably shocked. "What's wrong with Marigold's place? She's got a great new apartment not far from the clinic."

"See?!" I interjected. "Told you!"

"Mari, what's going on?" Parker's words were tinged with concern. "What have you done this time?"

This time? Really?

"I apologize for the misunderstanding," the officer said. "Maybe I got a little confused."

"Marigold tends to have that effect on people, sir," Parker said. "It's a common problem."

Wonderful. If I ever wanted to know what my friend thought about me, there it was.

"Right." Dennison paused. "I guess her story lines up, after all. So, I suppose that means her car is really missing and the key to her apartment is MIA too. Can you come and get these ladies, or should I bring them to you?"

"Bring them to me?"

"Okay, I'll do that. What's your address?"

"My address? You're actually bringing them to my house?"

"Isn't that what you told me to do?" Exasperation laced the officer's words. "By the way, I hope you're okay with the dog. Kind of a mangy-looking little thing, but they tell me you're good with animals. Maybe you can fix him up."

"I'm so confused." Parker's exasperated tone carried the truth of those words. "Mari doesn't have a dog. Her Corgi passed away six months ago."

Great. Thanks for bringing that up, Parker. Just when I'm at my lowest.

"She's got a new one. Kind of a mangy-looking thing. And he stinks to high heaven." The officer paused. "Look, my shift ends at ten and I'd sure like to get home to my wife. Can't wait to tell them this sordid tail. Get it. . .*tail?* Dogs?"

"Got it."

"You should see this poor thing, Parker," I chimed in. "He's gonna need a lot of work. But he's so cute—except for the smell, anyway—and I really think—"

"Bring them to my place, Officer," Parker interrupted. "I've got a key to Mari's apartment."

"You do?" I squealed.

"Yeah, remember you gave me your spare the day I helped you move? You said, 'Keep it just in case.'"

"Whelp, the *just in case* was a good prediction on my part." I laughed. "But I'm glad you can let me in. Want to just meet me at my place, then?"

"Sure. Just let me grab some shoes and a jacket."

"Thank you, Parker. Cassidy can spend the night with me. She's locked out of her place too."

"Of course she is."

Officer Dennison ended the call, and I turned to face Cassidy. "Parker to the rescue."

"Again."

"What do you mean, again?" I squirmed on the uncomfortable seat.

"Don't you remember last week when you left your debit card at home? He bought you lunch. Fajitas from Mario's, your favorite."

"Oh, right."

"And the week before that when you needed an oil change and he saved you the money by doing it for you?"

"True."

"And right before that, when you moved? He showed up with his truck and did the heavy lifting while we ate chips and salsa? And he obviously kept a spare key, so he's coming to your rescue again."

"Right." I nodded. "He's a great guy."

"He's a cutie." Cassidy's voice now had a nervous energy I hadn't picked up on before. "Don't you think?"

"Parker?" I hadn't really thought about it. "I guess."

"He sure is," she countered, her voice now sounding fairy-tale dreamy. "Prettiest eyes in town. And he's a great guy who's always looking out for others, which is a bonus."

Did my friend Cassidy have a crush on Parker, perhaps? Intriguing.

"Always good to have friends who put others first," I said.

"He does oil changes?" Officer Dennison asked from the front seat. "If so, my truck is overdue for one."

I gave the pup a little tickle behind the ears. "Sweet boy! That's the kind of friend I'm going to be to you."

"The kind who does oil changes?" Cassidy asked, and then laughed.

"No, the kind who tends to his needs." I snuggled the stinky little thing, not even caring about the odor. Not much, anyway. "As soon as I check to make sure he doesn't have a microchip." The reality settled over me. Someone might be looking for this sweet boy. Maybe, under all this matted fur, he would shape up to be a handsome fellow. The docked tail clued me in to the fact that he might just be a pedigree pup. Stranger things had happened.

As the patrol car pulled out onto the highway pointed toward my apartment complex, Cassidy released an exaggerated sigh from her spot next to me.

"You okay?" I asked, as I settled back against the uncomfortable seat.

"No. I'm just sad my phone is dead. I'd love to take a selfie of the two of us right now and put it on social media."

"I know, right?"

"Talk about a missed opportunity. When are we ever going to get to ride in the back of a patrol car again, Mari?"

"Never, I hope."

"Opportunities like this don't come around every day."

"Unless you hang out with me."

"Well, true. But we need to mark this date in history so we never forget. You know?"

"I doubt I'll ever forget. Besides, we're taking home a dog. That's better than a photo. He's a living, breathing thing." I patted the little pup on the head and then sniffed. Goodness, the smell was getting stronger. It seemed more exaggerated, now that we were cooped up inside the vehicle.

"Officer, can we borrow your phone?" Cassidy's words interrupted my internal thoughts. "We want to take a selfie."

"I'm sorry, ma'am, but I can't let you do that."

Cassidy pursed my lips and leaned back against the seat. "You should really give thought to getting cushioned seats back here. It's very uncomfortable. I would think the Brenham PD could afford better than this. You know?"

He adjusted his rearview mirror to better see them. "I'll tell that to the captain. I'll ask him to upholster them in a lovely shade of pea green."

Okay, that was funny. Before long we were all chuckling. Well, until the smell overpowered us once more. Hoping I could get the smell to dissipate, I reached over to roll down the window but quickly realized I couldn't do that in the back seat of a patrol car. Bummer. When I complained about it, the good officer came to our rescue.

"I'll put the front window down," he said. "It's a little rank in here."

"Yeah, the dog is a mess," I said as I stroked the pup behind the ears. "Sorry about that."

"I hate to tell you this, Mari, but it's not just the dog." Cassidy pinched her nostrils with her fingers. "You smell worse than a container of fish bait."

"Gee thanks."

"I haven't gone fishing since I was a kid," she added. "But I'll never forget that smell."

This, of course, led to a lengthy chat between Cassidy and Officer Dennison about fishing. Which led to a conversation about fried catfish. Which reminded me that I'd skipped dinner.

My stomach rumbled. Oh well. When Parker let me back into my place I could grab some leftovers from the fridge. If they were still edible. How long did nachos keep? Anyway, I'd swallow down some food and then shower and get a good night's sleep. Before long, this would all be a distant memory.

Yep. Tomorrow morning Tyler would patch up this pup's wounds. Together, we would give him a second chance, a new leash on life. Pun intended. And, if I played my cards right, my boss might just agree to link arms with me to create the city's finest animal rescue organization ever. He would be the perfect person to assist me, after all.

If I made it home without passing out from the smell.

A call came through on the radio, and Dennison responded. Seconds later, his voice far more animated than before, I realized something big was stirring in town.

He repeated the address back into the radio, and I startled to attention. Were my ears deceiving me, or did they just put out a call for a burglary in progress at 1507 Washington?

1507 Washington was the address of the Lone Star Veterinary Clinic.

CHAPTER THREE

There's a burglary in progress at our clinic?" I didn't mean to shout the words, but they came out in a heightened shriek.

"Apparently so." Officer Dennison turned on the lights on top of the patrol car, and off we went, sirens blaring and lights blazing, to the Lone Star Veterinary Clinic, my home away from home. My heart rate quickened as I thought about what must be happening there, and I ushered up a silent prayer, begging for God's intervention.

"Now I *really* wish my phone was working," Cassidy moaned from the spot next to me. "No one's ever going to believe this story when we tell it later."

She went off on a tangent about how exciting this night was shaping up to be, but I couldn't stop thinking about the clinic. Was someone really burglarizing the place? Tyler would be devastated. That clinic was his baby. Mine too, really. In the six months I'd worked there it had rooted itself in my heart, making itself at home. And no one messed with my home.

The patrol car whipped into the parking lot of the clinic a couple of minutes later, and my heart sailed straight into my throat as I took in the shocking scene in front of me. The large plate-glass windows that framed out the lobby had been shattered in multiple places. My heart felt nearly as shattered as I tried to imagine who could have done such a thing. What sort of heinous individual had caused this mayhem?

Cassidy gasped and immediately went into a panic, which got the dog worked up. His high, shrill barks rang out in rapid succession as he trembled in my arms. I did my best to silence him so that I could make out that strange shrieking sound in the background.

Yes, even with the doors and windows of the patrol car closed, I heard the unmistakable sound of the alarm going off. I knew that particular pitch quite well, having accidentally set it off a time or two in the months since we'd opened. Okay, three times, but who was counting? I'd never been very good with technology.

Before I could get control of my thoughts, the parking lot swarmed with patrol cars. Officers bounded from their vehicles in whirlwind fashion, much like a scene from a movie I'd recently watched. Thanks to the streetlamps overhead, the whole thing was framed in a shadowy light, which made me feel like I was having one of those weird out-of-body experiences.

Maybe I was dreaming all of this. Perhaps I wasn't really holding a barking, smelly dog in my soggy lap while seated in the back of a patrol car watching a movie scene play out in front of me. Maybe this was all just some sort of technicolor dream.

Or, maybe—as I watched Dennison swing his door open—it was real after all, and we happened to be thrust into the middle of it all.

I pinched myself, just to make sure. Nope. Not a nightmare.

The officer turned back to face us with a firm, "Stay in the car, ladies!" then slammed his door and took off to join the other officers, who were congregated near the front door of the clinic, which appeared to be locked.

"What other choice do we have?" Cassidy grumbled. "We're stuck."

We were stuck, all right. I tried the door a couple of times just to make sure, but we were definitely pinned inside the patrol car with no way to know the goings-on inside the clinic, which was now surrounded by armed officers. And we didn't have any way to contact the outside world, since both of our phones were unavailable.

I peered out the window and my body was wracked with trembling as I realized the extent of the damage to our clinic's windows. Our poor building! Shattered glass filled the lobby, covered the chairs where patients normally sat, and even lay in chunks across the walkway outside. My mind whirled at the possibilities. Who could have done such a thing? Everyone in Brenham loved Lone Star. After that recent write-up in the paper, we were their little darlings.

Or, so I thought. At least one someone didn't care much for us, if such a thing could be judged from the chaos in front of me. Knowing we had a very real enemy out there got me even more nervous than before.

The pup must've picked up on my fear because he finally stopped barking and nuzzled close. The precious little thing reached up to lick me on the chin. I patted him and calmed down as I held him tight. My Corgi, Watson, used to do that too. Gosh, I missed him. He always had that intuitive sense about him and knew just how to calm me.

Tears sprang to my eyes at once with the memory, but the pup in my arms snuggled closer than before. I could feel his heartbeat and it settled me down. Dogs always had that effect on me.

"This. Is Freaking. Me. Out!" Cassidy's staccato words reflected her concern, as did the trembling in her voice.

"Me too. I'm kind of glad we're in here and not out there, just in case whoever did this—" I gestured to the building but couldn't finish the sentence. I didn't want to think about whoever had done this or whether they might be lurking in the shadows.

Whoever had done this.

A shiver ran down my spine as I remembered an incident earlier this afternoon involving one of our groomers.

"Cassidy, remember what Isabel told us earlier today, right when we were leaving?"

My friend turned to face me, eyes wide. "About her ex, you mean?"

"Yeah. She broke up with him a couple of days ago and he flipped out on her. He was threatening her. Remember? She was so scared he might show up, and—" I didn't know the "and" part. She hadn't elaborated. But, if Isabel was worried, maybe we should be worried.

"Oh, I heard, trust me. Matt called the clinic repeatedly today, demanding to speak to her. He even cussed me out. Girl, I haven't heard language like that since I was in high school. But I was under strict instructions not to put the call through to her. She was avoiding him at all costs."

"You don't suppose he..." I shivered as the possibility flooded over me. Had Matt Foster done this? If so, was Isabel okay? I wanted to call her, to find out, but with no phone, that couldn't happen. Instead, I ushered up another silent prayer, this one for her safety.

"I don't know much about what's going on with the two of them, but I do know she was scared of him." Cassidy shifted her position in the uncomfortable seat. "I always thought he was kind of a creep, myself."

"Same. But you can't exactly tell a friend that her boyfriend is creepy, now can you?" I mean, if my good friend couldn't even tell me she didn't like the color of my sofa...

"Of course you can," Cassidy argued. "And I tried. But she was *way* too into him to notice the creep factor."

"Some girls are like that."

In my lap, the dog released a low growl in the back of his throat. He startled to attention, and his head tilted as he watched an area to the left of the parking lot. Did he see something I did not?

Ah yes. Another vehicle came screeching into the parking lot, nearly hitting the curb.

"Look, Cassidy! Tyler's here."

His Dodge Ram came to a halt in front of the shattered glass door leading to the lobby. Tyler bounded from the cab but was stopped right away by a female officer, who blocked the front door.

Cassidy leaned forward and rubbed her breath from the now-foggy window. "What's he doing?"

"Looks like he's giving her a key to the front door."

"They could go in through the busted windows."

"And get cut up? I don't think so."

Tyler took a couple of steps back as the officer took the lead and headed to the front door of the clinic. Another vehicle turned into the parking lot. I recognized the SUV as belonging to Dr. Kristin Keller, our newest vet. Straight out of the A&M vet program, she was new to the practice but had a solid head on her shoulders.

Only, not in a crisis, apparently. She rushed from her car, dressed in pajamas and fluffy slippers, her hair in a messy twist.

"Oh wow. Look at Kristin." Cassidy giggled. "Now, that's a photo op. Do you think she realizes she's wearing her puppy-themed slippers?"

"Probably not." I'd never seen the woman when she didn't look like the picture of perfection, so I found the sight in front of me fascinating.

Tyler and Kristin held some sort of a lengthy conversation and he gestured to the door, as if to explain something to her. Then they both leaned against her car and waited.

Okay, so I felt a little jealous. I don't mind admitting it. Ever since Kristin joined the practice, I'd noticed their camaraderie. I didn't want him to like her. At least, not like that.

Get your act together, Marigold. You're in the middle of a crisis.

I didn't need to be thinking about my love life. . .or lack thereof.

Moments later, a fire truck pulled in. Could things possibly get any more dramatic? Oh yes. Clearly, they could. The firefighters emerged, carrying all sorts of clean-up equipment, and swarmed the building. Through the broken plate glass, I could see them working inside to clean up the mess.

"We have some really hunky firefighters in Brenham, don't we?" Cassidy swiped at the window with her hand and then giggled. "I'm just saying. Did you see that really tall one?"

No. No, I didn't. I was too busy watching Kristin and Tyler, who were still engaged in conversation. Would this situation cause them to bond even more?

When things settled down, I rapped on my window to get Tyler's attention. He eventually turned my way and a beam of light hit me—for the second time tonight—and I realized he must be shining the flashlight from his cell phone at the police cruiser. He and Kristin rushed our way.

Tyler leaned down to my window, then hollered, "What are you doing in there?"

"It's a long story!" I hollered back.

His gaze shifted to the broken panes glass at the front of his beloved clinic, then he turned to face me once again, as if to ask, "Are *you* responsible for this? Is that why you're in the patrol car?"

"No!" I yelled through the glass. "I didn't do it." I pointed at Cassidy. "We didn't do it. We just got here."

As if on cue, Officer Dennison showed up. He paused to talk to Tyler and Kristin.

"Can you make out what they're saying?" I asked Cassidy.

"Nope. Not a word. They really need to speak up."

Dennison opened the front door of the patrol car and reached inside to grab a notepad.

"What's going on?" I asked. "Can we get out now?"

"The building is clear, so I'll let you out now, as long as you promise to stay in the parking lot until they let you all inside." He gestured to Tyler. "This man says he knows you."

"Yeah, that's my boss. Tyler," I explained. "The first call you made. The one who didn't pick up."

"Ah. Right. I'm guessing he was a little busy when I called."

"Clearly."

Dennison opened the back left door of the patrol car and ushered us out into the dark parking lot. In that moment, I felt like my prison doors had been opened. I bounded out, ready to stretch my legs. Only, they didn't want to cooperate. Apparently I'd really done a number on them in that drainage pipe.

The pooch in my arms let out a bark and tried to escape, but I managed to hang onto him, though the muscles in my arms were feeling a little weird too. I shivered as the cool October air hit my damp, smelly clothes.

"Thank you for setting us free!" Cassidy exclaimed.

Kristin looked back and forth between us. "I don't get it. Why were you arrested?"

"Yeah, what did you two do?" Tyler spoke to both of us, but his gaze landed squarely on me. He pinched his nose and then stepped back.

Hey, give me the benefit of the doubt, please.

"They weren't arrested," Dennison interjected. "I picked them up for their own safety. I was transporting them to someone named Parker, who's going to let them into Ms. Evans's place."

"It's a long story." I shrugged. "This very nice officer was giving us a ride. My car was stolen." The dog continued to squirm and then took a flying leap out of my arms to the ground below. I knelt down and held tight to him, worried he might try to run. Nope, he just needed to potty.

"Does anyone happen to have a lead handy?" I asked.

Kristin bolted toward her car—*bolted* being a loose term, since she lost one of her fuzzy slippers along the way—and returned a moment later with one of the blue leads we often used at the practice. Seconds later, she had it in place around the pup's neck.

Finally. I could relax.

Tyler crossed his arms at his chest, and his penetrating gaze seemed to sear right through me. "Mari, is there something you want to tell us?"

"Yeah, whose dog is this?" Kristin asked. "I thought your dog—"

I willed her not to say it.

"He's a rescue," I spit out. "I just got him tonight. I don't know anything about him."

Tyler leaned down to look at the dog, then used his flashlight to focus in on the pup's leg. "He's got a gash in his leg."

"Right. I saw that."

"Because of the broken glass?" He gestured to the shattered windows.

I could see how he might draw that conclusion, but no. I quickly explained the events of the past couple of hours, and he nodded. "Okay, gotcha. Rescue dog."

"Yep." I beamed. "The first of many, I hope. We just picked him up down at the big drainage pipe at 36 and West Main."

"That would explain the smell." Tyler waved his hand in front of his face. "From both of you."

Thanks a lot, dude.

"So you just happened to be coming by the clinic when the robbery happened?" Kristin asked.

"Burglary, ma'am." Dennison's voice sounded from behind us, and we all turned at once to face him. "It's only considered a robbery if someone is on-site to be robbed. No one was here, right?"

"Not that I know of," she responded. "Except whoever did this."

"Also, it's only a burglary if something is actually missing from inside the building. You'll have to do an inventory and let us know."

Tyler nodded.

I felt sick inside, thinking about what might have been stolen. A horrible chill caught me off guard, but it probably had nothing to do with the weather. Should I tell them about Isabel's ex or let that story wait?

"I'm afraid the damage wasn't limited to the windows." Dennison reached inside the patrol car for his phone. "There's more inside—in the lobby and one of the exam rooms. You'll see for yourself, once they let you in. Won't be long now. They're just taking photos and fingerprints."

Tyler groaned. "How bad is it?"

"No idea what's been stolen, if anything, but there's more than enough evidence of vandalism. Someone painted the word *Murderer* on the wall in one of the rooms."

"Murderer?" Kristin gasped. "Oh no!"

"Yep. First exam room on the right."

"I. . ." Her voice trembled. "I think I know who did this, Tyler."

"Who?" We all asked in unison.

"Maggie Jamison."

"Maggie Jamison?" I echoed. I knew the woman well. Leathered and tough on the exterior but a total pushover when it came to her little terrier mix, Jasper, who had recently lost his battle with diabetes.

"Why would you think Maggie did this, Kristin?" Tyler asked. "I've known her for years. She's never shown any signs of aggression."

I had to agree. She seemed like the least likely candidate, in fact.

"She blamed me for Jasper's death," Kristin explained. "I guess she's been holding some sort of grudge since it happened. I got a call from her, just yesterday, in fact. She went on and on about how I could have done more to save him. I tried to explain that I had followed the protocol, but—"

"You did everything you could." Tyler rested his hand on Kristin's arm. "You gave her the best medical advice possible. And Jasper was an older dog. Thirteen, right?"

"Right. But she still blamed me. Blamed us. . .the practice."

"But he had diabetes and it was uncontrolled," I chimed in. "That's not our fault."

"Exactly," Kristin agreed. "And I explained that to her, but she was so angry that I was actually worried she might flip out on me."

I found this hard to believe, knowing Maggie the way I did. "Are you saying she was upset enough to do something like this?" I asked.

"I don't know." Kristin's voice trembled. "I just know she was in a terrible state of mind. She even mentioned filing a lawsuit against me. Against *us*."

"Lawsuit?" Tyler asked. "Why didn't you tell me?"

"Because I was hoping it was just the grief speaking. She just lost her dog, after all."

"I'll let the investigator know your suspicions." Dennison shoved his phone into his pocket. "In fact, I'm headed to the station now. My shift ends at ten, and I still have some paperwork to take care of before I head home for the night. But I need to get going."

He wished us well and then climbed in his patrol car.

"Thanks, Officer Dennison!" I called out after him. "Let me know if you decide to adopt the dog."

"Will do," he called back. "But talking my wife into it might not be easy. She's more of a cat person."

I did my best not to respond with my true thoughts. Cats were fine. In moderation. If a dog wasn't available.

CHAPTER FOUR

I watched as Officer Dennison's patrol car pulled out of the parking lot, and then I turned my attention back to the dog. Tyler knelt on the ground beside the pup to examine his leg.

"As soon as they let us inside, we've got to get this dog's leg stitched up. Otherwise we're going to be looking at a pretty serious infection from all that sewer water."

"You don't think it'll wait till morning?" I asked.

"Not if we want to prevent infection. And I think we should get him started on a round of antibiotics, just to be safe. I'll do a full exam when we get inside."

My hero!

He turned his flashlight on the wound, and the pup whimpered. "Let me see if I have anything to clean it up with."

"On your person?" Cassidy asked.

"In my truck."

"Oh, right. A vehicle. Some people have one of those." I sighed as I remembered my car was long gone. Would I ever see it again?

Tyler ventured off to his vehicle then returned with some sort of canine emergency kit. In that moment, I knew. I knew we were destined to be together. The two of us, working side by side to save Brenham's abandoned animals. Tyler, with his first aid kit, and me with my. . .

Well, my crazy ambition to save the helpless dogs. And the unbelievable stench now coming from my shoes, which were completely saturated with water from the drainage pipe.

Before he could go to work, another vehicle entered the parking lot.

"Oh, look!" Cassidy let out a squeal. "It's Parker!"

My coworker's Ford F-250 pulled up next to us, and Parker rolled down his window. "I was at Mari's place, waiting. But no one ever showed up. Then I heard sirens."

"Yeah, sorry," I explained. "I was trapped in the back of a patrol car, so there was nothing I could do about it. I didn't have a way to call you. My phone is missing."

"How do you do it, Mari?" He shook his head.

"Do what?"

His gaze shifted to the building. "I was starting to get worried when no one showed up at your place, so I decided I'd better follow the sound of those sirens, just on the off chance that they had anything to do with you."

"Well, technically, they didn't."

"What happened?" he asked.

"Vandals broke in," Tyler explained. "Cops are still inside, taking pictures. But I'm about to patch up this dog Mari rescued. He's injured."

"I'll help." Parker pulled his truck into the spot nearest us and hopped out. He walked to the back of his truck and dropped the tailgate. "We can use this as a table." Parker grabbed a blanket from the truck's cab then spread it out across the tailgate. Was everyone on the planet prepared for this rescue? Sure looked like it. He scooped the dog into his arms and lifted him to the tailgate, now a surgical station.

Moments later Tyler and Kristin went to work on my sweet pup.

Okay, not mine, exactly. But the pup my heart had suddenly latched onto.

"You're not gonna help?" Cassidy asked.

I pointed to the back of the truck. "Are you kidding? They've got this under control. And how many people can you fit around a tailgate, anyway?"

"Is this a trick question?" She quirked a brow. "You're in Aggie country, honey. You should know the answer to that."

Okay, that got me tickled.

They had it under control, all right. In fact, Kristin and Tyler looked like a well-oiled machine as they worked side by side.

Lovely. Weren't they just the cutest duo? And didn't they look adorable, tending to the dog I'd risked my life to save?

"We'll have to check to see if he's chipped," Tyler called out.

"Yes, maybe he has an owner," Parker added as he stepped into the place next to Kristin and handed off a bottle of saline. "You had this in your car?"

"Of course." Tyler took it from him and squirted it onto the dog's leg. "I always keep stuff like this on hand, just in case."

"Me too," Kristin chimed in. "That's what we were taught to do. You never know when an emergency will come up, after all. Like this one. Just proves that our training taught us well."

They really were two peas in a pod, weren't they? Ugh. My heart twisted as they carried on about all the amazing things they'd learned in the vet program at A&M. Tyler laughed as Kristin shared old memories from days gone by.

Not that I had any claim to the man. He was just my boss, after all. But what an amazing man he was, especially in moments like this. Watching him work was always a joy.

Tyler cleaned and wrapped the pup's leg and my admiration for him went even higher, if such a thing were possible. Did he have any idea how wonderful he was? As he tended to this poor pup, I caught a vision of what it would be like to work alongside him.

Oh, wait. I already worked alongside him. Every day.

But, not with rescue dogs. If I got my way, if Second Chance Ranch became a reality, I wouldn't have to look far for medical care for the pups. I had the best of the best right here, at Lone Star.

My heart swelled with joy at the possibilities, and I felt the sting of tears in my eyes. Maybe God was really bringing my dreams to reality, right in front of me. After all I'd been through this year—losing Mama, moving from my childhood home—I needed something to go right. Was this it, perhaps?

Please, God. . .let it be so!

When they got the pup fixed up, Parker lifted him from the bed of the truck and placed him back on the ground, then knelt down next to him. "Kind of a cute guy. Definitely a spaniel."

"Agreed." Kristin nodded. "Based on the shape of his head, I mean. And his tail is docked, so someone thought he was a pedigree pooch. I guess we'll see when we get him bathed and groomed. Those mats are something awful."

"Yeah, maybe Isabel can fit him in tomorrow after we get him stitched up," Tyler added.

Isabel.

Matt Foster.

A chill ran down my spine as I remembered my earlier conversation with Cassidy. I needed to mention it to Tyler.

Only, not right now. Something else vied for our attention. The officers exited the building and called out to Tyler. He crossed the parking lot for what appeared to be an intense conversation.

We eased ourselves in his direction, hoping to hear. As we approached the front of the building, the detective in charge took several steps in our direction and introduced himself as James Phinney. He gave us the all clear to go inside, with the instruction to use caution.

"The firefighters swept up the glass as best they could, but you're going to need to be careful, especially if you plan to open up to clients anytime soon."

"Right." Tyler sounded defeated. "Not sure how that's going to work."

"I can give you the name of someone in the glass business," Detective Phinney said. "We see this a lot. But that's specialty glass. It'll need to be ordered. They'll board things up for you in the meantime, though."

He passed off the information to Tyler, who called the number right away. Minutes later, he was heavy into a conversation with Bob from

Crystal Clear glass company. I couldn't make out much of what he was saying, what with the officers now emerging from the inside of the building and congregating in the parking lot around me. On the ground at my feet, the pup settled down next to me on the pavement.

"Good boy." I leaned down to scratch him behind the ears. "Thank you for not reacting."

He chose that moment to bark at Parker, who took several steps my way.

"You okay, Mari?" He rested his hand on my arm.

I nodded, but a yawn escaped. "Yeah. Kind of tired."

"Why don't I go ahead and take you home? I can come back and help Tyler and Kristin with whatever's going on inside."

"No." I shook my head. "I want to help."

"You sure?"

"Mm-hmm." Still, the events of the past few hours were catching up with me. The idea of a hot bath and a good night's sleep sounded pretty divine right about now. But I wouldn't let the others down. We needed to stick together at a time like this, and I wouldn't bail on them, no matter how tired.

A couple of minutes later, the detective led us inside. I gasped as I saw the chaos. Chairs had been flipped, and the reception counter where Cassidy usually met with clients was covered in debris—everything from shredded papers to broken glass.

"No!" Cassidy stood in shocked silence, her hand now covering her mouth. "My computer! It's gone!" She ran behind the counter and started tearing through the debris, as if she thought it might magically reappear. I'd never seen her so worked up before.

Not that I blamed her. Cassidy always took such great care of everything at the reception desk. It was her pride and joy. Now it was a hot mess.

I shifted my gaze to the dog. Now that we were finally in the light, I got a really good look at him. The poor boy was as big a mess as the room. Still, underneath the matted fur, I felt sure we would find a gorgeous dog. He had rich brown eyes and chestnut and white coloring. Something about the shape of his face put me in mind of another dog I'd seen recently. Oh, right. Mrs. Moynihan. Her beautiful spaniel, Chelsea. This little guy had a similarly shaped face. Only time would tell, I supposed.

"Wasn't sure what to do with all the papers everywhere," Detective Phinney explained. "Figured I'd better leave it to you."

"I'll deal with it." Cassidy took her usual spot behind the counter and got to work, but I made my way into the examining rooms. Only one was in bad shape—the first. That's where we found the word *Murderer* spray-painted on the wall.

Kristin erupted in tears the moment she saw it. "This is the room where Jasper died," she explained. "I'm telling you, it had to be Maggie who did this, y'all. She was so upset."

"You really think she's physically capable of that?" I asked.

"Maybe she had help?" Kristin shifted her gaze back to the walls.

"Or. . ." I decided this would be the appropriate time to share my news. "It might've been Matt Foster."

"Who's that?" Tyler and Kristin asked in unison.

"Isabel's ex. She just broke up with him a couple days ago and he called the clinic multiple times, demanding to speak to her. But Cassidy was under strict instructions not to let him anywhere near her. Apparently he's shown signs of violence in the past."

"That's awful." Kristin's gaze traveled the room. "But, why would he write the word *Murderer* on the wall. Isabel never murdered anyone."

"No idea. To make us look bad, maybe?"

Tyler pivoted on his heels toward his office. "You guys check the rooms to see what else is missing. I'm going to take a look at the security footage of the building and see if we can make out anything."

"After you stitch up Beau Jangles' leg?" I suggested.

"Beau Jangles?" Parker's voice sounded from the open doorway, and I turned to face him.

"Yeah. At least until we know if he's microchipped. He just looks like a Beau Jangles to me."

"Let's settle the microchip question once and for all." Parker headed off to the back to grab our scanner and seconds later we had our answer. Beau Jangles was not chipped. We could move forward with his care, at least for now. But finding the owner was going to be a lot tougher.

"It won't take more than ten minutes to get him stitched up," Tyler said. "I say we go for it and then send you two home to rest."

I agreed.

We spent the next several minutes in the surgical suite, far removed from the debris, with Tyler quickly stitching up the gash in Beau's right back leg. He found another small cut on his front left leg and a tiny laceration on his side.

"Do you think he was attacked?" I asked as I reached for a package of gauze.

"I don't think so, but I'm going to treat him with antibiotics, like I said. I don't want him to end up septic, and that's a real possibility with all that sewer water."

As Tyler gave Beau his first injection of meds, my admiration for him soared. This man really was the best, wasn't he?

Parker set a rectangle of gauze in place and then wrapped the pup's leg with more. He finished up and then lifted the dog down to the floor.

"He needs a bath, but I think he's been through enough trauma tonight," Tyler explained. "We'll see if Isabel can work him in for a solid grooming. Until then, I think the poor guy needs a good night's sleep."

"We all do." I yawned again.

"Let me take you home, Mari," Parker insisted.

I started to argue, but the smell from my clothing wafted up and made me feel a little nauseous. Only then did I remember that I still hadn't eaten. Was the room spinning, or was I just feeling discombobulated from the chaos surrounding me?

"You don't look so good," Tyler observed.

"Gee, thanks."

"Go home, Mari," Kristin added. "We'll take it from here."

They didn't need me. Fine. I'd just go home. With my smelly dog. The one who was suddenly looking hyped up and ready for some fun. Beau began to dance around the room with the cutest skip in his step. I'd given him the perfect name, apparently. This dog was a dancer.

Tyler headed to his office to check the cameras with Kristin on his heels. Parker led the way back out into the lobby where I found Cassidy sweeping the floor. "They didn't get all of the glass," she explained. "So, I'm going to sweep and mop. Then I'm probably going to sweep again, just to be safe."

"It's so heartbreaking." I gestured to our beautiful lobby. It was such a spacious, bright place—a welcoming area where our clients could congregate with their pets.

But not tonight.

Parker leaned down to pick up the dog. "Okay, you. No walking in here for a while." He turned to Cassidy. "I'm taking Marigold home. Don't you want to go back to her place to sleep and deal with this in the morning? You're locked out of your apartment, right?"

"I really want to stay here and finish up. Maybe I could hang out at your place when I'm done, Parker?" She shot him a hopeful glance and I wondered about her motivations. Was Cassidy looking for an excuse to have some alone time with Parker? What was up with that?

He shrugged. "That's fine with me. I've got a guest room. You're welcome to it. I'll come back and get you once I drop Mari off at her place."

"Thanks, Parker." She flashed him a warm smile then went straight back to cleaning.

Yep. The girl clearly had something up her sleeve. Strange, that I'd never noticed before.

He led the way to the front door. Before he could open it, Isabel came bursting through it. She took one look at the chaos inside of the clinic and let out a cry.

"I knew he was going to do something like this! I knew it!"

"Matt did this?" Parker asked. "Are you sure?"

She shook her head. "I'm not a hundred percent sure, but he threatened to hurt me. Earlier today he said he was coming back and that I would be sorry. That we would all be sorry! And now look around you. The broken windows. It's something he would have done."

I felt a shiver run up my spine. Had that creep come in here and done all this damage to prove some kind of a point? If so, we'd see him locked up in jail to pay for it!

"I feel horrible!" Moisture dribbled over her lashes. "I never meant to put you guys at risk. I thought I could get away from him without any drama. I should've known better. He's been bad news from the very beginning. I'm so sorry, y'all!" Her tears flowed in earnest now.

In that moment, my sisterly affections for my coworker kicked in, big-time. I threw my arms around her neck and offered a warm hug. The poor girl. Getting free from him was the key thing, especially if Matt was capable of something so heinous. We would handle the fallout. We just needed to protect her at all costs. If he would do something like this to prove a point, what might he do to her in the days ahead?

"Not on my watch," I spoke in my most calming voice. "We're a team, Isabel. We won't let him hurt you."

"I'm just *so* sorry." Isabel plopped down into one of the oversized chairs in the lobby.

"No!" Cassidy hollered. "I haven't wiped those chairs down yet!"

Isabel came springing back up and brushed at the back of her pants. "He's a terrible, terrible man." She paused and then shook her head. "No, he's a good man with a terrible problem. He's addicted, y'all. And it's affecting everything."

"We don't know for sure that it was Matt," Tyler countered. "But we'll know soon. The police took some prints. They'll figure it out. In the meantime, please don't blame yourself." He gazed into her tear-stained face. "You're safe, and that's really all that matters. I mean that, Isabel."

"You're not mad?"

"How could I be?"

I almost swooned at his kindness. My hero, ready to forgive and forget!

"I still don't get why he—or whoever—wrote the word *murderer* on the wall," Cassidy interjected. "That's the last thing we do around here.

We're in the business of saving lives, after all."

"Murderer?" Creases formed in Isabel's brow. "That's weird. Why would he say that?"

"I don't know," Cassidy countered. "But it really irritates me. It's one thing to vandalize a building, another thing to make an accusation like that. And that's what it is, a full-out accusation. I sure hope no one saw it."

"The alarm went off at some point," Tyler explained. "So, I doubt anyone happened by in the dark to see anything."

"What about the cameras?" I asked. "Did you check, Tyler?"

"Yep." He nodded. "They were working fine until around nine o'clock. I could see a shadowy figure with some sort of hoodie and white ski mask on, then everything went black."

"Anything special about the ski mask?" Parker asked.

Tyler's gaze narrowed and he appeared to be thinking. "It was white with some kind of stripes on it."

"Do you think he—or she—taped over the camera?" I asked. "I saw that in a movie once. Bad guys do things like that when they don't want to be seen."

"Probably. I'll go back and watch it more carefully when things settle down. But whoever did this came in with a plan and executed it flawlessly, so we're looking at someone with really bad motivations, not just a random last-minute decision on someone's part."

"It was Matt. I'm telling you." At this proclamation, Isabel started crying all over again.

In the middle of the weeping, the clinic's phone began to ring. Cassidy was busy with a broom and dustpan in hand, so I raced over to grab it before it went to our service. I answered with the words, "Lone Star Veterinary Services!" and was startled to hear Officer Dennison's voice on the other end of the phone.

"Miss Evans?"

"Yes?"

"Officer Dennison. Glad you picked up. I just wanted to tell you, we've located your car."

CHAPTER FIVE

I could hardly believe my ears. Unbridled joy flooded over me at the proclamation, "Wait, you found it? Really?" Hallelujah!

"Yep," he explained. "Turns out, it wasn't stolen at all. Apparently, someone called it in as an abandoned vehicle on the side of the road, so a city wrecker towed it to an impound lot. I thought you might want the number to contact them in the morning."

"Oh, I see." Ugh. "It wasn't abandoned. Not exactly."

"I understand, but it's been towed and marked as such, regardless."

That explained some of the highway noise Cassidy heard, anyway. I felt a lump in my throat as I posed the next question. "What about our purses and the rest of our stuff?"

"Everything was in the car, just like you said. The wrecker driver says he didn't touch a thing except the keys. Oh, and he told me to thank the ladies for leaving them on the dash in the unlocked vehicle. Made his job much easier. He was grateful for that."

Good grief.

Officer Dennison chuckled. "Hey, when I got home I told my wife the whole story about the sewer and the dog rescue and all."

"Drainage pipe."

"She didn't quite believe me. But she wants to see pictures of the dog after you get him cleaned up."

"Oh? She's a dog lover too?"

"If we're being honest, I'm the one who wants to see the pictures. She tolerates dogs, but I love them. Can you text them to me? Just use the number I'm calling you from. This is my cell."

"Wait, you really want me to text pictures of the dog?" I perked up at this news. "Do you think you might be interested in him, if we can't track down the owner? He's not microchipped, by the way. We checked."

"Sure. I have a heart. I love animals. And once you and your Aunt Trina start that animal rescue organization, let me know. I'd like to donate."

"So, you believe she's my aunt, now?"

He chuckled, and I could almost envision the look on his face. "After I told my wife about your claims, she looked it up on the web. You can find out just about anything you want from the internet. I had no idea Trina was from Brenham. I've only been here a couple years, myself. Transplant from Austin. But, apparently your story checked out. You even look a little bit like her."

"You think? She's got all of that gorgeous hair and I'm just so—" I wanted to say plain, but he cut me off.

"Yeah, you've both got freckles."

Gee, that's all he noticed about me? Most people commented on my natural platinum locks, but maybe—being covered in ditch water and all—he obviously hadn't noticed my hair.

I glanced across the room and noticed Parker had started mopping. He must've given up on me. Or, he just wanted to help Cassidy out.

"Trina was born and raised here," I explained. "She just left for Nashville a few years back. Ripped my grandma's heart out."

"Yes, that checked out. She wrote a song about your grandma."

" 'Don't Mess with Mama'." I chuckled. "It may or may not be rooted in actual truth. My grandmother can be a little. . .testy."

"Well, this is the South. Anyway, I figured the rest of your story must be true."

"It's good to be believed."

"Yeah, sorry it took me a while. Strange circumstances. I actually thought you were homeless. Anyway, your car's at an impound lot and you can't get it until morning. And I think there will be a fee of some sort to pay the wrecker driver, so be prepared for that."

"Okay." I prayed it wouldn't be much. "Thanks again for everything."

"You're welcome. Sorry I doubted you. It's the nature of my job. And hey, I wasn't kidding about that dog. I might try to talk my wife into adopting him. Wouldn't that make a great story, to be able to say that I played a role in rescuing him from the sewer line?"

I sighed.

"He's kind of a cute little thing. So, keep us in the loop."

"Um, sure. I'll keep you in the loop. Hopefully it'll work out."

"Hope so. Fingers crossed."

We ended the call, and I put the phone back on the hook, but not before jotting down the number that had come through with it. Now, to formulate a plan. I turned to face the group but directed my words at my good friend. "Parker, can I ask a favor?"

He stopped mopping to glance my way. "Sure, what's up?"

"They found my car. It's at an impound lot just a couple miles away. I'll need to get it in the morning, along with my purse and phone and Cassidy's things. Is there any chance you could—"

"I'll pick you up bright and early. We'll stop off on our way in to work."

"Parker to the rescue!" Cassidy said. "Once again. If you go on rescuing folks, Parker, you can start your own 501c3. You can call it Second Chance People Rescue. You can pluck us up out of the gutters of life and help us walk the straight and narrow."

"Hey, that's kind of what I already do." He shrugged. "With the ministry I'm involved in, I mean."

"You're in a ministry?" This was news to me.

"Yeah, we go into Houston once a month to a rough area where we feed the homeless and hand out clothes and stuff. There's usually worship and some sort of message. It's been pretty life-changing. I could tell you all kinds of stories, but not tonight." He wrung out the mop and put it back in the bucket.

"Wow." I had no idea. So, he really was in the rescue business.

I thought about what he'd said as he drove Beau Jangles and me to my place. Then again, as he used my spare key to open the door of my apartment. When I stepped inside, I felt a wave of relief wash over me. It felt so good to be home.

Apparently the dog liked my place too. He tugged at the leash, ready to investigate, but I wasn't ready to let go of him just yet. No telling if he was housebroken or not, after all.

"You gonna be okay?" Parker asked.

I nodded and yawned. "Mm-hmm."

"Okay. If you're not—if you need anything at all—just. . ." He paused. "I guess you can't exactly call me, can you?"

"I can go to my neighbor's and use their phone if it's a true emergency. But the only emergency at the moment is that I need to use the bathroom."

"Okay then." With a nod of his head, he accepted that bit of information. "I'll just head back up to the clinic to pick up Cassidy, and I'll see you bright and early to go get your car and the rest of your stuff."

"How early do you think? I'm not sure when the lot opens."

"Tyler told me that he's pushing back the first surgery until nine thirty. So, sleep. I'll pick you up at eight fifteen and take you to get your car."

"I can't thank you enough, Parker. For everything. Coming to my rescue like you always do, being willing to make sure I made it home okay. I'm super-grateful. I'm just so glad you had my key." I released a yawn.

He passed the key to me and then gazed at me with compassion in his eyes. "Of course, Mari. I'm always here for you. I hope you know that."

As I gazed into those concerned blue eyes of his, I felt the weight of his words. He meant them, from the heart. Man, this guy was great, wasn't he? Kind of like the big brother I never had. Someone to watch over me. He glanced in the direction of my sofa and smiled. "Hey, love the new sofa."

"Really? You like the color?"

"Yeah, I really do."

"Interesting."

As soon as he left, I realized the dog was probably starving. I didn't have any dog food on hand, but I did have plenty of lunch meat, so the pup got a few nibbles of that. And a slice of cheese. He seemed thrilled beyond belief at both.

After getting him settled onto an older blanket on my bedroom floor, I took the world's fastest shower, jumped into some pajamas, and headed to bed.

I found the contented pup curled up at the foot of my bed, his stinky fur nestled against my pretty cream-colored blanket. Oh well, it would wash. I hated to move the little guy, especially after the day he'd had. He had that comfortable snore that said, "Please leave me alone."

So I did. I settled into the bed and glanced at my clock. Almost one in the morning. Ugh. What a day.

When my alarm went off six hours later, I groaned. It didn't seem fair, to have to wake up so soon after falling asleep, but what choice did I have? I pushed back the covers and swung my legs over the side of the bed, ready to face the day. Only, I felt completely out of whack. Every muscle ached. Every joint felt locked up. And what was up with that weird smell?

It took a moment to figure that last one out. Then I saw the matted little pooch, snoring at the foot of my bed. Oh, right. Beau Jangles. I gave him a pat on the head and prayed he would wait until I'd dressed to go outside to do his morning business.

I rushed through my routine, knowing Parker would be here soon. When he arrived at ten minutes till eight, I met him at the door with wet hair and mismatched shoes.

He glanced down, laughed, and then turned his gaze on me. "I brought a collar and a better leash for Beau."

"Aw, you called him by his name."

"Of course." He knelt down and fastened on the collar, then attached the leash. "Has he been outside yet?"

"I was just about to take him. I had planned to use the lead, but this is much better."

"Yeah, safer. I'll take him out while you dry your hair."

"I'm drying my hair?"

He nodded and then took off out the door.

So, I dried my hair and touched up my lipstick. When he got back I realized the collar and leash were a matched set. "Oh wow. Those are so cute, Parker." I had to smile when I saw the cute tropical design. Parker knew how much I loved the ocean. Did he make an early morning run to the store to buy them? If so, I really owed him!

"Yeah." His nose wrinkled. "I bought them for Watson a while back. Had planned to give them to you for Christmas this year."

"Oh, Parker. Really?" I felt the sting of tears. To think he'd planned something like that made me a little weepy. Or maybe the tears were just from the pain I was currently experiencing in every joint and ligament.

"Yes." He plopped down onto my sofa, looking very much at home there. "But after he passed away, I wasn't sure what to do with them. Now I see they were meant for Beau all along. I hope you like them."

"I do." I flashed a warm smile in his direction. Parker really was a great friend, wasn't he? The very best.

But I still had one friend-test left for him.

"Hey, Parker."

"Yeah?"

"What do you think of my breakfast table?"

He glanced over at it and shrugged. "What about it?"

"Do you think I should paint it?"

"Paint over that beautiful cherrywood? Are you kidding?"

Okay then.

We spent the next few minutes driving to the impound lot where I paid the $175 fee. After hearing about my work with the dog, the lot owner cut that fee in half. Turned out, he was a dog lover. And I was beyond thrilled when he handed over my belongings—my purse, phone, and sweater, along with Cassidy's purse and keys.

Finally. I felt like I could breathe normally again. Strange, how being without my personal belongings had made me feel so off-kilter.

Now, with my struggles finally over, I could move forward with my day, putting all my angst behind me.

I hoped.

CHAPTER SIX

A s we left the impound lot, I thanked Parker profusely. He did that thing he always did when I praised him—looked completely and totally embarrassed. And even more when I threw my arms around his neck and gave him a big hug.

Not that he argued about the hug. Was it my imagination or did he hold onto me a little longer than I would've expected? Weird.

Afterward, I got behind the wheel of my own vehicle to drive to the office. I arrived at 8:40 and my heart went to my throat as I saw—in broad daylight—the boarded windows across the front of the building. The scene ripped my heart out. Hopefully it wouldn't be long before the glass could be replaced.

I buzzed inside and went straight to the reception area, where I found Cassidy in a tizzy.

"I don't know how much work one girl can do!" she exclaimed. "This morning has been nuts."

"Sorry I'm late. What did I miss?"

"The glass repair guy came." She gestured with her hand to the windows. Er, what used to be windows. "He's boarded everything up, as you see."

"How long before we get new windows?"

"A few days." She shrugged. "If we're lucky. They might be on back order. But here's the scary part, Mari. He said whoever did this knew what they were doing. The rocks were thrown at the bottom corner of the windows. He said that's significant because the glass shatters in a different way when it's hit in a vulnerable spot like that."

"Whoa."

"That's exactly what I said." Her eyes widened. "It's a special kind of glass. I didn't really understand it all. But apparently, to get it to fall like that you would have to throw with a lot of force, straight at the bottom of the glass. They hit in the corner, which caused the rest of the window to fall straight down the way that it did. So, yeah. . .definitely someone with some skills."

"And a cute white ski mask with stripes," I added.

"And a roll of duct tape to cover the camera."

It creeped me out to realize that whoever had done this was actually skilled in the art of window-breaking. Would he—or she—come back? I prayed not. If it really was Matt Foster, we'd have to be on our guard, come up with some sort of a plan if he showed up again.

I got Beau settled into a crate in the boarding area and went about my usual morning routine. I had a break around 9:20 and decided to spend a few minutes scouring the web pages of our local shelter to see if anyone was looking for a missing dog in Beau Jangle's size. I found nothing. At least that freed me up to begin looking for a new home for him. Perhaps Officer Dennison would end up being Beau's adopter. How cool would that be? It would make for a great story, as he said.

Story. Maybe I should contact the local paper. They always loved feel-good stories.

Still not convinced about the lack of a current owner, I turned my attention to a couple of local rescues, but no one knew anything about him. Then I checked with the paper, to see if any ads had been placed for a missing dog that looked like Beau. I even asked my friends to post in their neighborhood groups.

If this little guy had an owner, we would find him. Of course, figuring out what he really looked like was key, and that would require a bath and a solid grooming. No telling what we were looking at under all that matted hair. And if he didn't have an owner, then I would call Officer Dennison.

I stopped by the grooming room to see if Isabel had time to add my pooch to her lineup. She agreed to take care of him by midmorning, and I offered her my profuse thanks. I couldn't wait to see how my matted little fellow would shape up.

At 9:30 I assisted Dr. Tyler in surgery—first, a terrier with a dental extraction and then—after adjusting the table to accommodate a larger dog—a pit bull with a hernia repair. As he worked, I shifted the light overhead so that Tyler could see his patient more clearly. Anything I could do to help. And it didn't hurt that the light put Mr. Tall, Kind, and Swoon-Worthy directly in my line of sight.

After the pit bull, I assisted Dr. Kristin with a spay, followed by another dental, this one more simplistic than the first. By the time we finished, it was well after noon. I was exhausted but anxious to see how Beau's grooming turned out.

I gasped when Isabel brought my gorgeous boy into the lunchroom for the big reveal.

"What? No way!" Standing before me was the most gorgeous Cavalier King Charles Spaniel I had ever seen—tricolored with touches of black and brown around the eyes, intermingled with white across the rest of his body. I couldn't believe my eyes. This guy was a knockout!

Obviously, the others couldn't quite take it in either. Within seconds the room filled with my coworkers, who greeted the pup with squeals and words of glee.

"I knew he was a spaniel!" Kristin exclaimed. "The shape of the head was a dead giveaway." She turned my way. "And the docked tail was a clue too. Mari, this is an expensive dog. Purebred, I'm sure."

"Right?" I felt my eyes bugging. Who would have guessed it? This little gem was probably worth a couple thousand dollars. Maybe more. Surely someone out there was looking for him. Pedigree dogs didn't just roam the streets unless there was some sort of backstory. Hopefully we'd figure it out sooner rather than later.

"Are we sure he's not chipped?" I asked.

"I checked again," Isabel explained. "Once I realized we were looking at a dog with such a high-dollar value, I figured someone must be on the prowl for him. But there's no chip."

"And I've checked every shelter, every one of our usual sources," Cassidy added. "I can't find anyone searching for him."

"And he's super thin," Kristin observed. "Which tells me he's been on his own for a while now."

"He's fifteen pounds," Isabel said. "I weighed him."

"He could stand to be a couple pounds more than that." Kristin folded her arms at her chest and observed the dog jumping up and down. "But he appears to be in pretty good shape, all things considered. And his dance moves are stellar. No one can argue that point."

I couldn't help but laugh. She was right. He had the cutest little moves, pouncing up and down, then circling her like a buzzard.

Kristin knelt down and gave him a kiss on the head. "I'll give him a thorough examination and make sure he's had his shots. I think I've got an opening at two o'clock, Mari. Let's get it done then and go from there."

"Thanks."

See there? Working as a team we really could take care of Brenham's lost dogs.

Still, I couldn't quite get past the notion that someone might be missing this sweet top-of-the-line boy. Was someone pining for him, even now? That notion broke my heart.

After my lunch break, I decided to take Beau out for a walk in the fenced-in yard behind the facility. We often walked dogs here, especially those we boarded. I'd always loved the space, which was nestled between the back wall of our clinic and the tax office on the property behind ours. Before heading out I stopped off at the front desk to let Cassidy know my plans.

"You're brave to go out there." She shivered. "I had a terrible run-in with Beckett a couple weeks ago."

I cringed as she mentioned the name of the CPA whose property butted up to ours. This wasn't the first time we'd had a run-in with Wayland Beckett. The snarky businessman had a long-running history with our clinic. But, hey? Was it our fault we happened to build on the lot directly behind his place of business? We were zoned for animals. He needed to chill.

"I still haven't recovered from that tongue-lashing he gave us a couple weeks ago." Cassidy looked my way, bug-eyed. "Were you in the lobby when he came by to tear me up?"

"No, but I heard him through the door. He was loud. And I wasn't a fan of his language."

"Hey, it's not our fault a client let her dog loose on his property. They hadn't even made it into the clinic yet when it happened."

"What happened, exactly?"

"The dog went tearing across the side yard and straight onto the back of Beckett's property. I guess he started digging or something? I don't know. I didn't see it. I just know that he flipped out on me and said he was going to call the cops if it happened again, so watch Beau closely."

"We'll stay in the chain-link fence," I assured her. "No worries."

I led the pup out to the yard and unhooked his leash once we were safely inside the fenced area. I couldn't help but laugh as Beau Jangles ran with reckless abandon around the yard in silly circles. Apparently he enjoyed being rid of the matted fur. Round and round he went, enjoying the warmth of the sun overhead. He started a crazy yapping routine, and I ended up chasing him around the yard, enthused by his joy. He let out another bark, and I laughed as I watched him jump up and down like a yo-yo.

This precious boy was so much fun. I loved his enthusiasm and the sound of his adorable little yap-yap-yap. How sweet was that?

I knelt down in the grass next to him to give him some undivided attention. From this angle I could take in every detail of his gorgeous spaniel face. Quite a contrast from the dog I'd seen through the glow of my cap light in the pipe last night. Oh, no! The cap light! And the catch pole. I needed to go back to get them.

Or not. Maybe I'd seen enough of that drainage pipe for a while.

Regardless, the boy standing in front of me was show dog material. His coat was silky and smooth with the tiniest bit of wave to it. I loved the tricolored look—black, brown, and white—like a beagle. Only, the proportionally square body was definitely all spaniel. There was no denying that now. And the tiny docked tail wagged nonstop. Talk about a lovebug!

"You're just the cutest thing ever!" I said, and then wrapped my arms around his neck.

He went into a crazy fit of hyperactivity, running around the yard and barking at a squirrel in a tree on the corner nearest the business behind us.

A couple of minutes later, Mr. Beckett appeared opposite the chain-link fence. Creases lined his forehead, and his jaw was tight as he approached. Uh-oh.

"What is wrong with that dog?" He jabbed a finger in Beau Jangles' direction.

"Oh, I'm so sorry. Is he bothering you?"

"I'm trying to meet with a client, but all I can hear is the eternal yapping. It's distracting. I've told you people that the noise has to stop, especially when I'm with clients. Are you trying to destroy my business?"

Wait. . .you people?

Be gracious, Mari. You'll catch more flies with honey.

"I'm sorry, Mr. Beckett. Beau Jangles is brand-new and he's acclimating to the place."

"A new dog?" The man groaned. "I hope you're not saying that this one's going to stick around. You're just boarding him like the others, right?"

"Actually, I rescued him last night from a drainage pipe. But don't you think he's cute? He's a spaniel. Cavalier King Charles. They're worth a lot of money."

"I don't care how much he's worth. He's costing me money right now. I can barely hear myself think, for all the yapping."

Seriously? Was it really that bad? Ugh.

"I'm trying to run a business over here. I don't know how many times

I have to tell that boss of yours before someone finally takes me seriously. I've been on this corner lot for thirty-two years. And everything was just fine until you people. . ." He waggled a finger in my direction. "Until you people moved in and took over with the nonstop noise. And the traffic! I can't even get into my own driveway because your customers block me."

Who was he to talk? The man's parking lot was overflowing most days.

"We've asked them not to do that," I explained. "And as for this dog, he's probably not going to be here long. We'll find a home for him or locate his original owner. He was lost and alone in the drainage pipe."

"Should've left him there. Would've made my life easier."

Ouch.

"Thanks for checking on us," I managed. "Very neighborly of you. Poor little Beau Jangles has been living on his own for so long he has no social graces. But he'll get there, with help from people like you and me. I'm Marigold, by the way. And you are. . . ?"

"Tired of saying the same thing repeatedly." The older man glared at me. "So, don't make me—"

"Now, don't you fret over us making any more noise. I'm going to take him in now, I promise. We'll be as quiet as church mice over here."

"Sure you will. Sure you will." He walked back into his office, and I snagged Beau Jangles, giving him a gentle scratch behind the ears. I couldn't get away from Beckett soon enough. Ugh.

I'd just headed back into the boarding area to crate him when my cell phone buzzed. I was puzzled to see Cassidy's name on the screen. I picked up right away.

"Hey, Cassidy!" I shifted the phone to my other ear. "What's up?"

"I'm in Victoria's office."

"Still playing office manager?"

"No. I had to get out of the reception area in a hurry. Are you still out in the yard?"

"Just wrapping up. Girl! I had a little run-in with Old Man Beckett." I groaned. "You don't want to know. But what do you mean? Why did you have to get out of the reception area? What's happening?"

"Mari, get in here. You're missing all the action."

"Like what?"

"A truck just pulled up in the parking lot."

"Oh?"

"Um, yeah. It's Matt Foster. Isabel's ex."

CHAPTER SEVEN

A shiver ran down my spine at the mention of Matt Foster's name. "Cassidy, call the police."

"I need to tell Tyler first, to make sure he agrees we need to go that far," she said. "He's in with a client so I'm waiting it out in here."

"Skip that. Just call the police. I'm coming out to lock the front door. Don't move from where you are. Promise you'll call them. Now."

"O—okay."

I raced into the lobby and barreled past her, slipping past the plethora of clients and easing my way toward the front door, which I locked at once.

My heart rate picked up as I glanced through the only plate glass windows that weren't boarded up. Matt Foster's truck sat in the front spot, pointed straight at the windows, and I could see him glaring at me as I looked his way. Oh boy. I ushered up a prayer that God would protect us, then made my way back over to the reception desk and tried to think of what to do.

Cassidy looked downright panicked as she reached for the phone.

"Stay calm," I instructed with a forced smile. "We don't want to alarm our clients."

"You don't understand, Mari. This is the last thing I needed today. While you guys were in surgery this morning I was on the phone with

Maggie Jamison. She's threatening to hire an attorney to file a lawsuit against Kristin. And she's totally serious."

"What?"

"Yeah, she was very worked up. I did my best to calm her down, but I don't think it worked."

"Did you tell Kristin yet?" I asked.

Cassidy shook her heard. "I haven't had the nerve, but it's all about to blow up. And now *this* happens?" She gestured to the parking lot. "I picked a terrible week to play office manager."

"Good point. But stay calm."

"How can I? Ugh! I'm ready to call Victoria and tell her she has to come back." Cassidy's brow knitted.

"No way. I wouldn't want to bring her or that sweet new baby into the mix. Can you imagine? Things are scary enough already."

"True. And this jerk showing up right here?" She pointed to the window. "It's the last thing I needed."

"It's the last thing *any* of us needed."

Off in the distance I heard the distinct sound of an engine revving, and I wondered if Matt would come crashing through the windows and into the lobby. Maybe we should all vamoose.

Isabel came racing from the grooming room, covered in dog hair. "Is that—" She peered out of the window. "Oh no!"

"Okay, I've waited long enough." Cassidy reached for the phone. "I'm calling the cops right now. I can't wait for Tyler to finish up."

Hello. Didn't I already say that, along with "Call them now!"

She dialed 911, and we all waited with bated breath as the officer on the other end of the line said he would send someone right away.

Cassidy put her hand over the receiver and whispered, "He said to get everyone to a safe space but not to alarm anyone. How are we supposed to do that?"

Good question. I glanced around the room and assessed the crowd. Three humans, two dogs, one cat.

"I'll call them into examining rooms, like it's an ordinary day," I said, doing my best to keep my voice steady and calm. "They'll never know."

I quickly put a plan into action, and with Parker's help we ushered the clients in their respective rooms lickety-split. A couple of them were curious about the noise coming from outside and one had a lot of questions about the goings-on last night. She confronted me about it as soon as I had her settled in the farthest examining room near the back of the building.

"Your poor windows! Looks like a tornado blew through."

That might've been easier, I wanted to say, but didn't.

She gripped her little Yorkie-Poo like a security blanket. "I heard you had a break-in?"

"Yes."

"Any idea who did it?" She stroked her pup's head and he responded by nuzzling into her.

The engine revved once more, followed by the repetitive honking of a horn.

"Um, maybe."

"Should I be worried?" Her eyes bugged.

Um, maybe.

Only, I didn't say so. Instead, I clung to my phone and prayed Tyler would take control of the situation.

A text came through from my grandmother, something about pies. I texted back with a quick, PLEASE PRAY. IN THE MIDDLE OF AN INCIDENT.

This began a barrage of messages from her, demanding more information from me. Unfortunately, I wasn't able to comply with her demands right now, what with my friend's angry ex-boyfriend in the parking lot and the Yorkie-Poo, who had taken to barking at the noise. That certainly wasn't helping anything.

Minutes later I heard pounding on the front door, followed by yelling. Safely tucked in this tiny room with my anxious client, I wondered if Matt would come busting through the door of the clinic and attack us all. I reached to lock the exam room door, just in case.

"Okay, now I'm really worried," the woman said. "What aren't you telling me?"

I gave her a quick rundown and she backed herself against the wall with a quiet, "Oh, help."

Exactly.

Fortunately, the banging on the door was the police. I peeked out of the exam room and saw that the officer was talking to Tyler at the front door. I stepped out into the lobby and noticed Cassidy was missing. She must be back in Victoria's office, hiding out. I didn't blame her.

Tyler turned to face me. "They've got things under control now, Mari. But I'd stay in there, just in case."

"Are they going to arrest him?"

"Looks like it. They've got him cuffed."

"Good. They need to lock him up and throw away the key."

I went back into the exam room and made small talk with the client about our unusually cool weather, then heard the sound of a car engine.

Tyler knocked on the exam room door, and I opened it and stepped into the lobby.

"Well?" I asked.

"It's okay now," he said. "They got him."

At this point everyone flooded into the lobby, clients and employees alike. We were all talking on top of each other, but Isabel's woes carried the weight of the conversation.

"Everything's all right," Tyler explained, a forced calm lacing his words. "They've taken him in."

I had to give it to him. Tyler had a great "We're going to be just fine" vibe going on. Just one more thing to admire about him.

"Is Matt the one who—" I pointed to the boarded-up windows. "You know?"

"That didn't come up in conversation, but likely. He's in custody now, so they'll take care of it and let us know." Tyler spoke to the clients now, urging them to return to their various exam rooms. Then he gathered the staff for a quick pow wow behind the counter, far from listening ears.

"Y'all, we need a plan for days like this. I can't believe I'm saying this, but we've got to have a strategy for break-ins and other threats, and we need to figure it out ASAP."

A shiver ran down my spine as I thought about his words. I didn't take a "How to ward off an attack" class in vet tech school. I wasn't psychologically or physically prepared.

The clients were skittish too. Hopefully this wouldn't be enough to put them off. There were other vets in town, after all. Probably with less drama. And less broken glass on the floor. We were still sweeping up pieces of it.

We spent the next several minutes doing our best to calm things down. I managed to get the Yorkie-Poo's nails clipped and anal glands expressed. Not fun. Then, with Parker's help, I got Mrs. Miller's crazy Rottweiler under control. He was moderately aggressive on a good day, but with the current goings-on, the over-the-top pooch responded to everything with teeth bared. And it was his teeth we needed to deal with today. The pooch was one of our few clients in braces.

Somehow, Tyler still managed an exam of the crazy pooch. How the man kept himself steady with all the chaos swirling, I would never know. But he did.

So did Parker, who took charge of the Rottweiler like he was a cuddly Golden Retriever pup.

When the police left we somehow settled back into a routine, though Cassidy decided to lock the front door of the building, only opening it when a client arrived.

"Hey, it's safer this way," she explained.

Tyler wasn't keen on the idea, but with current circumstances being what they were, he didn't argue, at least not for long. Okay, so he did mutter a quick, "Matt's been arrested, right?" But Cassidy would not be persuaded.

I didn't really blame her. We still didn't have proof that Matt was the one who'd vandalized the building last night. Sure, he looked like the most logical candidate at the moment, but looks could be deceiving.

At some point, when things settled down, Cassidy shared the news with Tyler and Kristin about Maggie Jamison's lawsuit.

"You don't really think she's going to carry through, do you?" Kristin asked. "That would be horrible, Ty. I'm so sorry!"

"I don't think she stands a chance," Tyler interjected. "No court is going to side with her, since she turned down our treatment options. It's not our fault her dog didn't make it."

"Are you saying it was her fault?" I asked.

He shook his head. "No, I'm saying we're looking at a thirteen-year-old dog with uncontrolled diabetes. I doubt his spleen would have lasted much longer, even with all the meds we'd recommended. We truly did everything we could, but the dog was too far gone when we took him on as a client. We've only been in business six months, remember? He's been sick a lot longer than that." Tyler paused, and I could see the concern in his eyes.

"What is it?" I asked. "What aren't you saying?"

"Well. . ." He released a sigh. "I finally went back through the camera footage and saw something that concerned me. I wasn't sure if I should mention it."

Kristin turned his way, her brow wrinkled. "What did you see?"

He released a slow breath. "Right after we closed last night, Maggie stopped by. Must've been less than an hour before the windows were broken."

"Are you sure it was her?" I couldn't imagine she could be capable of such a thing.

"Yep, she came to the door and tried to open it, but we had just closed. Then she stood outside for a while on her cell phone. Making a call."

"Ugh. Probably to her attorney." Kristin pinched her eyes shut. "Do you think she—"

Tyler shrugged. "I can't even believe I'm entertaining the possibility, but she's on the short list."

We wrapped up the conversation and got back to work, though my nerves were shot. We somehow finished up the day without further incident. I was so happy to get into my car to head home. Beau Jangles seemed happy too. He jumped into my lap as soon as I took my spot behind the wheel.

"Oh no you don't, boy." I nudged him to the passenger seat. If we kept up this car-riding routine, I'd have to invest in one of those car seats for dogs.

Not that I was keeping him, of course. But, just in case I ended up fostering for any length of time.

I stopped off for some fast food on the way home. Just as I got into line to order my double cheeseburger and jumbo fries, my cell phone rang. Grandma Peach.

I started to avoid the call, but then I remembered what happened the last time I'd done that. Oh boy. It took weeks to get past that guilt trip.

So, I answered with a chipper, "Grandma Peach."

"What's this I hear about you being arrested?"

"Oh, I wasn't arrested, Grandma, I promise. I was just in a drainage pipe trying to rescue a dog when the police officer misunderstood."

"Oh, you rescued a dog?" Her tone changed at once, from worry to curiosity. "What breed?"

"You're never gonna believe it, Grandma. He's a purebred Cavalier King Charles Spaniel." I couldn't help myself. I reached over to pet Beau Jangles on the head. He seemed to know I was talking about him and licked my hand. My goodness, but this little boy was a doll, wasn't he? I could fall in love with him, right here and now.

Grandma let out a little whistle. "No way. Those sell for over two thousand dollars."

"I know."

"He's got to have an owner out there somewhere."

"Likely, but he's not chipped. We're putting a notice in the paper tomorrow, and we've put a flyer on the wall in the lobby at the clinic. We've also been checking the local shelters to see if they've got any leads. Without a chip or any tags, it's hard to tell."

"People should take better care of their animals," she said.

"Agreed."

"Was that handsome young doctor with you when you caught him?"

"Tyler? No."

She clucked her tongue. "I don't mean Tyler. I mean the other one, with the really pretty blue eyes. The one who's always saving your bacon."

"Saving my bacon?"

"Yeah, like that time your car broke down on the side of the road and he drove over to help you out. And then, didn't he help you move?"

"Ah, you mean Parker."

"Yes, Parker." His name practically danced off her tongue. "Such a kind young man."

"Right, he's super nice. But he's not a doctor. He's a tech, just like me."

"Same thing." She paused. "You know, Marigold, I'm not getting any younger."

"O–okay." What did she mean by that?

"One of these days you're going to take a look at a nice young man like that and see him as something other than just friend or coworker material."

Oooh, so *that's* where she was going with that. I would have to put a stop to that notion, and the sooner, the better.

CHAPTER EIGHT

P arker's one of my best friends, Grandma," I explained.

"Exactly. Now, tell me more about this dog. What color?"

"Oh, he's a tricolored spaniel, so pretty! Black, brown, and white."

"No, what color should I make his Halloween costume? I need a new sewing project. What about a hot dog? That's always a cute Halloween costume for a dog, though it might be a bit overdone."

"I appreciate it, but he's not a wiener dog. And since when do you make dog costumes?"

"Since Curtis Elban asked me to make a superhero cape for his Chihuahua, Tripod."

"Tripod?"

"Well, that's his new name, since the amputation. But, between us, I didn't think he looked very good in it. He's put on weight, by the way."

"Curtis?"

"No, the Chihuahua. He's really gotten fat since the surgery. But that doesn't surprise me. I've been taking a ton of pies over to Curtis since his wife died."

"The dog's wife died?"

"No, Curtis's wife died, smarty britches. Six months ago. I told you that when it happened. Don't you remember? I baked a pie for the funeral."

"You bake a pie for every funeral, Grandma." I slipped the car into drive and inched forward a couple of feet as the car in front of me moved forward in line.

"True." She laughed.

Though, something she'd said had raised my antennae. "But, now you're specifically baking pies for Curtis Elban. And his dog. Who, if I'm understanding correctly, is actually eating your pies." I slipped the car back into PARK.

"I can't prove it, but there's been a direct parallel. I've been feeding Curtis pie for six months, and Tripod has put on five pounds in that time. For that matter, Curtis has too. When we went to the fall festival at church on Saturday the buttons on his flannel shirt were threatening to pop."

"And yet you keep baking for him."

She sighed. "It's my way of ministering to others. From my kitchen, straight to the heart."

I had a feeling she was trying to get to Curtis's heart, all right. She was sure talking a lot about him lately. Did Grandma Peach have her eye on him as a potential love interest, perhaps?

The idea of my seventy-four-year-old grandmother dating someone gave me the willies, so I changed the subject. "I think a costume for Beau Jangles would be lovely, thank you. Anything you like. He's about fifteen pounds, so judge accordingly."

"Wait. . .Beau Jangles?" A ripple of laughter sounded from her end of the phone. "Like in the song?"

"Yep. Only, it's Beau. B-e-a-u."

"As in, the only 'beau' in your life right now?"

I skipped over that question and just kept going. "I don't know why, but he just looked like a Beau Jangles to me. He's got a lot of spring in his step. He does the cutest little dance-like-thing when he gets excited. He starts hopping up and down like a rabbit."

"A bunny rabbit costume, then?"

"Um, no."

"Okay then. I'll think of something cute to make for your beau. I'll surprise you. But we don't have to wait for Halloween for him to wear it.

You can show it off at the clinic. Maybe I'll get more customers that way."

"You're looking to make dog costumes as a business?" It didn't surprise me, really. Grandma Peach was always trying to turn a profit on her goods. Everything from pies to crafts. The woman made—and sold—it all. She'd probably end up with a booth at the local flea market. She spent more than her fair share of time there, anyway. Buying, not selling.

I peered out of the car window as the line of traffic inched forward once again. I was almost to the spot where I would need to order.

"Well, I would be remiss in not trying. A girl's gotta earn a living, you know."

She said things like this a lot, but I knew better. Trina sent money every month. Lots of money. Grandma didn't need to work. Her little house was paid off, and she was sitting on quite the nest egg.

Unless she'd baked it all into pies and given it to Curtis Elban.

"Besides, I've had years of experience sewing costumes for your Aunt Trina," she added. "I've sewed enough sequins to make Liberace green with envy."

"Who's Liberace?"

She groaned. "Now, what's this I heard about someone robbing the clinic? Is that what you were referring to when I texted you today? The big incident?"

"It wasn't a robbery, it was a—"

"I want you to know that I pray a hedge of protection around you every single day, Marigold."

"Oh, thank you."

"But if you're going to go climbing in drainage ditches, I'll have to up my prayers, maybe change the tone a bit."

"Well, I don't plan to make a habit of—"

"And if that clinic of yours turns out to be in a high crime area, I'll really have to kick it up a notch. I've always thought that particular corner of town was questionable."

"Why?"

"Because of that horrible Beckett fellow." She clucked her tongue.

"The man sends a shiver up my spine. You don't even want to know what he did in church one Sunday a few years back. Let's just say the congregation at First Presbyterian won't ever be the same."

That's what I got for attending a different church, I supposed. I'd never know what Wayland Beckett had done at First Prez.

"He's just plain mean," Grandma Peach added. "He's always been a harsh man, but we witnessed it firsthand that day."

"I agree that he's mean. He just about took my head off earlier. Ugh."

"Wouldn't be the first time." She clucked her tongue. "If I were a charismatic—which I most certainly am not—I would swear the man had a demon. My friend Hattie is full-gospel and she finds demons under every bush."

"There are plenty of them to be found, that's for sure."

"Well then, someone call for a priest, because this fella needs deliverance. He did a lot of damage to our little church back in the day. Almost brought it down, in fact. I've always said he could start an argument in an empty room. Did I mention he's mean?"

"You did." But, how did I not know this? I slipped the car back into drive and approached the microphone to order. Any second now I would need to pause the conversation.

"Yes. When he turns on you, he turns on you. He knows how to bring out the big guns, to cause real damage. And he's sly. You can't trust him as far as you can throw him."

"Wow." I had no idea.

"We tried to pray it through, as Hattie likes to call it, but that man's so mean even our prayers couldn't reach him."

I wasn't sure that comment was theologically sound, but didn't say so. If Grandma wanted to believe Wayland Beckett was beyond help, I wouldn't argue with her. The idea that he had such a deep backstory did make me plenty nervous, however. And I did wonder what he was up to over there in that office of his. He did a good business; that was sure and certain. His parking lot was nearly as full as ours. Few CPAs boasted a following like that.

There were so many questions I wanted to ask, but Grandma was on to the next topic before I could even ask.

Halfway into her dissertation about Wayland's penchant for lying, a voice came over the loudspeaker, welcoming me to the restaurant.

"What's that noise, Marigold?" Grandma Peach asked. "Sounds like you're with someone."

"Hang on a second, Grandma Peach." I put my hand over the phone and placed my order, then went back to the call as I waited in line.

"Marigold Evans, did you just order a double cheeseburger and fries?"

"Yes ma'am, I did. I've had kind of a stressful day, and I'm just drowning my sorrows in a cheeseburger."

"A double cheeseburger and fries."

"Yes ma'am. With pickles. Pickles are a vegetable, right?"

"Hardly. Fast food is toxic to your intestines and has absolutely no nutritional value whatsoever. How many times have we talked about this? If you're in need of a good meal, just let me know and I'll stock your fridge. I've got some yummy cabbage soup made and I just whipped up a batch of those homemade fiber balls. They'll keep you as regular as a clock. I can bring them over later this evening."

"No, that's okay, Grandma. Really. I'm fine for now."

"Well, all right, but remember—keeping your intestines healthy is key to a long life. And every cheeseburger you consume moves you in the opposite direction."

"I see." At least I was moving that way with a smile on my face.

"I have to let you go, honey. I've got a pie in the oven, and I can't let it burn."

"Wait, what kind of pie?" I asked.

"Apple, of course. It's October, Marigold."

Of course. How silly of me. I'd almost forgotten that Grandma themed her pies for her vast array of customers. She carefully strategized a plan to coordinate with the local ice cream factory, with their seasonal offerings. Next month it would be pumpkin pie, just in time for Thanksgiving. Then pecan, the month after. God forbid, I should ever ask for a peach pie in the fall. She'd probably go apoplectic on me.

As I eased my car forward in the line, she carried on about the benefits of fiber. I tuned her out, the whole conversation making me feel a little nauseous. Still, I had to give it to her for trying. It proved just how much she cared about me. A person would have to care, to fret over my health like that. And Grandma was nothing, if not a fretter. She could win awards for her fretting, in fact.

Not that I minded. Not one little bit. She played a pivotal role in my life, and I wouldn't change a thing—except maybe that green drink she forced me to chug down the last time I was at her house. I never wanted a repeat of that one.

But one thing was undeniable. Grandma Peach was the source of all wisdom. If I ever had a problem of any kind—be it health-related, relational, or spiritual, she knew just what to do.

I pulled up to the window and paid for my food, then took the bag that the teenage boy offered me.

"Do me a favor and don't go climbing into any more ditches unless you call me in advance." Grandma's stern words interrupted my thoughts. "That way I can contact the prayer chain, okay? When it comes to keeping you safe, I think we're gonna need backup."

"Okay, Grandma." I pulled into a spot and set the bag of food on the seat next to me then nestled my soda cup into the cup holder to my right. "And just for the record, it was a pipe, not a ditch. One of those great big ones. Only, it got narrower as it went along."

"Odd, I could've sworn Myrtle Mae said it was a ditch."

"Myrtle Mae Caldwell? How did she hear?"

"Well, from Estelle, of course. Estelle is Kennedy's aunt."

"Kennedy?"

"Yes, that sweet redheaded girl who works at the front desk at the vet clinic. The clumsy one."

Ah. Cassidy. I took a swig of my soda, then set the cup back down.

"The one who's up for office manager."

I almost choked on my soda. "Wait, who told you that? Has Victoria decided not to come back?"

"You didn't hear that from me," Grandma said. "But I know Kennedy will do a terrific job. She just needs to work on her people skills a little bit."

"She does?"

"Yes, she's always overreacting when I bring Hector in."

I cringed as Grandma mentioned Hector, her feisty tabby. There were very few animals on the planet that I would speak ill of, but that cat made the short list. I'd met mountain lions with a better temperament.

Grandma cleared her throat. "That reminds me, Hector is due for an appointment. I think I'd like to see that new vet. I'm not a huge fan of that one guy, the one you're always carrying on about."

"Tyler? Why not?"

"I don't believe he and Hector got along last time, and Hector is a good judge of people, so. . ."

"Grandma, to be fair, Tyler is still nursing the scratches from last time you brought Hector in."

"Let's try someone new."

"Fine. I'll have Cassidy set up an appointment for you with Kristin. She's the new vet."

"You do that." A dinging sounded in the background. "I've got to run, Marigold. The timer is going off. I want to get this pie over to Curtis while it's still warm. He likes 'em best that way."

"I see."

Only, I didn't. Not really. Was my grandmother just being neighborly, or did she have her eye on a certain Curtis Elban?

"You really need to call your Aunt Trina," Grandma interjected just as I prepared to say my goodbyes.

"Oh?"

"Yes, I think she's homesick. I'm working on getting her home for Christmas but need backup. Promise me you'll call her and talk her into coming, honey. Now, I'm not telling you to twist her arm or anything, but if she hears from both of us, maybe that baby girl of mine will finally get her tail back home where she belongs."

"Maybe." Though I doubted it.

"I'm not unrealistic," Grandma added. "I know that daughter of mine won't be the one plucking my chin hairs when I'm in the nursing home."

Okay then.

"That'll be you, honey bun. But I will want her to come home every now and again. A woman my age needs to see her family, and now that your Mama's gone. . ." She paused and I wondered if she was trying to keep from crying.

"I know, Grandma. I'll call her. I promise."

We ended the call and I settled back against the seat, ready to fill the empty spot in my stomach. Eating in the car wasn't exactly what I'd planned, but right now I just needed to get some food in me.

I reached to grab the bag and shoved my hand inside.

And came up empty.

My gaze shifted to the passenger seat. Beau Jangles licked his lips, then grabbed the empty bag from my hand and tore it to shreds, right in front of me.

Well, terrific.

CHAPTER NINE

On Wednesday I decided to slip over to the feed store to pick up dog food for Beau Jangles during my lunch break. I didn't want to say aloud what I'd been feeling in my gut for the past day or so, but this little guy was settling into my heart like he'd belonged there all along.

I'd taken to calling him the office mascot. Tyler didn't respond very well. His elderly cat, Aggie, held that honor, after all. The fourteen-year-old had been our mascot from the get-go. But Beau Jangles was giving Aggie a run for his money these days, stealing a lot of the attention from our clients, who couldn't seem to get enough of him.

I couldn't get enough of him either. Every moment I spent with the little doll tugged on my heartstrings a bit more. Even if he had eaten my double cheeseburger. Even if he had gotten into Cassidy's files and shredded a few. Even if he chewed my favorite socks and ate my tooth-brush. I couldn't blame him for that last one. I'd left it on the edge of the bathroom counter while I ran to grab my phone. Apparently he liked the minty toothpaste.

In short, I adored him. And while I had done my due diligence by placing an ad in the local paper and hanging flyers in the clinic lobby, everyone at Lone Star secretly prayed an owner wouldn't show up. We'd fallen in love with Beau, and he with us. And now that I thought—hoped—he was sticking around, I had decided to hold him even closer by giving him everything he needed to thrive.

And Bubba's Weed & Feed just happened to have a sale on my favorite brand of high-end dog food, which we'd run out of at the clinic. So, off I went on my lunch break, to purchase enough to get me through a few weeks.

Hopefully he'd still be around a few weeks from now, but if not I'd pass the food off to his owners.

I made the drive from the clinic—which was in town—to the feed store, which was a few miles away, just past Blinn College off Highway 290.

I thought about my quaint little town as I drove. I'd lived here all my life and loved every square inch of Brenham, from the ice cream factory to the old-fashioned storefronts downtown, to the tiny diner at our local airport. I loved the homes in the historic district, where Mama and I had lived for years. And I adored the boutiques and shops.

Mostly, though? I loved the people. We were Texans, through and through. . .and unapologetic about it. Country music blared from our radios and conservative bumper stickers trimmed out our vehicles. Local businesses waved the Stars and Stripes, of course, but the Texas flag hung nearby, as if to remind passers-through that we considered both of equal importance.

And we did.

There was a reason our state carried the "Don't Mess with Texas" motto. We dared anyone to try. As Cassidy was prone to say, we were a little bit country, a little bit hood. Okay, a lot hood.

I was feeling the country part as I tooddled down the highway toward Bubba's Weed & Feed that morning. I didn't often hang out at the feed store—though, there was that one infamous time I'd come with Grandma Peach to purchase a bottle of Mane and Tail—a horse shampoo that she swore made her hair the shiniest in town. I was only sixteen at the time and thought my elderly grandmother had lost her marbles. In the years since, I'd come to rethink my former position on Mane and Tail, having seen its benefits in my own life.

These days, though, I bought my hair products online. Or at Curl Up & Dye, our local hair salon. I'd left the horse products to the horses. And to the ladies like Grandma Peach, who found it hard to give up on a good thing once they'd found it. Did I mention we Texans were loyal?

This morning, as I pulled into the parking lot of the feed store, I couldn't help but notice that it was fuller than usual. That probably had something to do with the multiplicity of sales going on inside. Bubba knew how to throw a sale soiree, that was sure and certain. And, from the looks of things, I wasn't the only one taking advantage of his generosity. Half the town of Brenham had arrived, and boy, did they show up and show off.

You know you're in Texas when you pull into a parking lot and see nothing but pickup trucks. Ford F-150s and -250s dotted the perimeter, along with a handful of Dodge Rams. Wedged between them, a couple of Chevy Silverados, most all of these vehicles presenting in a dazzling display of red, white, and deep blue. We were a patriotic—if not predict-able—bunch of rednecks. And I couldn't be prouder.

Off in the distance a food truck boasted our local ice cream brand, Blue Bell. I'd grown up on the stuff. . .was weaned straight from Mama's milk to Blue Bell as a toddler. Same with everyone in Brenham. Ask any one of us about our heritage and we'd talk your ear off about three things—bluebonnets, Blue Bell, and BBQ. And we'd share about those things with as much pride as any Texan dared.

Maybe my stalwart spirit came from living in Washington County all my life. It was the birthplace of Texas, after all. The place where the Texas Declaration of Independence had been signed in 1836. We were a hearty, rebellious bunch, known for our tenacity and our ability to shovel down BBQ at record speed.

And, apparently, our discounts on manure by the yard, which Bubba's Weed & Feed boasted today. If I owned land, I'd be tempted. Though, I might've moved the manure display a little farther away from the ice cream truck.

Not that we worried about such things in our neck of the woods. Nope, we swallowed down the good with the bad, and all of it with smiles on our faces and country songs in our hearts.

Country songs.

My heart twisted inside of me as I thought about Aunt Trina. No doubt she was working on that next big hit for her upcoming album. My aunt seemed to be knocking them out, right and left, these days. But I wondered if she'd ever give up on crooning songs about broken hearts and come back here to help mend mine.

Since Mama died. . .

No, I wouldn't think about it. Not today. I had to focus on my little project. My Beau.

I bounded from my car with Beau Jangles at my side, carefully leashed. I knew from experience that he would bolt at the drop of a hat, so I'd need to keep a close eye on him. Still, I couldn't resist the notion that bringing him with me would be fun.

And boy, was it. We barely made it inside before the oohing and aahing began. First, a woman with a bag of fertilizer slung over her shoulder. She glanced down, let out a whistle, and said, "That'uns a beaut!"

I had to agree.

Then came the fellow with the missing teeth. He was pushing one of those jumbo carts loaded down with manure, and the smell was enough to knock a buzzard off a death wagon, as Grandma Peach liked to say. He froze in place when he saw Beau Jangles. A hint of moisture filled his eyes as he carried on about his dog Roy—a cocker spaniel—who had passed away a few years back, and how much Beau reminded him of "that sweet ole boy."

Before long I was telling this stranger the whole story about my passion to start a rescue organization, about how I was hoping and praying for a piece of property where I could build a proper facility to care for the animals. . .everything.

Decker agreed to pray and even scribbled down his phone number on his Bubba's receipt for me so we could keep in touch. I promised I'd let him know if we got any older dogs in need of a place to live out their final years. Maybe Decker and his wife Corabelle would end up fostering for me. Stranger things had happened, right?

By the time I got to the dog food aisle, I was completely overwhelmed with people fussing over Beau Jangles. And he didn't seem to mind the attention. He appeared to be a real crowd-pleaser, and easygoing with strangers, which was always nice. He didn't snap or snarl once.

After I loaded a couple of bags of food into my cart, I rounded the corner, landing on the horse supply aisle. Standing directly in front of me was a woman I recognized at once.

I'd seen her dozens of times before, but Maggie Jamison had never appeared as weathered or tired as she did now. The woman standing in front of me had that haggard appearance one would get after missing out on sleep. Lots of sleep. She'd never been one to pay much attention to hair and makeup, but the disheveled hair—grayer than her former auburn—was in need of a thorough washing. And the tattered cowboy hat, her signature look, had seen better days. What really threw me, however, was the torn, wrinkled T-shirt.

Maggie was a woman with money. Lots of money. In fact, she was probably one of the wealthiest women in the county, thanks to the success of her Double J ranch. But this woman standing in front of me today looked more like someone you'd see shopping the thrift aisle at the Dollar General.

Or, someone who might actually live in a drainage pipe.

Perhaps her husband's death had caused her to age prematurely. I knew she couldn't be much older than Mama had been, in her late fifties, at best. But, the dark circles under her eyes? The sagging around her mouth. Something had gone terribly wrong.

Maggie glanced my way and her brow wrinkled at once. I knew she recognized me. We'd spoken dozens of times over the past few months, after all. Jasper was a regular at the clinic. But, today? She scowled at me like I was some sort of demonic entity and then turned on her heels and bounded away like a horse barreling from the gate.

Okay then. So much for trying to smooth things over. Looked like I'd have to wait for another day to attempt that.

CHAPTER TEN

I purchased my dog food and then headed back to my car. Beau Jangles stopped at the curb to sniff the edge of the Blue Bell truck. I was tempted—my stomach still empty from skipping lunch—but I didn't give in.

Just as quickly, the sweet pup gravitated to the manure display. I tugged at his leash and urged him to keep going. We didn't need that scent in our lives, thank you very much.

Just as I reached the aisle where I'd parked my car, I saw Grandma Peach and Curtis Elban walking toward me. What in the world? What were they doing together at the feed store?

I looked back and forth between them. I'd known Curtis for years, but not well. He and his wife Ginger had been semipermanent fixtures at several of Grandma Peach's events over the years. Like her annual Fourth of July party and the big Christmas shindig.

But I'd never known Curtis apart from Ginger. Since her death earlier this year he'd been hanging around a lot more than usual. Seeing him here, in the parking lot of the feed store, side by side with my grandmother, I had to wonder what they were up to. This relationship had apparently moved to a new level. Was I the last to get the memo? She used to tell me everything.

One thing could be said about my grandmother today. . .she was definitely dressing to be noticed. She looked darling in her matching blouse and slacks, like a woman who was taking this dating experience seriously. Then again, her clothes were always as themed as her pies—appropriate for the season. So, maybe she hadn't dolled herself up to entice him.

Of course, there was the issue of the pink lipstick. She only pulled out the pink when she needed to call on the big guns.

Curtis needed to pick up some clothing cues from Grandma. He wore tattered jeans and a faded flannel button-up. Just as my grandmother had said, the buttons were threatening to pop across his extended belly. But, other than that, the man looked as pleased as punch to be leading my grandmother across the parking lot of the feed store, arm linked through hers.

"Grandma Peach?"

"Marigold!" Grandma Peach released her hold on Curtis's arm and extended her hands in my direction. I obliged by giving her a hug. Her gaze shifted down to the dog. "Oh, my stars and garters! This is the dog you were telling me about?"

"This is Beau Jangles."

"Your beau." She gave me a little wink, and I caught her double meaning. I was falling for him, so the point could not be argued.

She leaned down to pet him, and before long the dog was jumping up and down, loving the attention. Knowing the arthritis issue in my grandmother's back, I decided to make things easier on her. I picked the dog up and held him so she could fawn over him with ease.

"Oh, Marigold, he's just beautiful. You've got to bring him over to meet Hector."

Um, no thanks.

"You're bringing Hector in to the clinic soon, right?" I countered. "They can meet then."

"Yes." Her nose wrinkled. "But Hector always seems to be such a naughty boy at the clinic. I think it's the stress of the place. He knows he's about to get jabbed, so he tenses up."

"You're still working at that clinic?" Curtis asked.

"Of course. I hope to go on working there forever. I love my job."

"Your grandma brags on you day and night." He flashed a winning smile and won me over in an instant.

"Of course I do. She's a peach, this girl of mine." Grandma gave me a little wink and my heart melted. "Which is why I want to keep her around awhile. Which reminds me"—she fished around in her jumbo-sized purse and came out with a bottle of supplements—"I bought these for you."

"Oh?" I took the bottle she pressed into my hand.

"Yes, I bought them a couple of weeks back. Had planned to give them to you for Christmas, but after hearing about your cheeseburger incident, I decided not to wait."

"Thanks?" Should I tell her that I had a full bottle of them at home on my dresser? Nah, better not.

"Start on them right away," she instructed. "I've been taking them for months, and my intestines have never operated more smoothly."

Curtis cleared his throat.

I shoved the pills into my purse.

"How are things at the clinic?" Curtis asked.

"Typical morning." I shrugged. "I did a few blood draws, set up the surgical suite, induced vomiting for a German Shepherd who ate a chocolate bar, and sanitized some kennels."

"Oh my." Grandma's voice reflected her thoughts on all that. "Well, in that case, you'd better double up on those supplements, honey. You're coming in contact with more than your fair share of bacteria. Those pills are a natural antibiotic. None of that Big Pharma stuff with all of its side effects."

"You're jealous of my life, wishing we could trade places." I gave her a little wink.

She laughed. "There are times that I envy your ability to be doing something so productive with your life." She turned to face Curtis. "Have I told you that Marigold is starting a dog rescue?"

"Yes, you have." He flashed an admiring smile—though I couldn't tell if it was meant for her or me.

"Grandma Peach is a little prideful when it comes to the family."

"Pshaw." With the wave of a hand, she appeared to dismiss my accusation.

"Remember what you always taught me, Grandma," I said. "Swallowing your pride rarely leads to indigestion."

"Maybe I *am* a little prideful," she confessed. "But who can blame me? I mean, not every woman in Brenham has a country western star as a daughter and a superstar animal rescuer as a granddaughter." Just as quickly, the light faded from her eyes, and she seemed to disappear to a darker place. I knew she was thinking about Mama.

"Thank you for that," I said. "I'm pretty proud of you too. You're the best matriarch in town."

"Thank you." Grandma rested her hand on my arm. "You know, Marigold, I was awfully proud of your Mama too. She was a star in her own right. She did such a good job raising you after your daddy—" Grandma cleared her throat. "Anyway, she kept you fed and clothed, and in church on Sundays. Even if it wasn't First Prez. She was an amazing woman."

"Agreed."

"And you, my sweet girl, are just like her."

"I. . .I am?" I'd never heard my grandmother say anything like that before.

When she nodded, I burst into tears, right there in the parking lot of the Bubba's Weed & Feed.

Curtis's eyes widened, and before long he'd swept me into his arms in grandfatherly fashion.

"I'm so sorry," I said after I dried my tears. "It's been a rough few days, what with the break-in and the dog rescue and all. I think I'm just emotional."

"No doubt you're exhausted too." Curtis gave me a fatherly look. "You need some rest."

"And some good food. You come on over to my place soon, and I'll give you a proper meal." Grandma reached into her purse and brought out a bottle with some tiny white pills inside. "Pop one of these under your tongue, honey. It'll fix you right up. I'll tell you all about it later, maybe send you a brochure."

I didn't even bother asking what I was putting in my mouth. I just did as I was told and dissolved the pill under my tongue, hoping it wouldn't kill me.

"Can you take the rest of the day off?" Grandma shoved the bottle back into her purse. "We're headed to the rose emporium after this. Come with us."

"The rose emporium? In October?"

"Oh yes. They've got a sale on their Texas Pioneer roses. And then we're headed to the Blue Bell creamery for a tour."

"Grandma, you've been on that tour a million times."

"Yes, but they're sitting on some sort of top-secret flavor they're about to reveal, and I figured if I did the tour they might give us a little hint. You know, I like to theme my pies to their new flavors, so I've got to stay ahead of the game."

Yes, I knew.

"She brought me the tastiest apple pie." Curtis rubbed his belly. "Tripod and I are both putting on weight."

So I'd heard. But I didn't mention it. Instead, I glanced at my watch and gasped as I saw the time. No way. I needed to get back. We had a full schedule this afternoon. Was it my imagination or was that pill starting to give me some kind of weird buzz?

Out of the corner of my eye I caught a glimpse of Maggie Jamison pushing a cart toward a white F-250. Grandma must've noticed her too. She offered a wave, but Maggie kept right on walking without responding.

"That's odd," Grandma said. "Maggie's usually so friendly."

I decided to spill the beans, so my grandmother wouldn't think Maggie's behavior had anything to do with her. "Her dog died a couple weeks back. Apparently she blames one of our vets."

My grandmother looked duly shocked by this notion. "Oh no. Tyler or the new gal?"

"The new one. Maggie is claiming neglect, but that's not true at all.

Kristin had the dog on exactly the right protocol, but apparently he was too far gone when the condition was diagnosed, so the meds didn't work. Now Maggie's threatening a lawsuit. Can you believe that?"

"Sue-man-sue." Curtis laughed. "That's the way of things these days. If you get irritated at someone, you file a lawsuit or lash out at them on that internet thing."

"Sad, isn't it?" Grandma's gaze shifted to Maggie, and we all watched as she climbed up into her truck. "Maggie used to come around, until her husband died. Then we lost touch."

"Really?"

"Yep. She was a friend of your mama's growing up."

"Oh wow."

"She lives all alone out there on that big old piece of property of hers out off Round Top Highway. She's got sixty-three acres. Lots of cattle, goats, chickens. . .the whole thing. Apparently the ranch was her husband's passion, but she was left with it after he died."

"That's sad. How did he die?"

"I'm not sure. I just remember that she would bring pot roast to our community potluck. Everyone always looked forward to that. The woman can cook."

"Ginger was always asking for recipes," Curtis added.

"Oh yes. And remember Maggie's chicken pot pie?" Grandma practically swooned. "It was the best I'd ever tasted."

Pot roast. Pot pie. Potluck. There seemed to be a theme going on. Then again, we were in Brenham.

My thoughts were interrupted by Grandma's penetrating gaze. "Did you call your Aunt Trina yet?"

I startled to attention. "Oh no, ma'am. But that was just yesterday that you asked me to. I haven't really had time to—"

"Please don't forget. I'm really hoping she'll come home for Christmas." Grandma sighed. "It just won't be the same without your mama here. And if Trina doesn't come. . ." Her eyes brimmed with tears. "Who will eat all of the Christmas ham? And the pumpkin pie?"

Curtis cleared his throat. "I was kind of hoping for an invitation."

Her frown tipped into a smile at this proclamation. "Well, of course, Curtis. And you bring Tripod too. You two are always welcome at my place. You know that."

From the smile on his face, I had the sense he *did* know that.

I offered grandma a hug and then said my goodbyes, but not before she clucked her tongue and pointed down at my shoes.

"Marigold, what have I told you about wearing white after Labor Day?"

"Yes ma'am, but these are tennis shoes," I responded. "I have to wear them for work. I'm on my feet all day."

"I understand, honey, but they don't have to be white." A thoughtful look settled over her. "I just figured out what I'm going to get you for Christmas."

Oh boy. I could hardly wait.

We said our goodbyes, and I opened the door to my SUV. Beau Jangles jumped inside without any prompting from me. He went straight to his spot in the passenger seat, and I climbed in and took my spot behind the wheel. After giving the clock a quick glance, anxiety kicked in. Hopefully I wouldn't be late.

Before I could text Cassidy to give her a heads-up, my cell phone rang. I saw her name on the screen and answered right away. "Hey, I'm on my way. I was just—"

"Guuuuurl!" She crooned. "You're gonna wanna get here as quick as you can. The most handsome fella I've ever seen in my life just waltzed through the door, some friend of Tyler's from A&M. We're talking Hollywood material here."

"Oh?"

"Mm-hmm. He's been talking my ear off. And best of all? There's no ring on his finger! You'd better get here quick, before he leaves!"

CHAPTER ELEVEN

I rushed back to the clinic, not because of the handsome stranger, but because we had a full schedule and I didn't want to disappoint Tyler. These days, I lived to make him happy. Though, when I took the time to examine my motivations, they weren't entirely pure. I had this vision in my head of the two of us working together with my rescue pups—me, saving them from harm, and him, patching them up and nursing them back to health. Like he'd already done with my sweet Beau Jangles.

Okay, so Tyler wasn't the only one who'd jumped in to help with Beau's care that first night. Cassidy had gone with me for the actual rescue, of course. And Kristin had assisted Tyler later that night. And Parker had been right there, taking excellent care of me, as always. He was always present for such things, wasn't he? But Tyler was my go-to guy, and I'd do anything to make sure he knew it, so keeping him happy was key.

I got back to the clinic in record time. Beau and I rushed inside to discover Cassidy behind the reception desk, showing off her new cell phone to a very handsome man who looked to be in his early thirties.

True to her word, he was a looker. His blond, wavy hair was what I'd call sensibly shabby. Grandma Peach would cluck her tongue at the length, but I didn't mind it. It suited that ruggedly handsome face. And my goodness, was it a ruggedly handsome face.

He had a great style about him as well. The classic jeans. The fitted button-up shirt, snug against a muscular body. Oh my. A girl shouldn't ogle, but Mr. Tall, Blond, and Handsome was making it difficult not to.

Something about the guy seemed vaguely familiar to me, though I couldn't quite place him. But I had the weird sensation that we'd met before.

Cassidy made introductions, and the name Cameron Saye jumped out at me. Where had I heard that name before? He turned to face me, all smiles.

Okay, I could definitely see the draw, now that we were face-to-face. Those sparkling brown eyes. His firm features. The confident set of his shoulders. The impressive height. The nice lips. Wow. Either he'd been schooled in the art of smiling, or this guy had the most naturally positive personality I'd ever seen. His lips curled up, as if always on the edge of a good laugh. And where did one have to go to get a tan like that in October?

Then again, this was Texas. Maybe he worked out in the field? A rancher, maybe? No, he was missing the obligatory cowboy hat. What did he do for a living, to look like that? And, how could I get a degree in that?

Before I could ask any of these questions, the door to Tyler's office opened and my boss stepped out. His usually easygoing posture stiffened the moment he clamped eyes on the stranger behind the desk. Was it my imagination or did Tyler's jaw flinch?

"Cameron."

"Tyler! Dude!" Cameron extended his hand, as if expecting Tyler to shake it. "Long time no see, man."

"Not that long." Tyler's gaze shifted to the rest of us and then back to the man. Why did this guy make him so uncomfortable?

For the first time I noticed the bandages on Cameron's arm. He tugged at his sleeve to cover them up.

"What happened to your arm?" Fine lines creased Tyler's brow as the question was voiced.

"Oh, weirdest thing. I was helping an elderly neighbor with her fence and the broken board slipped. Next thing you know I've got a gash in my arm. So, I had to make a run to urgent care for some stitches. It's a fresh wound, so I'm bandaged up for now."

"I'm sorry to hear that," Tyler said.

"Yeah, remember that time—I think it was our freshman year—when I tried to change the oil on your truck to save you some money?" Cameron tipped his head back and laughed. "Aw, man. I remember it like it was yesterday. The filter got stuck so I shoved a screwdriver through it to pry it off. Ended up getting a gash in my hand." He lifted his right hand to show it off. "Dumb move on my part, but I still have the scar to prove it."

"I remember the doctor at the ER said it would've been cheaper to go to Jiffy Lube," Tyler said.

"Yep. Not much has changed." Cameron tugged at his sleeve once again to cover the bandages. "Except I'm not as accident prone these days."

"Couldn't prove it by me." Tyler gave him a knowing look. "So, what brings you by?"

"Just came for another chat, man. I miss you." Cameron's gaze traveled around the lobby, and I could read the admiration in his eyes. "This place has really shaped up since I was here last."

Okay, so he had been here. That would explain why he looked familiar. But when? I couldn't place it.

"Thanks." Tyler nodded and reached to brush a crumb off the reception counter.

Was it just me, or was this whole thing kind of awkward and weird?

"What's up with the windows?" Cameron gestured with his head to the boards covering the spot where windows once stood.

Tyler flinched. "We had an. . .incident. . .a couple of nights back. We're getting the windows replaced soon. It's specialty glass, so it had to be ordered. We'll be boarded up until then."

"Sorry to hear that, man. Must've been some incident. Hey, I was hoping we could talk. Maybe finish what we started on the phone the other day?"

"I told you on the phone—" Tyler must've realized he had an apt audience because he stopped abruptly. "Anyway, come into my office. We can talk in there. Okay? But we've got a full afternoon, so I don't have long."

"Anything you can give me, I'll take. I'm at your mercy, dude. You know that. Things are tough for me right now."

Tyler glanced my way. "Mari, can I ask a favor?"

"Sure. Anything."

"Mrs. Joslin is already here in Exam Room 2. She's wanting Pico's nails trimmed and he needs a fecal. I would ask Parker to do it, but he's busy with a blood draw in Room 3. I'll be in to finish his exam when I'm done."

"Of course. And I'm sorry I was late getting back. I took Beau to the—" Never mind. There wasn't time to explain. And he didn't need my excuses. Right now I just needed to get back to work.

I kept a watchful eye on Cameron as he followed Tyler into his office. When they disappeared from view I reached to pick up Beau Jangles. I'd need to get him kenneled before heading in to Exam Room 2.

"Did I tell you, or what?" Cassidy whistled as her gaze followed our visitor's backside. "Cameron's a cutie, huh?"

I nodded, my gaze still on Tyler's office door. "Yeah, but something about him seems off with Tyler. I get the feeling there's bad blood between the two of them."

"You don't even want to know." These words came from Kristin, who walked behind the desk to grab a clipboard.

This certainly got my attention. Kristin lowered her voice as she took a couple of steps in my direction. "They were roommates their freshman year at A&M. But, Tyler got the scholarship that Cameron wanted, and things kind of went south in the years that followed. Though, to his credit, Tyler tried to be a good friend. But Cameron didn't always make it easy. He's had some issues over the years."

"Oh wow."

"It's kind of been like that between the two of them all along," Kristin explained. "Tyler graduated at the top of his class and started his own practice. Cameron, well. . .let's just say he's had a harder time of it. And he's a little bitter that everything seems to come so easy for Tyler but not for him."

"Tyler's had to work hard to get this place set up," I countered. "It hasn't all been easy."

"Exactly." Kristin nodded. "Try telling that to Cameron. From his point of view, Tyler's always been the Golden Boy and he's been the underdog."

She headed into Exam Room 1, and I went into the room next to hers to deal with the nail trim and fecal. But, as I worked I couldn't help but worry about Tyler. If what Kristin said was true, then Cameron might be holding onto some sort of grudge. That was never good. People with grudges wanted to get even.

Hmm.

I tried not to let my mind go there. Still, something about this guy really troubled me.

I held off Mrs. Joslin for as long as I could, making small talk, but wondered if I should go get Tyler so that he could wrap up the exam. Usually he didn't keep the clients waiting like this. The anxious woman kept looking at her watch and referencing the time. Ugh. Yep, we were definitely about to lose her. And if she left today, would she come back next time? Maybe not. We couldn't afford that.

I walked to Tyler's office and observed the closed door. Was he still in there with Cameron? I leaned in to listen before knocking, not wanting to interrupt. That's when I heard my boss's voice, and he did not sound happy.

"Cameron, we've been through this before, man. You know I can't hire you. I can't. I'm not in a position to—"

I pulled away from the door, realizing I'd already heard more than I should have. Ack.

The next words were so loud I didn't have to strain to make them out. "You think you're so high and mighty, don't you, Tyler?" Unbridled anger laced Cameron's words. "I tell you what, things don't always turn out like you think, bro. The higher you climb, the more it hurts when you fall."

"What are you saying?" The tension in Tyler's words was palpable.

"Just saying you might not want to get too high up on the ladder or hitting the bottom will cause more pain, man. Guard yourself."

Whoa. I leaned in closer, dying to hear Tyler's response. This was sure to be a doozie.

CHAPTER TWELVE

G uard myself?" Now Tyler really sounded angry. "Is that some sort of threat, Cameron? Because if it is—"

"Me—threaten you?" Cameron's laugh was anything but humorous. "No, man. You know me better than that. You're the one who's always been the bigger threat in this relationship. I'm just. . .here. As always. In the background."

"Not true."

"Just saying you can't always be the one on top while the rest of us grovel at your feet, below you. That's all. One day you'll probably understand what it's like to struggle."

"I'm already struggling, Cameron." Tyler's tone took a definitive shift. "I've got an office full of employees counting on me for their paychecks, and I'm just getting this practice up and running. I can't afford for anything to go wrong. And ever since the break-in. . .." His words drifted off and I couldn't make out the rest.

Man. Was he struggling to make ends meet? If so, this was certainly news to me.

"And hiring me would make things go wrong? Is that what you're saying?"

"I'm just saying I can't afford to take on another vet right now. I don't have the clients yet to justify that. Maybe if the practice grows. . .but not now."

Cassidy approached, eyes wide. "What's happening in there?" She whispered. "Is he hiring him? 'Cause I'd love to see that face every day, wouldn't you?" A tiny giggle followed, and her thinly plucked brows elevated. "Might be a bit of a distraction though, huh?"

I shook my head, unwilling to say more. Tyler could share the news if and when he felt like it, but I wouldn't be spilling the tea. This was none of my business. I scooted out of the way and turned back toward Cassidy, making small talk about the new windows, which were scheduled to arrive soon.

A few minutes later Tyler and Cameron emerged from the office. Cameron offered a flirtatious wave to Cassidy and then dove right back into a conversation with her.

Tyler shot a stern gaze her way. "Cassidy, I need to talk to you in my office. Now, please."

"O–okay." She shrugged and followed behind him, pausing only to give Cameron an impish shrug.

Oh boy. This conversation was sure to be a doozie.

I turned my attention to Cameron, hoping to send him packing. I don't know how the guy did it, but before I could help myself, he'd engaged me in conversation about how I had rescued Beau.

"You're the one Cassidy was telling me about?" When I nodded he flashed a toothy grin. "You rescued that dog from the drainage ditch."

"Drainage pipe."

"Right. And you almost got arrested, right?"

"Yeah." I sighed. "That's me."

Happened the same night as the robbery?"

"Burglary. It's only a robbery if—"

"There's a victim."

At least he knew his terminology. Still, something about his response set my arm hairs on edge. I'd better get back to work and stop gazing into his rich, brown eyes.

They were very pretty eyes, weren't they?

Snap out of it, Mari! Get ahold of yourself.

Parker must've picked up on my addled state too. He cleared his throat and then disappeared into the lab. I excused myself and followed behind him.

"I see he's trying to cast his spell on you too," Parker said as he went back to work loading supplies into the cabinet.

"Yeah? Well, I'm not falling for it."

"Anymore." He paused, and then went straight back to what he was doing, not even looking my way. So weird.

"What do you mean?" I planted my hands on my hips. "I fell for nothing."

"It's none of my business."

Only, the way he said it made it sound like Parker thought it was his business.

So. Weird.

I went to work cleaning off a piece of equipment, my thoughts a million miles away. My thoughts gravitated from the handsome stranger to my Aunt Trina. I wondered what she would say about him.

"You okay over there?" Parker asked.

Sure. Now he looks my way. "Yeah."

"I'm not sure if you noticed but you just used window cleaner to wipe down the lens."

"Did I?" I jerked back, embarrassed that he'd caught me making such a foolish mistake. "I must be distracted."

"Yeah. Noticed that."

"For your information, I was thinking about Trina." Sort of.

"I understand. Is she coming back for the holidays?"

The question brought tears to my eyes right away. I brushed them away and hyper-focused on cleaning the lens properly. "I'm not sure. This Christmas is going to be weird. With Mama gone. . ."

"You know, I'm here for you, Mari." He rested his hand on my arm and gazed into my eyes with such compassion that I felt a lump rise to my throat.

"I know. And I'm grateful, Parker. I really am. It's just weird, now that

Mama's gone and Trina's so far away. I know that I have my grandmother, but she's busy baking pies and searching for a new beau."

"A new beau?" He smiled and I realized the irony of my wording.

"A new fella," I said. "My point is, it's just going to be weird this holiday season."

"Brenham is your home and we're still your people. Don't ever doubt that."

"Right."

I pressed past him, heading back to Mrs. Joslin. Thank goodness I found Tyler with her and she was all smiles. He, on the other hand, was not. I could see the tension in his face and I didn't blame him, not after what I'd heard.

He rubbed at the back of his neck and then popped it. Several times. I couldn't help but notice the sheen of sweat on his cheeks, chin, and forehead. It definitely wasn't hot in here, so he must be worked up over his conversation with Cameron. Man. There was definitely more to this story than what I'd heard. Hopefully things wouldn't escalate.

We forged ahead with other clients over the next couple of hours and I did my best to mind my own business, though I wanted to ask Tyler all the questions running through my head. Instead, I did the bloodwork on a labradoodle to check his kidney values, drawing blood from his jugular vein like a pro. While it spun down in the tube I pondered the events of the morning, starting with grandma and Curtis, then the situation with Cameron. One thing was for sure—my days, of late, weren't boring.

When we wrapped up with the labradoodle, Kristin took an emergency case, a dachshund who'd gotten ahold of some cherry pits. Oops. We induced vomiting, and less than a minute later. . .voilà. Eleven cherry pits, exactly the number the client had said we would find. When I wrapped up there, I finally managed to take a break in the lunchroom, where I found Parker gobbling down what looked and smelled like a tasty late lunch.

"I'm so sorry you had to cover for me after my lunch break," I said as I plopped into a chair. "I made a run to Bubba's Weed & Feed on my lunch break and was late getting back."

"Bubba's Weed & Feed?" He quirked a brow. "Do I even want to know why?"

"Dog food."

"Ah. So, what did *you* eat?"

"Eat?" I paused to think it through. "Oh wow. Nothing."

"You need to stop doing that, Mari." He gave me that concerned big brother look I so often got from him in moments like this.

"Oh, I—"

He pushed a food container my way. "I've got plenty of fajitas left over from Mario's."

"I love Mario's fajitas."

"I know. You're welcome to them."

I eyed them, now drooling as hunger pangs kicked in.

"I don't want to take your food, Parker."

"I ate too much already. Please take them. I want you to take care of yourself." He rested his hand on my arm and gazed intently at me. "You're always rescuing everyone else, but you need to take care of you too. Remember that whole airplane thing."

"Airplane thing?" I grabbed the container and pulled it toward me, then opened the foil wrapper housing a couple of flour tortillas.

"Yeah, that thing they tell you on the airplane about putting the oxygen mask on yourself first. Otherwise you're no good to others."

I grabbed a tortilla and didn't even bother looking for a fork. I used my fingers to stuff pieces of chicken into it. "And in this analogy, your fajitas are the oxygen mask?"

"Yes." He smiled. "But you get the point."

I did. He cared about me and wanted me to take care of myself. And, with my stomach rumbling I couldn't argue the point. So, I pressed some cheese in on top of the chicken and rolled it up, then took a giant bite.

"Oh. Yum."

"See? Told you." Parker grabbed a chip from the container and jabbed it into the salsa. He chomped down on it, a reflective look on his face.

"So, talk to me about that guy who came to see Tyler earlier," I said as I licked salsa off of my fingertips and leaned back in the chair. "Do you know him?"

"Why do you want to know?" He crossed his arms at his chest, lips now pursed. "So you can swoon over him like Cassidy?"

"Um, no."

Parker chomped down on another chip then shrugged. "Cameron Saye. He went to school with Tyler. Graduated in the same class. I met him last time he showed up."

"I was trying to place him. He looks familiar."

"You were here when he stopped by. It was after hours but we were just closing up. That's when Tyler was looking to hire a second vet."

"Oh." It was all coming back to me now. "And he was up for the job?"

"I guess he thought he was. But Tyler hired Kristin, instead."

"Ah. I see. Actually, I overheard a little of their conversation today and I don't think this guy poses any risk to Kristin."

"Risk to Kristin?"

I turned as I heard the familiar female voice and did my best not to gasp aloud when I saw Kristin standing there, a perplexed look on her face. Oh boy. Talk about getting caught red-handed!

"Kristin, I'm sorry. I—" I reached for a tortilla chip and shoveled it in my mouth as I tried to think of something brilliant to say.

She took a seat next to me and reached to grab one of the chips from the bag. "It's okay. I know everyone's worried about Cameron showing up. The guy would like nothing more than to take my job. But I have it on good authority that's not going to happen."

"Good." But her comment also clued me in to the fact that she and Tyler had already talked about this, so she clearly knew a lot more about this guy than I did. Why that made me uneasy, I could not say. But it did.

"I know that Tyler's been worried about him, ever since the last time he stopped by. He's persistent, if nothing else." She leaned back against the chair. "Cameron gave him some sort of ultimatum last time, I think."

"Ultimatum?" Parker and I echoed together.

"Yeah." She released a sigh.

"You don't suppose..." I paused to think through my words carefully. "I mean, do you think there's any chance he's the one who broke in?"

A thoughtful look settled on her face. "I can see that as a distinct possibility. I've known him since we were in school together, and he was always a force to be reckoned with. Problem is, he's so stinking handsome."

"Yeah, I know how that feels." Parker grabbed another chip, and his eyes took on a faraway look. "It makes my life so difficult." He popped the chip in his mouth and crunched it a little too loudly.

"Hey, just so you know, my grandmother thinks you have the prettiest eyes in town," I said.

"Gee, that'll make a guy feel good. Somebody's grandma has the hots for me."

"Oh, and someone else we all know and love went on and on about how handsome you are," I threw in. "So, my grandma's not alone in her principles."

Parker's eyes widened. "Back to Cameron..."

"Right." Kristin grabbed another chip. "I've learned that the beautiful people of this world get away with more. People don't always suspect them, simply because they're just so, well..."

"Beautiful?" I tried.

"Yes."

She nibbled on her chip and thought through what she'd said. Cassidy had fallen for Cameron's charms right away, completely swayed by his good looks. He could be an axe murderer for all we knew, but, hey... he was a handsome one.

A few minutes later we rose to get back to work and Parker stopped me when we reached the doorway. "Hey."

"Yes?"

"You said someone else thought I was handsome. Just curious. Who?"

"Oh." Should I tell him? An awkward silence rose up between us before I finally worked up the courage to say, "Cassidy."

His brows arched and he looked pleased by this news. "Cassidy thinks I'm cute? Really?" He squared his shoulders.

"Yeah. She told me so, the night we were in the patrol car."

"Something about being in the back of a patrol made her think of me?" He laughed. "Explain, please."

"We were talking about what a great friend you are, how you always come to my rescue."

"Ah." He gave me a pensive look.

"How you're always making sure I'm okay. Feeding me. Changing my oil. Helping me move. Stuff like that."

"And in the middle of all that, she popped up with a line about my handsomeness?"

"She did."

He looked intrigued by this.

Maybe a little too intrigued. Suddenly the idea of my two friends becoming an item sounded too off-putting. So, I dampened his enthusiasm by adding, "But, boy. . .you should've seen how she swooned over Cameron today. She called him Hollywood material."

I watched the air go out of Parker like a tire blowing on an 18-wheeler.

Great job, Marigold. Kick his knees out from under him.

I wanted to apologize, to take back what I'd said. But, it was too late. The damage was done. Parker grabbed another chip, then headed out of the room, saying something about helping out in the boarding area.

Perfect.

Wasn't I just the most wonderful friend in the world? He fed me, drove me here, there, and everywhere, and I responded by knocking the wind out of his sails.

Still. The idea of Cassidy and Parker? A couple? Nope. Nada. Not on my watch.

CHAPTER THIRTEEN

Thursday was my scheduled day off. I spent the morning tidying up my apartment and dealing with bills. Big girl stuff. I got distracted looking at social media, and ended up pinning a couple of recipes and posting pictures of Beau Jangles on my news feed to see if anyone recognized him.

I hoped they wouldn't. By now, my heart was fully wound around those silky paws. He'd won me over, hook, line, and leash, and I had to wonder which of us would mourn the most, if he did have to leave. The sweet pup dozed at my feet but woke a couple of times and gazed up at me, as if to say, "I'm glad you're mine." Then he fell back asleep.

Sometime around ten I decided he needed a walk, so I grabbed the cute leash Parker had given me and hooked it onto Beau's matching collar. We headed out to the center of the complex, to the trails around the small lake with a pretty fountain. This lake was the primary reason I'd chosen this complex. That, and the fact that my best friend lived just three doors down in an apartment that matched mine in nearly every way. Except the pea green sofa, of course. And the cherrywood table. Having Cassidy nearby was an added blessing, even if she did wear me out, carrying on about Cameron Saye's handsomeness.

Turned out, Beau Jangles was pretty good on a leash. He loved the crisp fall breeze, which sent the leaves tumbling down from the trees overhead. A couple of times he tried to tug to chase them, but I kept him under control. Still, the weather was beautiful, so who could blame him for being so frisky? Usually October in Texas was still pretty warm, but these past few days had brought with them a cool snap.

I walked down to the park and took a seat as the dog chased some leaves blowing up around my feet. He played like a young pup, though we'd already established—through his dental exam—that he was probably at least three years old. Still, he had a lot of puppy left in him, and that was fine by me. I enjoyed watching his antics.

An older couple walked by with their schnauzer on a leash. I recognized them from the clinic as the Millers. They paused to let the two dogs get acquainted, then headed off around the lake. I watched them from a distance, wondering what it would be like, to have a partner to walk through life with.

Maybe I'd never know. With Tyler always so preoccupied, he certainly didn't appear to be looking my way. At least, not the way I'd hoped.

Maybe I'd end up being one of those gals who fell so in love with her job and her dog that she didn't have time or inclination for romance, anyway.

Her dog.

Hmm. I'd better rethink that. Beau wasn't exactly my dog, was he?

On the other hand. . .I reached down to pet him and he nuzzled up against my leg. I was his caregiver, the one who fed, walked, and cared for him.

Guard your heart, Marigold.

I didn't want to fully give it away, in case a true owner showed up. And even if one didn't, the ultimate plan here was to get this pooch settled in a proper forever home. That was the goal, right?

Staring into those big brown eyes, I wasn't so sure anymore.

Maybe this would be a good time for a quick call to my Aunt Trina. Yes, it would make a happy diversion. And I'd be ticking one thing off my to-do list for the day. Not that I had to make room for family. Oh no. They were already top of the list. But Grandma would be happy that I'd reached out to Trina with the big "Are you coming for Christmas" question.

I glanced at the time on my phone. Trina was an hour ahead in Nashville. Surely she would be up by now.

The phone rang four times before she picked up. Her opening words made me laugh. "Mama Peach told you to call."

"Well, hello to you too. And yes, but you didn't hear that from me."

"Of course not. And I know how persuasive she can be. Is this the part where you're supposed to convince me to come home for Christmas?"

"Yeah," I responded. "Should I go there or just skip it?"

"Skip it."

"She means well, Trina. And she misses you." I paused and then added, "We all do."

"I miss you too." A lingering sigh filled the space between us. "It's so good to hear your voice. Southern drawl and all."

"Hey, now."

"I've got one too," she said. "Comes in handy for a country singer."

"I'm sure." I kept a watchful eye on Beau Jangles, who tugged on the leash, hoping to chase after a nearby squirrel. I managed to keep him from doing so, and turned my attention back to my aunt. "I have so much to tell you, I hardly know where to start."

"Oh, me too. I've been on tour for weeks but I'm finally back at my place in Nashville." She yawned. "It's so good to be home. You have no idea how worn out I am."

"Aw, I'm sorry. Speaking of home..." I worked up the courage to voice the question, knowing Grandma would press me on it: "Won't you come home, pretty please with sugar on top? It really would be nice to see you for Christmas. It's just not going to be the same this year, especially if you're not here."

"I know." She spoke the words with a tremor in her voice. "Sweetie, I miss home so much." She paused and seemed to drift away. "I miss your mama so much. This old world's just not the same without my sister in it. Vanessa was my rock."

"Agreed." An unexpected lump rose in my throat, and I did my best to shove it down. Every time I talked to Aunt Trina I felt this way. I wondered if I always would. Then again, she reminded me so much of my mother—a much younger version, of course—but similar in so many ways.

Okay, so Mama couldn't sing a note. And she didn't have that same shock of gorgeous red hair like Trina. And she'd never aspired to leave Brenham to follow the bright lights to Nashville.

But other than that, they were just alike. Two peas in a pod.

"I'm so ready for a break." Trina's words roused me from my thoughts. "This life is great, but. . ." Her words trailed off.

"Come home, Aunt Trina." I did my best not to resort to pleading, but when a girl felt as strongly as I did about this, what choice did she have? "We need you. I need you."

"I don't know, Mari. My life is here now." She sighed. "I mean, some of it is. Most of it is on the road these days. Have I mentioned that I've put on seven pounds since I saw you last? I've been eating my grief, I think."

"Me too. But if you get that ranch you're always talking about, I can give up apartment living and manage it for you while you're on the road. See? It'll be perfect."

In my mind's eye, I could see it all now. We would merge our two dreams—her childhood fantasy of living on a Texas ranch and my dream of rescuing dogs on a spacious patch of hill country land. Talk about a win-win! But, how would I go about broaching the subject?

"Hey, Trina, guess what? I rescued a dog the other night."

"You're still interested in doing that?"

Was this a trick question? She knew me, almost better than I knew myself, at times. "It's a calling, Aunt Trina. You know that."

"You think so?"

"I know so. From the time I was a kid. Remember? I've always loved dogs."

"I know your mama said she was exhausted, trying to keep up with all the strays you brought home."

"Nothing has changed. Only, now I think I'm in a position to actually help, not just take in a random stray or two, but to rehab dogs and get the medical care they need."

"Tyler is going to help you?"

I paused to think through my response. We'd never actually talked about it in detail, but I knew his heart for animals. Sure, he also needed to grow his business, but his compassion for the animals would win out over dollars and sense. I hoped.

"I think so," I responded at least. "I mean, I wish you could've seen him with the dog we rescued the other night, Trina. He was so great. He's such a terrific vet too."

"So, tell me about this dog. Where did you find him. Er, her."

"Him. In a drainage pipe. Oh, and I almost got arrested, but I guess that's another story."

"Marigold Evans!"

"It turned out okay. Except for the part where the clinic got robbed."

"Mari! The clinic was robbed?"

I paused to reword my statement, knowing Officer Dennison would scold me if he heard my version of the night's events. "Actually, burglarized. Did you know there's a difference? Apparently it's only called a robbery if there's a victim. And no one was in the building at the time, so I guess it was considered a burglary. It's really good that no one was there. But if someone had been there, we'd know who did this, so that would be helpful. Only, then it would be a robbery, not a burglary."

"I'm so lost right now."

"Yeah, I've been told I have that effect on people. But Trina, the point is, I was out rescuing a dog the other night and I brought him back to the clinic."

"Which was burglarized?"

"Yes, and Tyler was there and he helped with the dog and he was so great with him. I wish you could've seen them together. Did I mention how great he is with the animals? He's got a calling on his life too. So, see what I mean? It's going to be great."

"That's a lot of *great*." She cleared her throat.

"Anyway, he's going to help me. I know he is. Oh, and Cassidy and Parker too."

"Parker. He's that cute young tech you work with, right? The one with those gorgeous blue eyes?"

Okay. . .weird. "You think he's cute too?" I'd never stopped to think about it. To me, he was just. . .Parker. My friend. My fellow techie.

"Well, yeah. I would think it would be obvious to everyone. He's adorable."

"I think Grandma has a crush on him. Oh, and Cassidy. But I definitely don't think Parker and Cassidy would be a good match. She's a little. . .flighty."

"Why would you care, if you're not interested in him?" Trina asked.

That question stopped me cold, and I wasn't sure how to respond. Still, she'd struck a nerve.

"He's nice looking, Mari," she said. "But what were you saying about Cassidy?"

"Oh, nothing, really. Only, she was with me when I rescued the dog. Her phone died."

"And she almost got arrested too?"

"Yeah, she's still irritated at me."

"Why? Did you make her go when she didn't want to, or something?"

"No, it's not that." I shifted my gaze back to the dog, who tugged at the leash. "It's just that she wanted to take pictures of the two of us in the back seat of the patrol car, but the battery on her phone died because she had to use the flashlight when I was in the drainage pipe."

"Wait, you were actually placed in a patrol car? Like a criminal?"

"Yeah, but we couldn't take pictures, since her cell phone died and mine was in my purse in my car, which was stolen."

"Mari! Your car was stolen?"

"Don't worry, Aunt Trina! They found it! I picked it up the next morning on my way in to work and everything was safe and sound—my phone, my purse. . .everything. So, see? Everything works out in the end. And I guess that proves my point that everything with my dog rescue will work out too."

"I hope it's not that complicated, especially if it involves the police and stolen vehicles."

"Come home and see for yourself. I'll tell you all about it over Grandma's ham and pumpkin pie."

"Mama's a conundrum—baking up pies and ham while insisting we all get healthier."

"She's got a funny way about healing us, doesn't she?" I said. "But she means well."

"It all sounds tempting." She sighed. "And I can't tell you how much I'd love to see everyone again, especially you."

A lump rose in my throat at those words.

"I promise to think about it. You can tell her that much. I know she's going to ask."

"She is. But I really do want you to come too."

"I'll have to see if it's a possibility. We're headed to California in a few days. I've got a big show at the Staples Center. After that we're on to Seattle."

"When are you scheduled to come to Texas?"

"I'm playing the rodeo in Houston in February."

"That's forever away. It's not even November yet. We need you before then."

"I know." An exaggerated sigh followed on her end. "Sometimes I wonder if I picked this life or it picked me."

"Maybe both." I offered, doing my best to sound cheerful, in spite of the ache her words caused me. "You are über-talented. I mean, some people don't have a choice, I suppose."

Still, as I spoke the words, I wanted to add, "But you do have a choice. You could come home where you belong."

But I didn't. And honestly? I didn't really blame Trina for wanting to hang onto her life as a star. Getting out of the small town she'd grown up in had always been high on my aunt's list. Her wish had come true. Or, so it seemed.

I did my best not to feel too sorry for myself. With Grandma and Cassidy around I'd never really have to spend the holidays alone. But, with Mama gone and Trina out of town. . .

No, I wouldn't let myself go there. I'd make the most of things, just like I always did. I'd eat an extra slice of ham and two pieces of pie. And if this holiday was harder than normal, I'd suck it up and deal with it the best I could.

I suddenly remembered something that I needed to tell her, something important. "Hey, remember that older man at Grandma's church?"

"Which one? There are dozens."

"Oh, good point. I'm talking about Curtis."

"As in, Curtis and Ginger?"

"Ginger died several months ago."

"Oh. That's sad. She was a good friend to Mama."

"I know. Only now Grandma Peach has been spending a lot of time with Curtis. Baking him pies and such."

"Interesting."

"I saw them together today at Bubba's Weed & Feed."

Trina laughed. "Inquiring minds want to know what you were doing hanging out at a feed store, Mari. That's a very Texas thing to be doing."

"Buying expensive dog food. But my point is, I saw them together in the parking lot. They looked pretty chummy. I just thought you'd want to know what your mother is up to in your absence."

"You thought I'd want to know that my mama apparently has the hots for an old man who likes to shop at Bubba's Weed & Feed?" Trina laughed. "Stranger things have happened in my life."

"Like that one guy you dated last year?" I reminded her. "What was his name again? Chad something-or-another. You met him on a movie set? Right?"

"Ugh. Don't bring him up again. Promise?"

"Hey, the tabloids won't let me forget. He's dating that chick from *The Young and the Restless* now, right?"

"Gotta go, girlie."

"Mm-hmm." I'd struck a nerve. At least Trina and I had one thing in common. We were both blissfully single.

Well, single, anyway. Trina paused, and I thought I heard someone else talking to her.

"Really, gotta go, chica," she said after a moment. "We're headed into rehearsal, and then I have to lay down some tracks on a new song."

"What's it about?"

"What are they always about?" She laughed.

"Broken hearts?" I tried. "Not trusting men? Falling in love again, in spite of all that?"

"Yep. And cheating. Always cheating."

"Not another song about Grandma Peach?" I asked.

She laughed. "Nope. But that one was inspired, you have to admit. And boy, did it ever climb to the top of the charts fast. I think I struck a nerve."

"We all have a mama," I said. . .and then stopped cold.

I didn't.

Have a mama.

"Oh, honey." Trina's laughter faded right away. "I'm so sorry. I really am. And if it helps any, I feel your pain. I do."

"I know." It helped to hear someone say it, though. "Don't worry about me, Trina. Just please think about coming home for Christmas. We really, really miss you."

"I will."

We ended the call, and I realized I'd missed a couple of texts from Cassidy. The first had something to do with Maggie Jamison, though I couldn't quite make out what she meant by "trouble brewing with Maggie." But the next text? It almost took my breath away.

Matt Foster called Making threats.

I called her immediately and opened with the words, "I thought Matt Foster was in jail."

"They let him out after twenty-four hours," she explained. "He's free now."

"No way."

"Yep, can you believe it? Isabel told me first thing this morning. She's worried sick about it. He already showed up at her place at the crack of dawn and followed her here. Poor girl was shaking when she got here, and I don't blame her."

"That's awful. I can't believe they didn't keep him longer. Didn't they press charges?"

"I don't know that they have enough evidence," she explained. "The cameras were shut down, and we found out today that the fingerprints the police took match approximately twenty people—all of us and several clients."

"But not Matt Foster?"

"They didn't name him on the list," she said. "But maybe he was wearing gloves? He, or whoever else might be responsible. You know?"

"Yeah."

"So, they didn't press charges, and now he's free." A shiver ran down my spine as I thought that through. Horrible.

"Right, and Isabel was counting on the fact that he would stay in jail for a while," Cassidy added. "Now she's going to have to get a restraining order."

"That can't happen soon enough for me," I said. "In fact, I'll offer to go with her when she files it. I want that guy as far away from us as possible."

Still, I had the feeling Matt Foster wasn't going away anytime soon.

CHAPTER FOURTEEN

Friday morning, I arrived to find the window repairmen hard at work, installing the new plate glass. Finally.

I paused at the reception desk to drop a very excited Beau Jangles off with Cassidy, who couldn't seem to get enough of him. From there, I went straight to the grooming area, where I found Isabel in a puddle of tears while grooming a standard poodle. Not a great combination, since that particular breed required a keen eye and steady hand. Judging from the trembling mess in front of me, Isabel was neither of those things today.

I was tempted to take the electric razor away from her, but I didn't want to offend her. Besides, I knew very little about grooming. My razoring abilities were limited to surgery prep, and I wouldn't win any awards for my efforts.

Instead of further aggravating her, I drew near and spoke in what I hoped would come across as a controlled and comforting voice. "You're going to be okay," I assured her. "I'm here for you. And I'm going to go with you to get that protective order."

"You. . .you will?" She glanced up from her work, nearly losing a grip on the razor in her hand. "You would do that?"

"Of course I'll do that. I would never let you go through that alone."

"Thank you, Mari. You're a great friend. The best." Tears brimmed her lashes, and she brushed at them with the back of her hand.

To be quite honest, I hadn't always been the best friend to Isabel. She was one of the few people at the clinic I hadn't truly connected with. We were different in so many ways. And we both pretty much stayed in our own lanes, which didn't cross very often. But I would try harder. She was worth it.

"Let's go on our lunch break," I suggested. "I did some research last night, and I know just what to do when we get to the courthouse. You have your ID with you?"

"Yes." She turned back to the feisty dog, who had taken to squirming. "I do."

"Okay, I'm going to text you a link to a site online. Fill out the form, print it, and meet me in the lobby at noon and we'll head out. It shouldn't take long."

"Are you sure?" She kept working on the pooch, who tugged at the lead.

"Definitely. And remind me to grab some lunch while we're out. I always seem to forget that part."

"Okay. I'll do the best I can with the form, but I might have to print it blank and then fill it out while you're driving. I've got a busy morning ahead. Tyler asked me to help out in the boarding facility when I'm done with this grooming. So, I'm just not sure I can get that form done before noon, but I promise to try."

"Let me help you," I suggested. "My schedule is pretty loose this morning. What can I do to help?"

"We've only got a couple of dogs being boarded at the moment. One is set to arrive shortly—a Great Dane. The family is going out of town to some sort of convention."

"Oh?" People rarely boarded their larger dogs with us, so this came as a surprise.

"Yeah, she's going to require special care. She's got diabetes and has been having problems with her pancreatic levels, so Tyler decided it's safer not to board her elsewhere. Her name is Huntress, by the way."

"I hope that's not a sign."

113

"Me too."

The dog arrived a short while later, and I happened to be free. Isabel was hard at work on her protective order application, so I agreed to take the Dane out to the yard for a potty break before putting her in our largest kennel. I carried my umbrella just in case the rain started up again. We'd battled showers all morning long, and I didn't want to take the chance, especially not with a 120-pound dog in my care.

For some foolish reason I thought I could handle Beau Jangles and Huntress at the same time. Hey, it was a fenced area and they both seemed pretty chill this morning. At first. Besides, what sort of problems could two dogs get into in a spacious fenced-in yard, after all?

Apparently, a lot. Especially in a wet, muddy yard, fresh off a rainstorm.

The Dane, who didn't show any signs of ill health, took off across the yard, headed straight for the fence nearest Beckett's tax office. Beau—who must've taken Huntress's movements as an invitation to play—ran after her, yapping all the way. The Dane must've sniffed out something on the opposite side of the fence because she went to town, digging like mad. Beau got in on the fun, then ended up covered in mud in the process. I tried to take steps in their direction but stepped in a large pile of dog poop that had apparently been there from the day before, now mushy from all the rain.

"Gross!" I rubbed my shoe in the grass and lost track of what the dogs were doing while I attempted to clean my shoe.

When I finally gave up on that project, I realized the Dane had dug a hole under the fence large enough for Beau to slip through. And slip through he did. My precious little pooch took off across the tax office yard, yapping all the way. He went straight to the edge of the property and started to dig. And dig. And dig some more. Oh no! Beckett would have a fit if he saw him.

This, of course, got the Dane worked up even more. She began to dig underneath the fence in earnest now. The whole thing happened so fast, I couldn't think of what to do to fix the situation. Instead, I stood frozen in place.

And then the rain started. Naturally.

I needed help. Now.

I reached for my phone and called Cassidy, who responded with the words, "Parker to the rescue!"

Less than two minutes later, he was in the yard with me, catch pole and treats in hand.

He leaped over the chain-link fence and took off after Beau, still holding tightly to the treats. Thank goodness the catch pole wasn't needed. Beau—who always seemed guided by his stomach—responded to the smell of his favorite treats. He took one from Parker's hand and let a few happy yaps.

Which brought Wayland Beckett outside. In the storm. With an umbrella in one hand and a scowl on his face.

Oh boy.

I watched from a distance as he barreled toward Parker for a showdown.

Poor Parker. None of this was his fault, but there he stood, taking it like a man.

A couple of minutes later Beckett returned inside and Parker walked back over to the fence and passed a very soggy, muddy Beau Jangles my way.

"I'm almost afraid to ask but what did Beckett say?"

"You don't want to know." Parker made the awkward jump over the fence, landing on our side once again. He took hold of the Dane's collar. "C'mon, Huntress. Let's get you inside."

"You know this dog?" I asked.

"Yep. Her owner is my neighbor. I'm glad she didn't get out like Beau."

"Beau only got out because this one dug a hole all the way through."

"I see that. I'll be back out to fill the hole once the rain dies down. But for now, let's get in out of this weather."

I was overcome with relief at his kindness and did my best to convey it. "Thank you for showing up for me, Parker. And for helping Beau too, of course. You're really good at dog rescue. Want to come with me next time I get a call?"

"Sure." He shrugged. "That sounds pretty cool, actually. Adventurous."

"It takes someone special to win the trust of a dog on the run." And he might just be that someone special.

"Thank you, Mari." He turned to face me for a moment, his nose wrinkled as he sniffed the air. "What is that smell?"

I groaned. "It's my shoe. Don't ask."

"You might want to deal with that before helping Kristin with that incoming euthanasia."

"Oh, gosh. I forgot all about that."

"They're arriving any minute."

We went back inside, and I walked straight to the employees' restroom to deal with the icky shoe. I pulled it off and scrubbed the bottom of it until the smell was mostly gone. Then I put it back on, washed my hands, and headed back to work. As I passed through the lab, I heard a call over the intercom for Tyler to come to the front desk.

I stuck my head out of the exam room door, and my stomach hit my throat as I saw Wayland Beckett standing in our lobby.

Oh. No.

Tyler entered the lobby—completely oblivious to the scene Parker and I had just lived out in the yard—and took the brunt of Beckett's anger. Well, he and two of our clients, who happened to be seated nearby with their animals.

"I'm done with all of this noise!" Beckett turned red in the face. "And letting these dogs dig onto my property is not only dangerous, it's illegal. I told you that the last time one of your animals came snooping around. That animal was lucky he's still alive."

Tyler's gaze narrowed. "Now, I *know* you wouldn't actually hurt an animal, Mr. Beckett."

"Try me. Let another dog loose on my property when I'm in the middle of one of my busiest seasons yet and we'll just see what happens to it. I'm going to file a complaint with the city. I told you last week and the week before that. But you didn't listen then, and you're not listening now. Those dogs put my clients at risk, and I can't have that. I need to protect them."

"I'm really sorry." Tyler countered. "I don't know what happened, but I'll make it right, I promise. Why don't you come into my office and we'll talk about it."

"I'm not coming in your office, and I'm not talking about it. I've given every chance a person can give. It's your time to do the right thing. That mutt who barks all the time dug a hole next to my building."

"I'll come and fill it," Tyler said.

Beckett put his hand up. "You will not. You're not coming anywhere near my property. You hear me?"

Um, yeah. We all heard him.

"Just. Stay. Away."

I wanted to argue, "It's not that bad," but didn't. Honestly? I didn't think it was that bad. Sure, the occasional dog barked, and yes, Beau Jangles loved to run and bark in the play yard. But, the accusation about "constant yapping" simply wasn't true. And it wasn't like we let our dogs run his property on purpose. They just seemed drawn to it.

He stormed out of the room, breezing by a client who reached to quiet her yapping Chihuahua.

"My goodness," the woman said. "That's one mean man. How can anyone make such a big deal over a little barking?" Her pup continued to yap, as if to prove her point.

I walked over to Cassidy, who grabbed an armload of papers and headed toward Victoria's office with them. "That guy freaks me out almost as much as Matt Foster does."

"Me too. He's not a dog lover, that's for sure."

"He seems scared of them," I observed.

"Or maybe intimidated. You know? It's like they set him off." Cassidy rolled her eyes.

"Yeah, I've noticed that. And what was up with that comment about this being his busy season? It's October?"

"Clearly, you've never filed for an extension on your taxes, or you would know," Cassidy explained. "October 15th is the deadline to file your return if you asked for an extension back in April. And trust me when I say that lots of people file for extensions, especially these days. I did."

"Oh wow. Never thought about it."

"I'm guessing it's probably a crazy week for him, so that's why he's so worked up."

"He's always worked up," I countered.

"I just mean, that's why his parking lot is so full." Cassidy nodded. "And I can tell you, my best friend growing up—her dad was a CPA. And he got so stressed out during tax season. He came home one day and snapped at the two of us for laughing. And we weren't even loud!"

"Beckett's a snapping turtle, all right." I cringed. "But that comment about how he might actually hurt a dog that got loose on his property? Do you really think he'd do that?"

She nodded. "I do."

"Then I'm going to hold tight to Beau Jangles." Possessive feelings swept over me. That man would hurt my dog over my dead body.

Well, not my dog, exactly. But, anyway. . .

"Beau wouldn't hurt a flea," Cassidy interjected. "But did you see the way Beckett backed up when Beau came in the room, like he was scared of him?

I hadn't noticed that part. I'd been too distracted by the anger in the man's eyes as he stormed toward us. "Maybe he had a bad experience as a child. You know? Stranger things have happened."

She almost dropped the stack of papers but caught it on the way down. "I suppose anything's possible. Or maybe he just doesn't like dogs. Some people don't."

"Weirdos."

We both laughed and she kicked back with, "Right?"

"Let's just hope this day calms down," I said. "The very last thing we need right now is another reason to worry."

I did my best to focus as I walked into Exam Room 3 to aid in a euthanasia. An eighteen-year-old Siamese cat named Delilah. The owner was in meltdown mode throughout, and she probably didn't notice my shoe, but it was in the back of my mind the entire time.

Afterward, I retreated to the boarding area to check on the Dane. I heard another call go out over our intercom system, a 411.

"Ack." I knew the code well. Aggressive pet arriving. Just what we needed to round out the day.

I peeked out of the door and startled when I realized it was Grandma Peach with Hector.

Aha. She meant *that* aggressive pet. The one who responded gently to my grandmother but absolutely no one else on the planet.

I walked out into the lobby to greet my grandma but heard the cat hissing from inside his crate as soon as I approached.

"Don't pay him any mind, honey," Grandma set down the crate and reached to hug me. "You know how he is."

I knew how he was, all right. So did Cassidy, who stayed put on the opposite side of the reception desk. I didn't blame her. The last time Hector got out, he'd left scratch marks on several of the key players at the clinic, including Tyler, who usually calmed even the craziest of beasts.

Beau Jangles came close to the crate until Hector began a hissing fit from inside. Then the poor pooch took off running. He slid into a stand filled with heartworm products, which tumbled to the ground. From there, he rounded the corner and ran straight into the vitamin display, knocking several bottles of expensive product to the floor below. A couple of them broke open, and for a minute there I thought he might try to eat them. Nope, thank goodness, he kept going behind the counter, safely out of view.

Okay, then. Beau and Hector weren't going to be BFFs. This might be problematic.

Kristin didn't get the memo about Hector's aggressive nature. A few minutes later, after I'd ushered Grandma Peach and Hector into Exam Room 2, she entered with a jovial, "Who do we have here? Family?"

Before I could say "Spawn of Satan," Kristin unsnapped the door on the carrier and reached inside to grab that happy little ball of fluff.

CHAPTER FIFTEEN

Now, I'd witnessed a few miracles in my day. Like the time God provided funds to go on that mission trip during my sophomore year in high school. Or that one time when my Corgi, Watson, finally conquered the housebreaking thing. But I'd never seen anything like what I witnessed in that moment in Exam Room 2 at the Lone Star Veterinary Clinic.

Hector didn't react to Kristin. He not only let her scoop him into her arms, he actually nuzzled up against her and released a contented purr.

Even Grandma Peach seemed rightly astounded. "Oh my." She fanned herself, and those soft, wrinkled cheeks flushed a pretty pink. "Well, now. I do believe in miracles. I truly do!"

"Oh?" Kristin set the cat on the exam table and shot a look of curiosity my grandmother's way. "What do you mean?"

"He can be a bit. . .testy with most folks," my grandmother explained. "So, his behavior at this very moment is nothing short of astounding."

"It's Red Sea parting," I added. "Jericho walls falling down. David taming Goliath."

"Hey, now." Grandma glared at me.

"What? This old boy? Couldn't prove it by me. Seems pretty gentle." Kristin pried his mouth open to examine his teeth and Hector let her. Without wailing or biting or anything. Then he allowed her to examine his ears. And trim his nails. And give him a shot.

I didn't know what to say at this point. Any concerns I might've had regarding Kristin were washed away in that very moment as I saw her dealing with my grandmother's cat. She truly had some sort of anointing with cranky pets. She could calm the evil beast.

Kristin was also pretty remarkable with small talk as she worked. She engaged my grandmother in conversation—about the weather, Aunt Trina, church, and any number of other topics. After a while, I got the idea that they'd forgotten I was in the room.

Hello? Does anyone still see me?

Nope. They were too busy talking about Grandma's new passion for sewing dog costumes. At this point she pulled up a photo on her phone of the Halloween costume she was making for Beau Jangles. I gasped when I saw the police getup. She'd actually done it.

"I had to order the little cap online," Grandma explained. "But don't you think he's going to look darling in this? I figured the police theme would be perfect, especially after your break-in. You can tell folks that you've hired security."

This got Kristin tickled. She and my grandmother started laughing. Well, until Grandma brought up Maggie Jamison's name. Things kind of went south from there.

Grandma changed the topic a couple dozen times as she overstayed her welcome, but we'd all grown used to that. She seemed particularly interested in knowing whether or not the police had arrested the person responsible for the break-in at the clinic.

I wasn't sure how to respond. They hadn't actually charged Matt Foster, after all. And I'd started to wonder—call me crazy—if Wayland Beckett might have something to do with the break-in. Our cranky neighbor was becoming a real thorn in the flesh. I could see him trying to cause us trouble.

Then again, I could also envision Maggie Jamison causing trouble. She was filing a lawsuit, after all. And there was that camera footage of her on the night of the break-in.

Ugh. Lone Star certainly had its share of troubles right about now, didn't it?

When my grandmother left a short while later, I headed out to the lobby to pass Hector's file off to Cassidy. She had disappeared from the front desk. I found her in Victoria's office, where she'd been spending a lot of time lately.

"Hey there."

"Hey." She looked up from her paperwork. "Sorry, I'm preoccupied."

"Oh?" I stepped inside the office. "Something happening?"

"Yes, we just found out that Victoria's not coming back."

"No way." So, she had chosen the stay-at-home-mom route after all. Good for her! But, how would we ever survive without her?

"Yeah, apparently she loves being a new mama and doesn't think the baby will do well with a sitter. So, she's decided to stay home. Tyler was pretty upset."

"I'm sure he understands, though."

"Yeah, I think it's just going to take a minute to get used to the idea. He's already upset about Aggie."

"His cat?" This took me by surprise. "What's wrong with Aggie?"

"I'm not sure. I just know that he's been acting strange. I mentioned it to Tyler earlier and he's going to look into it."

"I had no idea." Good grief. Could anything else possibly go wrong for poor Tyler? My heart really went out to him. If anything happened to Aggie right now. . .

No, I wouldn't let myself think about it.

My thoughts shifted back to Victoria. "So, here's an idea: Maybe Victoria could work from home? I mean, her work could probably be done that way, right? And lots of people are working from home these days anyway, so it's not unheard of."

"Maybe. But I think Tyler's already talking about hiring someone to take her place. He's looking for a permanent solution. And with everything that's been going on around here, he thinks it would bring more stability to go ahead and get someone new in."

"Why would he do that?" I asked. "He just needs to give the position to you."

She shrugged. "I don't know. I didn't finish my degree, so I don't know that I'm qualified to be office manager."

"Are you kidding me? You're already doing it. I think you'd be perfect, and I'm sure Tyler will agree."

"You think?" She glanced my way with a hopeful expression on her face.

"If he hasn't already thought of it then I need to plant the idea in his head."

"But, who would take my place as receptionist?"

"We'll find someone new. Or maybe you could go on doubling up until we do?"

She groaned. "I'm already swamped, trying to do both. You can't imagine how many people I've accidentally hung up on today. It's been kind of a fiasco out there. But, hiding out in here?" She gestured to Victoria's tidy little office. "I love it. It's like my own personal refuge. You know? My shelter from the storm. My home away from home. My—"

"Got it. I'm sure it would be great to have a place to hide away, especially since you've been on full display at the reception counter for so long. For the record, I think you're doing a great job, keeping it all in balance, and I'm sure Tyler would agree."

"Thanks."

"You're welcome. So, pray about it, okay? Maybe Tyler will come around, with a little nudging." And I was just the person to nudge him. My friend deserved this boost. I would make sure she didn't get overlooked.

"I will." Cassidy flashed a warm smile. "And thanks for your confidence in me, Mari. I can always count on you to cheer me up or to bring a smile to my face. It's a special gift God gave you, to lift people's spirits."

"Thank you. That's very sweet."

"It's true. Oh, and by the way, I thought your grandmother looked adorable today in that colorful ensemble. She's pretty amazing, you know, and not just her over-the-top wardrobe."

"Yes, she's a Peach of a woman." I couldn't help but laugh at the play on words.

"She really is. And she matches her name in other ways too. That reddish hair, for instance."

"Clairol #13."

"That peachy complexion."

"Mary Kay. Light beige."

"That bright smile."

"Friedman's Dental. Caps. Don't even ask about the cost. She practically had to mortgage the house."

"Still, she matches her name. You know? I always think it's kind of fun when that happens."

"So, if I'm Marigold. . ."

"You. . ." Cassidy paused and gave me a pensive look. "Have a golden glow about you. Kind of like those Renaissance paintings of Christ and the disciples."

"Good try." I laughed. "I was kind of hoping you'd say that I was going to come into some money."

"Maybe you are."

"Not on a vet tech's salary." I sighed. "I'm not sure how I'll go very far on that."

"You sold your mama's house, though, right?"

"Yes. I put most of that money in savings. Paid off a couple of credit cards. Passed some of it off to my grandmother. But I need a long-term strategy for income beyond what I'm making now if I want to start this rescue. I'll need a place to house all the dogs. Wouldn't it be great if I had a large piece of property with an indoor facility for the dogs? And a big area for them to play and run? You know?"

I could read the compassion in her eyes as she offered a little smile. "Just pray about it, Marigold. God's got an answer for you."

"I know He does."

I thought about her words as I went back to my work. If this God-sized dream in my heart was really heaven-breathed, then the Lord really would give me what I needed to see it through. He'd always taken care of me in the past, right? Though, I had to admit, it seemed easier with Mama in the picture. Now that she was gone, my whole world was rocked. She had been the glue, holding everything together. And with her gone. . .

Honestly? I felt a little unglued. And I couldn't quite picture how things would be without her in the mix. My dream had always included her, after all.

We somehow made it through the rest of the morning. By the time noon arrived I was so overwhelmed that I'd almost forgotten my promise to drive Isabel to the courthouse. Unfortunately, she hadn't forgotten. She texted me at 12:01 with the words, IN THE LOBBY WAITING.

Oh boy. I couldn't weasel out of it now, even though everything inside of me wanted to run in the opposite direction. Instead, I joined her a couple of minutes later, pausing only to let Parker know my plans, just in case I was late getting back again. I also wanted to make sure someone knew to keep an eye on Beau Jangles in my absence. I didn't need him getting into any trouble around the office. Or, worse. . .getting out. I shivered, thinking about him ending up in Beckett's yard again. That couldn't happen.

Parker seemed worried that Matt might show up and offered to come with us, but I nixed that idea. One of us needed to stick around, just in case Tyler needed help. What if I got caught up at the courthouse and didn't make it back in time for the afternoon shift?

Still, Parker was not easily convinced I was doing the right thing by going. "But, Mari. . ." He shook his head. "I'd feel better if you didn't do this."

I couldn't really help how he felt, though, could I? I'd made a promise to Isabel, and I needed to follow through. She needed me, after all. And I know how I would feel, if I happened to be in her shoes. I'd want someone to stick close.

Isabel and I pulled out of the parking lot a short while later, and I pointed my SUV in the direction of the Washington County Courthouse.

"So, tell me what we're doing," she said, her voice trembling. "I've never had to do anything like this before."

"Me either, but it seems pretty straightforward. You're just dropping off the form and paying the fee to file it."

"How much?"

"I think it's a hundred dollars. But if you need help with that—"

"I don't. Money's not the issue. Matt is the issue. He's so—" She shook her head. "I honestly never dreamed I'd end up in this situation, Marigold. I'm the last person on the planet to get taken in by a guy like this. He's an addict who's skilled in the art of gaslighting. You can't even imagine what he's put me through. It's bad, though. And I let myself get sucked in. I feel like such a fool."

I couldn't imagine what she'd been through, but I wanted her to know that she wasn't going to have to walk this road alone. And so, I said so.

"Listen, Isabel. Your story doesn't stop here. You'll get past this. And I'll be here for whatever you need, I promise. And for the record, you didn't let yourself get sucked in. That's what these gaslighters do. They make you think things like that. And you know what? They know exactly how to prey on people. They're very skilled at what they do. But you're not alone here, I promise. We're all with you."

"You have no idea how much that means to me. Seriously." She leaned back against the seat. "I've felt like such an idiot. I can't believe I got caught up in a relationship with a guy like that. But he seemed so. . . normal. At least, at first."

"Sounds like his acting skills are stellar."

"They were, but at some point he stopped acting and the real him came out. At first I thought it was a fluke, like maybe he was just having a bad day or something. I'd never seen anyone flip out like that. But before long, he got really scary. He was following me around my house with a gun in his hand. Stuff like that."

"No way."

"Yeah." She shivered. "I can't believe I'm saying this, but it just became my normal. You know?"

"Um, no." I didn't. And I hoped I never would.

"I just have one thing to say about Matt Foster at this point. If his lips are moving, he's lying."

"Ugh. That's scary."

"Tell me about it."

I pulled up to the corner of Wilson and got caught in traffic. The weirdest sensation came over me as an odd noise from a vehicle behind me intensified.

In my rearview mirror I caught a glimpse of a large truck that seemed to be really close to my back bumper. Stupid driver. Why did he have to do that?

Seconds later, I heard the exaggerated sound of an engine revving. Someone was mighty impatient today.

"I can't exactly go anywhere," I muttered. "The light is red."

"Hmm?" Isabel glanced up from her phone, which she gripped tightly in her hand. "What did you say?"

"That guy behind us. . ."

He kept revving his engine, either an attempt to show off or. . .

I peered in my rearview mirror and gasped when I realized the man behind the wheel of the truck actually looked familiar to me. My heart raced to my throat as the reality hit.

Matt Foster.

And, judging from the anger in his eyes, he was out for blood.

CHAPTER SIXTEEN

The moment I realized Matt was trailing us, my whole body began to tremble. Isabel must've picked up on my anxiety because she turned around to see what had me so worked up.

"Oh no! Mari!" She started crying right away, her usual response to all-things-Matt-Foster related.

I felt like crying, myself, but didn't have the luxury. Someone had to maintain control, after all, if we were going to get out of this.

And we *were* going to get out of this, if it was the last thing I did.

"Stay calm." I did my best to keep my voice steady, but my hands shook as I gripped the wheel.

The light turned green, and I eased my way forward and prayed he would go around me. Maybe it was just a coincidence. Yes, he probably didn't even realize it was me.

He didn't go around me. In fact, he followed so close to the back end of my car that I wondered if he might hit me.

"He was watching us the whole time," Isabel whispered. "That's what he does, Mari. He's always watching. And hovering. That's how he knew when we were leaving work. He was right there, waiting for me to leave. I should have known!" The sobbing began in earnest now and before long had my nerves completely unwound.

Really, I could only think of one thing to do that made any sense at all. I called Parker right away. I explained the whole thing, doing my best to be heard above the sniffles coming from Isabel and the honking coming from Matt, who had pulled into the lane directly to my left. I tried not to meet his gaze. Instead, I stared straight ahead as I drove and spoke to Parker simultaneously.

By now, the idea of going to the courthouse seemed impossible. He would follow us there, and then what?

I didn't want to find out the "and then what" part. Not without backup, anyway. But, how could I avoid him now?

"What do I do, Parker? Come back to the clinic? Maybe you could call the police and they could be waiting?"

"Maybe," he responded. "But I'm more worried about what will happen before you get here."

"Me too. I'm actually scared he might try to drive me off the road." As if to prove my point, Matt swung dangerously close to my vehicle. My heart gravitated to my throat as I thought about the possibility of my car being hit.

"Stay in traffic, Mari. Stick to the center lane, if you can. Make sure you've got people all around you so there are witnesses, just in case."

"It's only two lanes going each way. And I sure hope this situation doesn't end with the need for witnesses."

"Me either. Maybe you should stay in the right lane so you can make a quick turn if you need to." He paused. "Hey, are you anywhere near the police station?"

"Just a few blocks, actually."

"Perfect. Stay on the phone with me, but drive straight there. I'm going to go get in my car and meet you there."

"O–okay." That sounded like a good idea. I glanced to the lane to my left and saw Matt's beady eyes staring at me. He made an obscene gesture and jerked his truck toward my vehicle. I flinched but managed to keep myself together.

I took a right at the next corner, but he somehow managed to do the same from the left lane. Ugh. This guy was relentless.

Then again, so was I. I wouldn't be taken down by an idiot like this. Not today, not ever. Where my courage came from, I could not say, but I found myself emboldened. Fueled by anger, perhaps. I wouldn't let him win. No way.

"Hold on, Isabel," I said. "I'm going to take a quick turn."

I managed to slip past him and turned onto a side road that cut through to Main Street. Unfortunately he must've figured out my plan because he was waiting at the corner. When the light turned he tried to block me in, but oncoming traffic forced him to move, thank goodness.

"Mari, I'm scared." Isabel gripped the door handle. "What can we do?"

"Oh, we're doing it. We're going straight to the police. He won't know what hit him."

I eased my way through the traffic at the next three corners until I reached the Brenham Police Department.

Now what? I weighed my options. Getting out of the car was a no-go. No telling what he would do before I could get inside and find help.

I wound around the side for the building where I saw several officers getting into their patrol cars.

"Thank You, Jesus."

I made a beeline straight for them, hyper focusing on the officers. Relief flooded over me the moment I noticed Officer Dennison getting into his patrol car.

I pulled up next to him and rolled down my window.

"Well, hey," he said, a smile lighting his face. "Long time, no see. Did you bring the dog by for a visit or something?"

"No, he's back at the clinic. I'm not stopping because of the dog."

"That's a shame. I was hoping to see what he looks like all cleaned up. You promised to send me pictures."

"I will, I promise. But that's not why I'm here. There's a man. He's been following us for blocks. Look behind me at the truck."

"A man in a truck?" The officer looked around, as if expecting a man to materialize.

"Yes, Officer," Isabel interjected from her spot in the passenger seat. "My ex. He's been stalking me. Marigold and I were just on our way to file a protective order." She held up the paperwork.

"You want the Washington County courthouse," Dennison explained. "You're in the wrong place, ladies."

"No, you don't understand," I explained. "He's been stalking us. Just now. Honking. Revving his engine. Tailing us. Making obscene gestures. All kinds of stuff. So we came here to get away from him."

Only, he was nowhere in sight.

I glanced in my rearview mirror and realized Matt's truck had disappeared from view. No way. He must've kept on going around the other side of the parking lot, once he saw my landing spot.

I felt an odd sense of relief, all mixed up with feelings of confusion.

The officer glanced my way. "You're saying there was a man following you just now, before you turned in here?"

"Yes, that's what I'm saying. He turned in, so he's in this parking lot somewhere. And trust me when I say he was looking to harm us. We also have reason to believe he's armed."

"So is half the state of Texas," Dennison countered. "What makes you think this one would hurt you?"

"Because he's done it before," Isabel explained. "He's hurt me before. And threatened me with a gun."

Dennison nodded. "Okay, I need a description of the vehicle. We'll search the parking lot."

Isabel and I both worked together to describe Matt's truck and a couple of the officers took off on foot to search for him while Dennison remained behind with us, taking notes in his laptop.

"I promise, he was just there," Isabel explained. "Matt Foster is his name. He's got a violent temper. He just got out of jail, and he wants me to pay."

"You're worried he will attack you?"

She nodded. "Yes. Yes, I am."

I was afraid too.

"You remember that mess at the vet clinic?" I reminded Officer Dennison.

"How could I forget it?"

"We have reason to believe Matt was responsible. And ever since that day he's been showing up at the clinic, stalking Isabel. We called the police a couple days back and they arrested him."

"For vandalism or for stalking?"

"Stalking, I guess. I really don't know. Maybe you could look it up? I just know that he was jailed overnight and then they released him."

"Ah. Give me a minute." He did some research on his laptop and came back a few minutes later with an answer. "He was picked up for trespassing, but they didn't charge him with vandalism. Must not have enough evidence that he was the one responsible for the break-in."

"Someone wearing a mask taped over the camera that night, so I don't know if we'll ever know who did it."

"We're still looking into it, I promise." He paused, and I could read the concern in his eyes. "So, what's your plan now, ladies? Want me to follow you back to the clinic?"

Isabel looked terrified by that idea. "We really need to get that protective order," she explained. "I don't think I'll sleep a wink until that's taken care of."

"I agree," I chimed in. "It's more important now than ever, since we know he's been released and is angry."

Isabel nodded. "I'm just so scared he's waiting around the corner for us."

I breathed the biggest sigh of relief when Parker pulled into the lot and came to a stop behind me. He jumped out of his truck and raced toward me.

"Did you get him?" he asked the officer.

"No." Dennison shook his head. "We've got officers looking. If he's close by, we'll find him."

Parker turned my way. "Mari, you're not going to the courthouse without me. I don't care if we're late getting back or not."

"Thank you, Parker." I wanted to throw my arms around him and give him the biggest hug ever, but this wasn't the time or place.

He turned to face Isabel. "We'll get that protective order signed. I'll follow you there and back."

I got back into my car and glanced down at my phone to find a text from Cassidy. Just four simple words, but they resonated way down deep.

PARKER. TO. THE. RESCUE.

CHAPTER SEVENTEEN

I received a call early Saturday morning from a reporter named Mollie Kensington, who wanted to interview me for the paper. Apparently, the story about Beau Jangles was really getting around. No doubt his picture in the local paper had stirred some interest, even though it had not turned up an owner.

Oh, we'd had applicants. Nearly a dozen people so far said they couldn't live without him. But, unfortunately, neither could I. And the words "foster fail" kept tripping across my tongue as I thought it through. It didn't exactly make sense to keep the very first dog I'd rescued, but this sweet boy needed me.

Or maybe I needed him.

Or maybe we needed each other.

But one thing was for sure—we were a match made in heaven, and I wasn't about to let him go, especially after what I'd been through over the past couple of days related to the chaos with Matt Foster. Having a dog in the house made me feel safer, especially with idiots like him on the prowl. I'd been a nervous wreck, knowing he was out there, free to do whatever he liked. My sweet pup brought a sense of security. Okay, so I wasn't sure Beau Jangles would come out swinging his fists on my behalf, but he could certainly bark with reckless abandon. That much, he'd proven time and time again—usually when Wayland Beckett was around.

I needed this little dog. It was undeniable. And having him filled another hole too, one I rarely spoke about. The death of my mother. The ache in my heart from losing her. Somehow, having that little dog to cuddle was ointment to that open wound. And now that I'd started applying the ointment, I couldn't very well stop, now could I? Of course not.

Not that I'd actually told anyone that yet. But I would. Soon. After this interview, perhaps. Then I would take care of the details, like getting a microchip transferred to my name. And registering him with the county. And asking Grandma Peach to make him a cute little Christmas outfit to wear when Trina came home.

If Trina came home.

Thinking of registering my pup with the county reminded me of all that had happened yesterday with Isabel and Matt. If it hadn't been for Parker, we would never have made it to the county courthouse so that she could file that paper.

But we did make it. And we made it back just fine too. And, thanks to a plan to have her stay at his place overnight, she had arrived safely at the clinic today. Hopefully Matt wouldn't show up when the reporter was here.

Of course, he wasn't the only one ready to cause trouble. I prayed Wayland Beckett would stay far, far away. His appearance could wreck this interview in a hurry.

I did my best to stay busy on Saturday so that I wouldn't worry about what I would say to the reporter. We saw a plethora of patients, and I found myself taking vitals, doing X-rays, running lab samples, prepping equipment, and ten thousand other things besides. I almost forgot to be nervous. Almost.

The reporter entered the clinic just as we were about close up shop Saturday. I invited her into the back office, where I found Parker wrapping up some work on the Great Dane's case. I made quick introductions, and Mollie flashed him a warm smile, then shook his hand. "Great to meet you."

"You too." He scooted out of the room with the words, "I'll let you two chat."

"Are you sure you don't want to stick around?" she called out after him. "I might have some questions for you too."

"So sorry, but I've got plans."

I knew his plans, of course, but couldn't reveal them. He planned to take Isabel back to his place and then invite his sister over to hang out. Hopefully they could distract her and keep her calm and safe. What he planned to do if Matt showed up, I couldn't be sure. I knew that Parker, like so many other guys in Brenham, was usually armed. Hey, we lived in Texas. It was pretty much the norm around these parts, like Dennison said. But, as for actually using that weapon? I couldn't picture it. He was such a softie. Did softies use guns? It wasn't something we'd ever talked about.

On the other hand, Parker-To-The-Rescue probably did know how to handle himself, should the need arise. He would likely sweep in and save the day, like he so often did. Hopefully this time he wouldn't have to, though. I whispered a little prayer to that effect as he disappeared from view.

My thoughts almost ran away with me as the reporter settled down at the desk and pulled out some sort of small recording device, which she set on the desk. She also flipped open a notepad and reached into her purse for a pen.

I grew nervous at once. I was usually free-spirited and carefree, babbling on about anything and everything. But with a recording device going? Not so much. Still, I wanted to share Beau's story.

The reporter introduced herself as Mollie Kensington. She was young, fresh, and apparently very anxious to have a story about my pup. I was happy to share the story.

She sat with her legs crossed and those dangly earrings hanging down as she smacked on a piece of gum.

"So, tell me about Beau Jangles." Mollie glanced up at me. "Start with his breed, I guess?"

I lifted the little pooch to my lap and scratched him behind the ears. "The best we can tell, he's a Cavalier King Charles Spaniel."

"Are you going to have his DNA done?"

"I guess we could." I shrugged. "But it wouldn't change anything. I've never been snobbish when it comes to breeds. Dogs are perfect, no matter their breed."

She scribbled something down, then glanced up. "And you found him in the sewer?"

"Not exactly the sewer, but close. I climbed in one of those large drainage pipes to fetch him. He was hiding up there."

"For how long?" She jotted something else down in her notes.

"No idea, but he was pretty hungry those first few days, so maybe awhile. And he was matted and stinky. In fact—"

She glanced my way.

"His matting was so bad that we weren't completely sure about his breed that first night. We were tickled to discover he's a diva dog."

"Diva dog?"

"That's what I call the high-end purebreds. But like I said, I'm not a breed snob."

"Some people are, though?"

"Oh, yeah. They wouldn't give thought to adopting a shelter dog, but they'd pay a couple thousand dollars to buy one with a pedigree." I did my best not to roll my eyes. After all, if I wasn't a snob, I couldn't be snobbish about people who cared about such things, now could I?

"And you've had offers for a home for him?"

Ugh. She would ask. "Yes, but the perfect situation hasn't presented itself just yet. To be honest, we've fallen in love with him. He's become our unofficial mascot."

"Why unofficial?" She scribbled down more notes.

"We've got a practice cat. Aggie."

"Practice cat? He's practicing being a cat?"

I laughed. "No. We're a veterinary practice. And we have a cat. That's all I meant."

"Cute." Mollie looked up and grinned.

"He's Dr. Tyler's cat. But he's 110 years old."

"The cat, or Dr. Tyler?"

"Oh, the cat." I laughed. "And he's not really 110. He's probably more like fourteen or fifteen years old. Not sure what that breaks down to in cat years. But he definitely rules the roost around here."

"Was he here the night of the incident?" she asked.

I shook my head. "Oh, no way. He goes home every night with Tyler."

She scribbled something down then looked up, pen dangling between her fingers. "Tell me a little about your work here at the clinic, Marigold. What's it like, being a vet technician?"

"Oh, well, it's pretty routine." I paused to think that through. "No, no it's not. I mean, I come in in the morning and do my usual things."

"Like what?"

"I usually set up the lab area when I first get here, then I check all of the exam rooms to make sure the necessary amount of supplies are on hand."

"Like?" She glanced up from taking notes to shoot a penetrating look my way.

"Syringes, supplies in drawers, and so on. Then I check in on the hospital patients, the ones who spent the night. They get their meds. And the heartworm positive pups get walked on a leash. We like to limit their mobility because of the strain on the heart caused by the worms."

She stopped scribbling and looked up. "Worms. Ick."

I couldn't help but laugh at her assessment of my job. No doubt, many would agree. "Yeah, there's a lot of ick in my job. Like poop. You can't be a vet tech without encountering lots of it. And vomit. And blood. But I'm used to all of that. It doesn't bother me at all anymore."

"Can't envision it, sorry."

She looked a little green, so I changed the topic. "Anyway, I sanitize the kennels, set up the blood machine in the lab area, do a quality control blood sample. Then we open for business and the clients start coming in."

"Any crazy ones?"

Should I mention my grandmother's cat? No, probably not.

"We've seen a few," I said. "But most are like family to us. It's usually pretty chill around here—my days are filled with rectal temps, vaccines, ear washes, and blood draws."

"How long did you go to school?"

Parker entered the room. "Hey, sorry to interrupt. I just need to grab something real quick."

Mollie's gaze shifted to him at once and I noticed her lips curl up in a smile.

"Oooh, you're back. Please join us." She flashed a coy smile his way. Wait, was she flirting with him?

"I can't, sorry. I'm with a last-minute patient. Just wanted to check in to see if you had any extra syringes in here, Mari." He walked to the drawer and looked around until he found what he needed.

"Marigold was just telling me about everything you vet techs do here," Mollie said. "For my article. Anything you want to add?"

"Sure." He paused and appeared to be thinking. "There are a lot of everyday tasks and you've got to go through the bad to get to the good, but when you've got a passion for the animals, it's worth it. And by the way, I've never"—and here, he flashed a warm smile—"never seen anyone as passionate or as caring as Marigold. She's the best." He grabbed the syringe and slipped out of the door.

My heart wanted to burst into song at his kind words. It felt good to be noticed.

"Wow, he really thinks a lot of you." Mollie sighed. "Lucky girl. He's a cutie."

Was I the only one who'd never really given much thought to Parker's looks? Weird.

"He's a great guy," I said after thinking it through. "And he's right about needing a passion for animals. That's what we're all about here at Lone Star. We've got a common goal—for the animals. And their owners too, of course."

"Since you brought up the owners. . ." Mollie looked a little nervous as her words trailed off. "Can I run something by you?"

"Sure."

"Off the record, I promise."

"Oh, okay." That made me nervous.

She leaned forward and lowered her voice. "So, rumor has it, a lawsuit has been filed by one of your clients. I'd like to ask you more about that, if you don't mind. How does it feel, knowing someone is out to get you?"

CHAPTER EIGHTEEN

W hat?"
Maggie had actually filed a suit? Already?

"Are you sure?" I asked, doing my best to keep my words calm and steady.

"It's not exactly common knowledge," Mollie said. "But I happen to have a family member who works for Henderson Law Firm. When I told her I was doing a story on the clinic, she let it slip about the incoming suit. Sorry if you didn't already know."

"Only rumors." Tyler would be devastated to know they were true. For that matter, I was too. That's all we needed, on top of everything else.

My heart twisted. Beau Jangles must've picked up on my worries. He reached up and licked me on the cheek, then nuzzled against me.

"Seems like a sweet little guy." Mollie reached for her camera and then snapped a picture of Beau Jangles showing me affection.

"Yeah, it's funny. I've been through it over the past six months. I lost my mom to cancer, and my Aunt Trina is so far away—"

"In Nashville. Recording hit songs. Like 'Don't Mess with Mama'."

"Yes."

"Which, if I'm understanding correctly, is dedicated to your grand-mother. Right?"

"Right. And she's mighty proud of it. But my point is, I haven't had

Beau Jangles for long but he's become like family to me."

"I can see how that would happen." Her nose wrinkled. "And I'm so sorry about your mom. I don't know what I'd do if I ever lost my mom. It's hard enough with her living in Austin and me here. It's so funny, isn't it? When we're in our teens we don't want anything to do with our mothers. Then we get older, and—"

"Exactly. And that's how I feel about Trina being gone too. I really miss her." Maybe I shouldn't go on and on about Trina. She might not like the fact that I'd brought up her name so many times.

Mollie jotted something down and then sighed. "I'm at a weird place right now in my life. It's kind of lonely in my one-bedroom apartment."

"I have a solution for that." A chuckle escaped. "I can add you as a foster. We'll be needing more of those soon."

"Oh?" She looked up. "You plan to rescue more dogs?"

"I hope so, if I can figure out where to house them."

"Once this story goes to print, I'm sure people will step up." She gave me an admiring look. They'll latch onto this idea of yours and run with it. You watch and see, Mari. You'll have volunteers. . .and financial support."

"You think?"

"Yep." She nodded. "If you haven't already set up a 501c3, you should probably start that process soon."

"I should." It sounded overwhelming, though.

"If you set yourself up with a nonprofit you can get all the help you need. And grants too. I can help you with that part. I did a little grant writing back in the day."

"Would you really?" Wow. Talk about a Godsend.

We wrapped up our interview a few minutes later, and I led the way back out into the lobby. I could hardly believe my eyes when I saw Cameron Saye behind the counter, gabbing with Cassidy, who seemed glued to his every word. Ugh. Tyler wouldn't be happy about this. Why did this guy keep showing up, anyway?

I drew near just as Cameron leaned over Cassidy's shoulder to look at something she was typing into the brand-spanking-new computer Tyler had just purchased to replace the stolen one. "You're really good at what you do."

Her cheeks flushed pink. "Thank you."

Good at what she did? The girl was typing, for Pete's sake, nothing more. But, from the look on his face, you'd think she had invented the cure for cancer.

"So, what's it like, working in a vet's office?" he crooned.

"It's fun." Cassidy went off on a tangent about some of the pets she'd checked out earlier in the day. "I mean, not everything is fun. All of that stuff the other night. . ." she shivered. "That was pretty awful. Getting robbed, I mean."

"Burglarized," I said under my breath.

"Yeah, I heard about that." Cameron leaned against the counter, arms crossed at his chest. "Scary stuff. Glad you're okay."

"Thanks." Cassidy seemed to lose herself in his gaze as they locked eyes.

Oh, brother.

Mollie froze up too. She stood, eyes wide, staring at Mr. Hollywood.

Good gravy. I'd never get out of here, from the looks of things. I took a couple of steps toward the door, but she didn't follow me, so I fussed with a microchip display on the counter to busy myself.

Tyler came out of his office and stopped cold when he saw Cameron behind the counter.

"Cameron." Just one word, but it was enough to convey his meaning. *Get out from behind my counter.*

Only, Cameron didn't move a muscle. Instead, he flashed a dazzling smile and said, "Hey, Ty."

Tyler walked behind the counter and grabbed a file, then gave Cameron a pensive look. "How's your arm?"

"My arm?"

"You know, the cut from when you were helping an old lady with her fence. The board fell on you?"

"Oh, *that* arm." Cameron laughed and then lifted his sleeve to show off several stitches. "I pulled the bandage off to let it air out. Stitches come out in a few days. I'll live. All's well that ends well."

That helping an old lady story didn't ring true to me. My gaze shifted to the plate glass windows, and I tried to envision how that gash might've really happened. A chill wriggled its way down my spine as I thought it through. The longer I stood here, the more likely it seemed.

Tyler's cat jumped up on the counter and made himself at home near the warmth of the computer. Cameron reached over to scratch him behind the ears, but the cat hissed at him and he pulled back.

"Whoa, Aggie!" Cameron pulled his hand back. "Don't remember me, eh?"

Tyler's brows arched. "As I recall, he always hissed at you, even back in the day."

"Yeah, well, he was about half this size back then," Cameron countered. "What do you feed this cat, anyway?"

"Hey, you know what they say about a vet and his pets. Do as I say, not as I do."

"He's not looking good, Ty." Cameron gave the cat an inquisitive look. "When did he start putting on weight?"

"A few months ago." Tyler opened a drawer and pulled out a pen, then reached for a scrap of paper. "Started pretty suddenly."

Cameron leaned forward to get a better look at Aggie. "Any other symptoms? Blood pressure? Thyroid?"

Creases formed between Tyler's brows. "Haven't slowed down long enough to check yet, but he has been more lethargic. I just chalked it up to old age."

"Renal issues." Cameron crossed his arms at his chest and leaned against the counter. "Remember that unit we did on older cats and renal disease? It shows up in more ways than just urinary symptoms. It can affect the heart, blood pressure. . .everything."

"Right." Tyler grew silent, and I could tell he was thinking it through.

"Do some labs, my friend."

Only, the way he said "my friend" felt a little. . .counterfeit. Tyler must've thought so too, because he grabbed the chart and turned to scribble something down.

I cleared my throat, then walked to the door, hoping Mollie would follow. She did. As she prepared to leave, the young woman turned my way. Her gaze shot to Cameron, then back to me.

She let out a little whistle. "My stars and garters, girl! Would you look at how the Lord has blessed him!"

"You think?"

"You don't?" She laughed, then turned back to stare at Cameron. "Are you blind, girl? Let's get those eyes checked."

"Maybe." Or maybe I just knew more than she did.

"So, who is he, anyway?" Mollie asked. "Does he work here? 'Cause, if he does, I might need to look into getting a dog. Or a cat. Or a hamster."

"We don't treat hamsters."

"Okay, a cat, then. Or a goldfish. What department does he work in? He sure sounds like he knows a lot about the medical stuff."

"He's not an employee. He went to school with Tyler, so that's how they know each other."

"Oooh, at A&M?" Her eyes lit up. "Maybe I could offer to do an interview about his training. He'd make a great candidate for an article."

"I don't know about that."

She fanned herself, her gaze never leaving him. "I can't stop looking at him. He's such a cutie."

"Right." *On the outside.*

"The other vet is nice too." She elbowed me then gestured with her head to Tyler, who was hunched over the file, writing something down.

"Yeah." I must've sighed because she laughed.

"Oh, I see. Please tell me *he* works here."

"He's the owner."

"Whelp, now I *know* I have to get a pet." She seemed to lose herself to her thoughts as she stared at the two guys. "Do you ever get so distracted looking at him that you forget to work? Because I could see myself totally doing that."

"Sometimes."

"He's buff. He's tall. He's the owner of the company." Mollie grinned. "Hey, he's pretty much Atlas, holding up the world."

"Well, when you put it like that. . ." Tyler did look a little like Atlas, with those muscular arms. "A girl would have to be blind not to notice."

"That other one, though." She stared longingly at Cameron. "He's the cat's meow." A laugh followed. "See what I did there? Cat's meow?"

Aggie chose that moment to jump off the counter and slink toward Tyler's office.

He had the right idea. With Cameron in the room, I wanted to slink away too.

I thanked Mollie for coming and waved as she walked out the door, then turned back to the reception desk just in time to see Cameron lean in close to Cassidy, who seemed over-the-top giddy at his nearness.

Oh no, girl. Not on my watch, you don't.

Something with this guy was off. Way off. And watching him schmooze his way into my best friend's heart? No sir. Cute or not, slick or not, I wouldn't let him lead Cassidy down a broken road.

This guy had to go.

CHAPTER NINETEEN

I had a standing date with my grandmother on Sundays after church. She wrapped up at First Prez, I wrapped up at Grace Fellowship, and we met for lunch at a local restaurant, usually at her favorite cafeteria, where she ordered the liver and onions and I ordered the fried fish plate. She always fussed at me for ordering what she called "processed fish flakes cooked in trans fats" but I usually just ignored her and ate the fish. And the mac-and-cheese. And the bright red gelatin with fake whipped cream on top.

We enjoyed our bantering. And, I had to admit, I only got the gelatin to irritate her.

It was what we did.

Today I'd had a hard time staying focused. Parker had invited Isabel to his church, and I was worried sick about them. Would Matt show up to cause trouble? When would that protective order kick in, anyway? Would it really make a difference? Would Parker know what to do if Matt stirred things up?

I struggled with these questions and more as Grandma Peach and I made our way through the lengthy line at the cafeteria to get our food. She gabbed with anyone and everyone in the line ahead of us, and I kept a watchful gaze on the plate glass windows behind us, as if expecting Matt to come barreling through them.

We got our food and settled at a table near the front of the crowded restaurant. I helped my grandmother get her plate and beverage situated on the table and then put the trays on a nearby holder.

When I took my seat, Grandma bowed her head and I followed suit. This was our usual routine. She spoke a quiet, sweet prayer, asking God to bless our food, and I ended with, "Amen."

Then we both dove in. Only, I didn't feel much like eating today.

"What's going on, Mari?" Grandma asked after she'd taken a couple of bites of her liver and onions. "You seem kind of distracted today."

"Do I?" My gaze shifted across the room. Would Parker and Isabel stop in for lunch after church, perhaps? This was one of his favorite places, after all.

"Yes, you do. Are you okay?" She set her fork down and reached for her glass of tea.

I decided to focus on her, so I offered a confident smile and said, "I'm fine, Grandma. I made the paper, by the way."

"Did you? For a good reason, I hope?" She reached for her knife and fork, then took another tiny sliver of the liver.

Sliver of liver.

Ha.

"Yes, a reporter showed up and asked all sorts of questions about the night I rescued Beau Jangles."

"Aw, that's awesome. You're a celebrity!"

"Hardly. But I suppose you could say I did get a few moments in the spotlight. Until the calls started pouring in."

"Calls?" She reached into her purse and came out with a little pill container, then dumped a bunch of supplements onto the edge of her plate.

"Yeah, I have a feeling everybody and their brother will have a dog they need—or want—me to rescue."

"Oh my." She took another nibble of her food and then dabbed at her lips with her cloth napkin before reaching for one of the supplements.

"I suspect that many of them will just be people who've grown tired of their dogs and want to rehome them." I managed a bite of the fish. It was just as yummy as I remembered. Hot. Flaky. Fake as all get-out, but so good. I took another bite.

"That's terrible, Marigold. What will you do?" She swallowed another pill.

"I'm not sure." I stabbed the prongs of the fork into the mac-and-cheese and took a big bite of the creamy deliciousness. Cheese made everything better. I could dedicate my life to eating more cheese.

"Why not take them to the local shelter?"

"Our shelter is fighting an ongoing battle with distemper. It's quite a problem. We're doing everything we can to keep dogs out of there. We're talking full-out epidemic at the one shelter and a high-risk situation at the other."

A supplement capsule dangled from her fingers, and I wondered if she might drop it. "Sounds like you're going to need a lot of help."

"I will. I know I can count on Cassidy. And Parker. He—"

"He's the one with those really pretty blue eyes, right?" She popped the capsule in her mouth and spoke around it. "The guy with the brown hair and nice smile?"

"Yes, Grandma." I shoveled a massive bite of fish into my mouth. "He's the other vet tech at Lone Star." *As we've already established.* "Anyway, I think he'll help me."

She chased her pill down with a swig of tea, then dabbed her lips once more. "I know his family from church."

"You do? They go to First Prez?"

"Yep. Not him, though. I think he defected."

Defected?"

"He was a Presbyterian as a child, but he's a Baptist now. Nearly wrecked his poor mother when he decided to pull the switcharoo. But it's okay now. They've ironed out their theological differences. And he still comes to the annual Christmas service, so his mama's happy. Well, one day a year, anyway. Not sure about the other 364."

"That's good." Though, I imagined there were worse fates than becoming a Baptist. "Now, tell me all about Curtis, Grandma. I'm dying to know what's really going on with you two, so spill the tea."

"Spill the tea?" Her gaze shot to her tea glass.

"That's a saying. It means spill your guts."

"Ah, I see. To be perfectly frank, my guts don't need to be spilled, especially not here at the cafeteria. So, I won't be spilling any tea, please and thank you."

"But..."

"No buts." Her gaze shifted to the table, and she fussed with her napkin. "This liver is so yummy, don't you think? Not quite as good as my version, and probably loaded with artificial ingredients, but still pretty tasty."

"I wouldn't know. I'm having the fish. But back to Curtis..."

She teased the tongs of her fork into what appeared to be a rather stiff piece of okra and sighed. "No one makes vegetables the way I do. Mine are so much better."

"Grandma, you're avoiding the subject."

"Yes, I am." She dabbed at her lips with her napkin once again, a nervous gesture, no doubt. "Would you pass the salt, please?"

"I thought the doctor told you to cut back on salt?"

"I only need a little. This okra is so bland. I could teach them a thing or two about seasoning."

No doubt she could. And right now she was teaching me a thing or two about how to avoid the subject. The woman had some serious skills in that regard. I had a lot to learn from her.

Not that I blamed her. Being put on the spot—especially with something as sensitive as a guy issue—was awkward, at best.

Fine. If she didn't want to talk about Curtis, I'd let her off the hook. I changed the subject and started talking about putting up the Christmas tree.

She flinched. "Mari, you know me better than that. I put up my tree on Black Friday. It's not even Halloween yet."

"I don't know why, but I just feel like Christmas needs to come early this year."

"Oh, that reminds me! I made another little costume for Beau Jangles, a Christmas-themed one. But I need to take his measurements to make sure it fits."

"What did you make?" I asked.

She pulled out her cell phone, and with a shaky hand, started thumbing through her photos. It took her a while, but she finally turned the phone my direction and I gasped when I saw the costume that looked like an elf.

"Oh, Grandma, it's perfect! I was going to ask you to make something for him for Christmas!"

"He's such a cute little thing, I figured this would be perfect."

"What makes you think I'll still have him at Christmas, though? Remember? I'm supposed to be finding him a home?"

"Pooh on that idea." She took a nibble of her liver. "You're going to keep that dog."

"I–I am?"

"Well, of course you are. I don't see how you could let him go now. I saw how he gazed up at you with so much love and affection that first day at the feed store. And at the clinic the other day. Everyone's in love with him. To let him go now would just be cruel—to them and to him."

"I have been giving it some thought. But, how did you know?"

"A grandmother knows these things." She lit into a carefree conversation about the special anointing on grandmothers to know all-the-things, but she lost me after a few seconds because I saw someone entering the cafeteria. The hairs on my arm raised as I watched Wayland Beckett cross the room ahead of a tiny little woman, head bowed low as she made her way across the room behind him. His wife, maybe? He paused when he saw me, his eyes narrowing to slits. Then he moved on to a table on the far side of the room. Thank goodness I wouldn't have to deal with him.

"Ugh." Grandma's nose wrinkled as she stared at him. "That man is enough to make a preacher want to cuss."

"Oh?"

"Yes, I feel so sorry for Mildred. Such a sweet little thing, to be stuck with a man like that."

I felt sorry for her too, and I didn't even know the woman. Still, her bowed posture as she tagged along behind him told me everything I needed to know about their relationship.

Grandma reached for another pill. "I told you what a troublemaker he was at the church. Griped about everything. Always had to have his way. And don't even get me started on the financial stuff."

"My goodness. Who has that kind of power?"

"The Wayland Becketts of this world, that's who. And we're the ones who give it to him. So, don't let him bully you, sweet girl. Be firm around him."

Easy for her to say. It wasn't her dog digging holes under the man's fence or disrupting meetings with his clients.

We dove back into our conversation, but a few minutes later Grandma was distracted by someone else entirely. Curtis Elban happened by with a tray in hand. He was followed by an older woman in a shiny pink blouse and black pencil skirt. She was probably in her early seventies, but her hair was as blonde as mine. Maybe more so. I wasn't sure which Lady Clairol gave you that particular color, but it was definitely found in a box, not nature.

Grandma Peach took one look at the two of them and dropped her fork. Her face turned so red I thought she might stroke out on me. She began to cough, and I wondered if she was choking on a supplement.

Curtis gave her a quick nod as he walked by but didn't really say much other than a muttered, "Howdy, y'all."

"Howdy, y'all?" Grandma said, after she got control of herself. "Howdy y'all? He walks by with that hussy, Donna Sue Specklemeyer, and all I get is a howdy y'all? After all the pies I've baked for that man?" She went into a tirade unlike anything I'd ever witnessed from her before. In fact, she got so loud that the people in the next booth all turned to stare. I wanted to crawl under the table.

"Maybe that's his sister?" I tried, when she paused for breath.

"No ma'am. That's Donna Sue Specklemeyer. I've known her since elementary school. She was flirty with the boys on the playground, and I see nothing much has changed. Can you even believe that hairpiece she's wearing? Who does she think she's fooling with that spare hair?"

I nearly spit out my sweet tea. "Just because they're having lunch together doesn't mean she's—"

"She's been through three husbands and is working on a fourth, from the looks of things."

"Oh my. A repeat divorcée."

"No, all of her husbands died."

"What?"

"Yep. And somewhere between the first and the second, Donna Sue got hooked on whiskey and started honky-tonkin'. You don't even want to know about those weeks."

"Weeks? She only waited weeks to remarry?"

"Yes, and that's another thing. She doesn't know how to take care of a man. She fed that last husband of hers fried chicken every Sunday after church. Can you imagine?"

I took another nibble of my fried fish and shook my head. "Terrible."

"Curtis can't afford to eat fried food." Grandma shot another glance his way. "Did you happen to notice what was on his tray?"

"Fried chicken, mashed potatoes, and corn on the cob."

"For the love of Pete. He won't make it till Wednesday." Grandma fanned herself. "She'll kill him before she gets him to the altar."

"But Grandma, you feed him pie."

"Only on occasion."

"Occasion? Like, morning, noon, and night?"

"There's a difference between an occasional slice of pie and a steady diet of trans fats. Besides, my pies are home baked. I know what goes in them—only healthy ingredients."

"Like sugar, flour, and butter?"

She ignored me and kept right on talking. "I know that Donna Sue has put on forty pounds since we were in high school, at least. Did you see how tight that ridiculous pink blouse was?"

"Grandma, I really don't think this is an appropriate conversation we're having. Can we change the subject?"

"Sure." She released a slow breath, as if willing herself to calm down. Then she looked me squarely in the eye. "Let's go back to talking about that cute young vet tech you work with. When are you going to admit that he's more than just a friend?"

Good grief.

The rest of the meal was a complete wash. Grandma couldn't seem to pay attention. Her gaze kept shifting to Curtis and Donna Sue. It didn't help that the woman's shrill laugh cut through the air like a bolt of lightning tearing across the Texas sky. It was that kind of high-pitched laugh that made you feel like plucking your eyes out.

Curtis didn't seem to mind. In fact, he seemed to be eating it up.

Well, that, and an entire plate filled with breaded, high-fat foods.

I managed to transition our conversation back to the story about the reporter coming to interview me. My article was supposed to come out in this morning's paper, but I hadn't had a chance to pick up a copy yet. Maybe I should do that now. Yes, there was a newsstand just outside the restaurant. I'd grab a copy and Grandma could celebrate me, her celebrity granddaughter.

Only, when I saw the article, I didn't feel like celebrating. First, the photo Mollie had nabbed of me was awful. I didn't look very good in black-and-white. And what was up with the double chins? I didn't have two chins. . .did I? No, surely it was just the angle.

And that headline! *Local Woman Goes to the Dogs.*

Really?

Okay, so the article was actually okay. I smiled as she described my take on the drainage pipe story. And I had to chuckle when she mentioned my love for Beau Jangles. But I could tell from the tone of the article that a lot of folks would think I was ready for more rescues. I wasn't sure that was the case, at least not yet. I had to find a place to house them, after all.

"Let me see, honey." Grandma shoved her plate aside, done with her meal. "On the other hand, maybe you'd better read it out loud. I don't have my readers with me, and you know how I am."

I'd just started to do so when Wayland Beckett rose and took several steps toward the door. He slipped his arm over his wife's shoulder and they marched past us, eyes straight ahead. The man was definitely avoiding me.

Well, he couldn't avoid me for long. Brenham was too small a town for that. And he would have to see me out walking the dogs in the yard, now wouldn't he?

"That man's slicker than a country road after a thunderstorm," Grandma muttered under her breath after they passed by.

Yes, he was. But I saw straight through him now. If he dared speak a word against my dog—or my clinic—I'd show him. Okay, so I wasn't sure how, but I would. No doubt about it.

Grandma got pretty riled up and forgot all about the article. She carried on and on about Wayland, about Curtis, and about that hussy, Donna Sue Specklemeyer.

I folded the paper and shoved it into my oversized purse, my thoughts in a whirl.

Then, just when I thought things couldn't possibly get any worse, a familiar duo passed by our table, trays in hand, searching for a clean table.

Tyler.

And Kristin.

Wasn't that just dandy.

CHAPTER TWENTY

"Mari, you're famous!"

I looked up from my work to discover Kristin standing in the doorway of the lab. "What?"

"Haven't you seen the article in yesterday's paper?" She waved a newspaper in front of me. "I got a copy first thing, and I bought another four this morning on my way in. It's going to be great for business. And you're a local hero, girl!"

"You think?"

"I know."

I felt my cheeks grow warm. I'd never done well with a lot of attention. Maybe I should've thought of that before agreeing to be interviewed. On the other hand, my rescue would need all the marketing available, so. . .

Kristin beamed with obvious pride. "Girl, they made you out to be a superhero. All of that stuff about passion for animals and rescuing dogs in need. And that whole story about climbing in the drainage ditch to rescue Beau Jangles."

Cassidy popped her head in the door and said, "Drainage pipe!" then stepped into the room.

"Whatever." Kristin laughed. "Point is, the reporter captured it all in living Technicolor. Well, in black print on a white page. But she did you justice, and then some. She brought a lot of attention to your rescue.

Doesn't that make you happy?"

"My unofficial rescue." I did my best not to sigh aloud as I thought about how far I still had to go before claiming I owned a rescue. Like starting a 501c3, for instance.

"Speaking of which, we just took in a call about a dog in need," Cassidy's nose wrinkled as she glanced my way. "I told them you would call back when you had a chance. I didn't realize you were already here or I would've put the call through."

"Yeah, I came in early. What's the story on the dog?"

"I'm not sure. But I think you need to brace yourself. You've got a big career ahead of you in the rescue biz."

"Just don't run off and leave us when you're famous, okay?" Kristin said. "Promise?"

"I won't. But how can I start anything when I don't have a place to put them all? I don't have a clue how to handle that part. I mean, I know Tyler would probably say it's okay to board them here temporarily, but if Beckett finds out. . ." I shivered. "Can you even imagine? He already gets worked up when I take the dogs out to the yard for a run."

"It's none of his business if we have dogs in the yard," Cassidy said. "We have a permit for that."

"Just ignore him," Kristin added.

"What if he ends up filing some sort of suit, like Maggie?"

"Maggie's filing a suit?" Kristin flinched. "Are you sure?"

Ack. I hadn't meant to let that slip out.

Think fast, Mari.

"I mean. . .she might. Right?" I shifted my gaze to Cassidy, hoping she would help. "Have we seen proof of that?"

My friend shrugged. "She's called a couple of times saying she plans to, but we haven't been served or anything."

Kristin looked genuinely ill over this conversation. "If anything comes through, let me know right away."

"I will. I promise." Cassidy shrugged. "But I'm still hoping she was just bluffing. You know?"

"Mm-hmm." Kristin turned and walked from the room.

"Ugh. That's my fault," I admitted. "The reporter told me on the sly that she'd heard about a lawsuit from someone in her family who works for an attorney."

"So, it's true?" Cassidy pinched her eyes shut. "That's all we need right now. I really was hoping it was a bluff on her part to scare us."

"I think it's more than a bluff."

"That's sad. But, speaking of Maggie, Jasper's paw print just came in today."

"Oh, she had that done?"

"No, we did it as a gift to her. I'll be mailing it tomorrow. Unless we get served." Cassidy groaned. "Then I'm not so sure. But, what brought up the lawsuit in conversation, anyway?"

"Oh, I was just telling Kristin that Beckett would probably try to file one too, if I opened up the clinic to rescue animals."

She waved her hand, as if to dismiss that notion. "He wouldn't have a leg to stand on. We're a veterinary business. We are supposed to care for animals, and animals make noise."

"I just can't figure out the 'where will I keep all of them once they're rescued' part."

"You'll find fosters. Just have faith, Mari. A teensy-tiny seed of faith the size of a mustard seed. God will take care of the rest."

"Yes, He will. I know He will." But it felt good to be reminded that I didn't need much.

"He'll give you the desires of your heart. That's what the Bible says. And I know you, Marigold. Your desire is to have a rescue."

"On my own land." I sighed. "Someday. And when that happens I'll have plenty of room to take in every one that I hear about. Until then, I just don't know how much I can manage. I mean, it was fun, going out that night and tracking down Beau. But it was a total fluke that I caught him."

"No it wasn't a fluke at all. You were prepared. You were ready. And I know you. . .you'll do it again. And again. And again. You'll go on doing it until you've saved every one you can save. But you can't let fear stop you from your calling. End of story."

Okay then. End of story.

I spent most of that day working an emergency surgery with Tyler, who seemed a little out of sorts. Something to do with Cameron, judging from the little bit he'd told me. I didn't press him on it. It wasn't my business. He did tell me that Aggie was getting worse, and that he'd done a blood draw to run tests.

"What are you thinking?" I asked.

"Maybe UTI?" He paused. "Or maybe Cameron was right. He is showing signs of the kind of renal failure we see in older cats sometimes."

"I hope not, Tyler." I rested my hand on his arm, hoping to console him.

"Regardless, I need to know so I can treat him. Parker told me that he had cleaned up after Aggie this morning because he didn't quite make it to the litter box."

"Ah. I'm sorry." Should I tell him that I'd cleaned up after Aggie for the same reason a couple of days back?

No, he might take my response as a complaint, and I definitely didn't want to come across that way. Cleaning up after the animals was part of my job description, after all. And taking care of that sweet old cat? No problem at all.

Still, the idea that something might be wrong with him made me nervous. He was fourteen, after all, and the sweetest thing ever.

Strange, the contrast between Aggie and Hector. Good cat, bad cat.

Kind of like the contrast between Tyler and Cameron. Good vet, bad vet.

Around four that afternoon I finally had a few minutes to return the call about the dog in need. He turned out to be a stray off 237, not far from the town of Round Top, a local tourist destination. It sounded like this poor pup—which she called Blacky— had been on his own for a while and was looking pretty thin and scraggly.

The woman on the phone shared a somber tale of a family that had moved away, leaving the lonely black dog behind.

"That's heartbreaking!" I responded, after hearing the details. "How could they do that?"

"I have no idea, but he's still hanging out near their property, even though a couple of weeks have gone by," she explained. "Trying to make it on his own. I've fed him from time to time but have my own dogs to take care of. The poor thing is looking really lost."

"No doubt." This story made my blood boil. Who would move away and leave their dog behind? That made no sense.

"The landlord is a cranky old guy, but he's aware of the situation. He's actually the one who wants the dog gone, so that he can try to rent the place out again. He wanted to call the county to pick up the dog, but after I saw the article in the paper about you, I convinced him that a local rescue was a better option."

"Gee, sounds like a great guy."

"He's not," she responded. "But you'll find that out soon enough. He's coming by the house this evening with a contractor to take care of some damage the renters did."

"Ugh."

Oh well. I'd dealt with cranky people before. I could certainly handle a testy landlord. I would fix this. Just like I fixed everything else in life. I'd find this pup and take him under my wing and then. . .

And then I wasn't sure. But Cassidy was right. I had a call on my life to do this. That's why such a fierce passion rose up inside of me when I heard stories like this.

God would help me figure out a plan of action, starting with a team of fosters.

And I knew just which foster to begin with.

I hoped.

I ended the call and headed straight to the kennel area, where I found Parker cleaning up. He looked up as I entered the room and flashed his usual welcoming smile. "Hey. Heading home?"

"No." I shook my head. "Headed somewhere else, actually, and wondering if you want to come with."

He stopped cleaning and faced me. "Where?"

"Before I tell you, can I ask a favor?"

"Does it involve a dog?"

"Maybe."

He picked up the bottle of cleaning spray and carried it to the shelf nearby. "What's the favor?"

"You've got a house."

"Right." He walked to the washing machine and opened the door, then tossed some dirty towels inside.

"With a yard."

"Right. Great yard." He dumped some detergent into the washer.

"And I'm in an apartment. No yard."

He turned on the washer, then turned to face me. "And. . ."

Just say it, Marigold.

"So, I've been thinking. . ." I tried to make my words sound positive and upbeat. "Maybe you could be my first official foster for Second Chance Ranch."

CHAPTER TWENTY-ONE

Second Chance Ranch?" Parker looked confused.

"Yes, that's going to be the official name of my rescue once I get my 501c3."

The look on his face was priceless. "But wouldn't that require, you know. . .a ranch?"

"Exactly," I concurred. "And that will come in time, Parker. I know it will. But I need to get some fosters lined up until I can find the right property to buy. So I was thinking—"

"Yes?" He gave me a pensive look.

"That maybe we could fix up the dogs and take them to your place to rehab until we find them homes."

His eyes widened. "You want to turn my house into a shelter?"

"Not a shelter, exactly," I explained. "More of a staging area. You know. . .someplace where the dogs can stay for a week or two until we find them homes."

"And if you don't find them homes? Then what?"

"Don't panic. I've been thinking this through and doing a ton of research over the last few months and I have just the thing. The local shelter runs a transport bus up north, to Michigan. They go up there once a month or so with harder-to-place dogs."

"Michigan?" He leaned against the washer and crossed his arms at his chest. "We're shipping dogs to Michigan now?"

"It's already happening. They transport dogs up north if they're unable to place them here. It's been a thing, ever since Katrina hit New Orleans in '05. Dogs from down south end up on transport buses, headed north to homes. People up there are desperate for dogs, and people down here are swamped with them. It's a win-win, especially for the dogs, who get great new homes."

"In colder climates."

"Well, yeah. There is that. But many breeds love cold weather."

"True." Just when I thought he might be upset with me, Parker flashed an admiring smile. "You've got this all worked out."

"I do. And I think I can get Tyler onboard to vet them as they come through."

Parker didn't look as convinced. "That's going to be costly, though. Right? You can't expect him to pay for all of their shots and meds and stuff. And what about the ones that are really sick? The heartworm positive ones? And the ones who are lame? Or needing surgery?"

"As soon as I get my 501c3, I can apply for grants and take donations. Who knows? Maybe we can do an annual fundraiser gala. Doesn't that sound like fun? Share stories? Testimonies? Put pictures of the dogs we've adopted out up on the screen? Folks will love that and give even more."

"Maybe. The whole thing might not be quite as dreamy as you're making it out to be, though. I just hope you're psychologically prepared, if you're going to start taking them in before you have a property. That's all."

I sighed. "Look, I know that some of these dogs will probably end up at the shelter. But we will do everything we can to keep them out. We'll work with other rescues, the breed specific ones, and make a difference. In other words, we'll do what we can. And sometimes that's all you can do."

"Oh, I get it, and I love the idea." He raked his fingers through his hair. "I'm just trying to picture my neighbors if I start bringing in all of these dogs."

"It might not be for long, though. Maybe they wouldn't even notice. Maybe you just bring them to your place until we can farm them out to other fosters. So, maybe hours. Or a day or two. You know?"

"That could work. If you had fosters."

"People loved that article about Beau. I'm guessing it won't be long before I have ten more people just like you," I said. "Maybe twelve. Or more. Permanent fosters."

"Now I'm permanent?" He gave me an inquisitive look.

"I'm just saying you don't have to be the only one, but I've got to start somewhere."

"And I'm that somewhere."

I didn't mean to sigh but couldn't help myself. I just wanted this to work out.

What I needed, was a place of my own. Not an apartment, with a microscopic patio area, but a real, honest-to-goodness patch of land to call my own, one with the perfect setup for dogs.

"Are you regretting selling your mom's place?" he asked. "I mean, it had a decent-sized yard. Not big enough for a plan like this, but something."

"Sort of." I sighed. "I loved our old house—emphasis on the word *old*. But the taxes were high. Running and upkeep..." I shivered, remembering how tight things were in the end.

"Right. I remember."

"After Mama died. . ." I let my thoughts drift off to a dark place. "Anyway, grief affected me in so many ways. I think that's what made me sell the house so quickly. I just needed to get away from the things that reminded me of what our day-to-day life was like in that house. I was there forever, you know."

"I do know. I'm still in the house I grew up in too."

"Oh, that's right. Honestly? I'm glad it was in the historic district so I was able to get top dollar for it. It felt good to put some money away for something bigger. I really need more space than what I had, anyway. I'm talking about several acres."

"I see." He seemed to be lost in his thoughts. "And where would these acres be, exactly?"

"I wish I knew. That part's up to God."

"It's *all* up to God, Mari."

"True." He had a good point. But then again, Parker always had a good point. "And right now God's not opening any doors. So, He's either asking me to give up on this dream or to trust Him with the timing."

"Pretty sure it's the latter. He's not going to ask you to give up on the dream of rescuing dogs." Parker rested his hand on mine. "He put that desire in your heart. And, in case I haven't said this to you yet, Marigold, I'm really proud of you."

"You are?"

"Sure. You went out there the other night to rescue Beau without any fear or worries about the risk to yourself. He probably wouldn't still be alive right now, if not for you. You swept in and saved him."

"Kind of like you do for people."

He looked genuinely perplexed by this. "What do you mean?"

"You might not do it on purpose. Chances are pretty good you don't realize what a great rescuer you are. But you're always there for people, Parker, kind of like I want to be with the dogs. Only, people are even more important, so what you're doing is the greater work." I laughed and then said, "Parker to the rescue."

"Huh?"

"It's what Cassidy and I always say about you. You're a rescuer too, but not necessarily dogs." I gave him a hopeful look. "Though, I hope—if this is really a God-idea—that you're in it somehow, helping me. Whether you keep dogs at your house or not. I really don't want to do this without you."

"Oh?" He quirked a brow. "Because. . ."

"Because. . ." I paused and gazed into those compelling eyes. Oh wow. They really were a nice shade of blue. Cassidy was right. "Because you're one of the best friends I've ever had, Parker. And we have a common vision."

"Ah, I see." He seemed to deflate at my words. I had that effect on him a lot lately, didn't I?

Time to make this right. I reached to grab his hand and gave it a squeeze. "I'm so happy God brought you into my world. I really am. And not just because you love dogs."

"I'm happy to be here." He paused but didn't release my hand. "So, tell me where you're headed when you leave here today so I can decide if I'm going too."

"Round Top. Or, rather, the road leading to Round Top. A dog was left behind by his family. They moved two weeks ago, and he's been on the property—or running the road nearby—ever since."

"No way." His jaw tightened.

"I know. It makes my blood boil too."

"Well, we have no choice. We have to go get him. And since we both get off early today. . ."

Please, Parker. Please.

He melted like butter. "Okay. I'm all yours."

Something in the way he said those words made me smile.

And wonder.

Twenty minutes later we were in his truck, headed out 290 west to the turnoff toward Round Top. Cassidy had agreed to take Beau Jangles home with her. Not that she minded one little bit. I suspected she'd hang on to him as long as I'd let her. It relieved me to know he was with someone who adored him.

When I realized the address for the property in question was close to Maggie Jamison's place, I decided to drop off Jasper's paw print in person. If I worked up the courage. I wouldn't mention it to Parker, just in case I changed my mind. But hopefully I'd manage to save a dog and a relationship.

As we headed out, I felt that same sense of anticipation I'd felt on the evening I'd gone to fetch Beau Jangles from the drainage pipe. Only, this time I wasn't wearing my scrubs. I'd taken to keeping spare clothes in my car, just in case.

Today was a just in case sort of day.

We stopped at a local fast-food joint to grab a burger for the dog.

Well, a burger for the dog and another one for Parker, who decided a cheeseburger sounded good.

By the time we got to the address the woman had given me, we were well into a conversation about several pieces of property we'd passed on the way. This was a beautiful part of the county—land as far as the eye could see. Gentle rolling hills with oak trees, pecans, lavender farms, and even vineyards. All nestled between ranches and bluebonnet fields. I could see myself here, on a lovely patch of land, surrounded by pups of every size and breed. Parker played along with my chatty conversations about how dreamy it would all be and didn't even challenge me.

He turned his truck down Marlboro Street, and I got creeped out at once as the road narrowed. No longer a traditional neighborhood, we now found ourselves in an area that was overgrown and run down. To our right, an old trailer home, dilapidated and rotting, sat near the edge of the road. Beyond that, just a couple of lots down, was a tiny broken-down house—if one could call it that. Really, it was more like a shack. Weeds had grown up around it, so high that I could barely make out the windows. When I did manage to see one, the cracks frightened me. Was this some sort of drug house, maybe? Sure looked like it. Ugh.

Parker tapped the breaks. "I don't know about this, Mari. Doesn't feel safe out here."

"Agreed." But if we felt that way, I could only imagine what this poor dog was feeling, especially if he needed food and medical attention.

We approached the property in question, and I saw a car in the driveway.

"I thought you said it was an abandoned house?" Parker said.

"Right. But the landlord is here with a contractor. Something about making repairs on the home so he can rent it back out."

"Oh, gotcha." Parker slipped the truck into park. "Looks like it needs to be demolished, not pasted back together. I've seen crack houses in better shape than this."

"Why are you hanging out in crack houses?"

He laughed. "On TV."

Before we got out, I decided to give him a heads-up about something important. "From what I've heard, the landlord's a cranky older man. He wanted to call the shelter and have them pick the dog up, but the neighbor talked him into calling a rescue, instead."

"Sounds like a great guy."

"That's what I said."

Parker came around to my side of the truck and opened my door. As I climbed out, burger in hand, a thin black dog eased his way toward us, tail tucked between his legs. My heart sailed to my throat the moment I saw how frail he was. I could see every rib sticking out, and he was missing patches of hair.

"Oh, Parker. This must be him. She said he was black." I knelt down to see if I could entice the dog with the cheeseburger and he came right away.

"Poor hungry guy." Parker patted him on the head.

I smiled at my ingenuity as I offered him another bite of the burger. "Works every time."

"Hey, a cheeseburger is the way to my heart too," Parker said. "But if you're really going to win me over, you're gonna have to bring me Triple B's."

"Oooh, yes!"

"You like Triple B's too?" he asked.

I gave the pup another bite of the burger as I responded with the words, "My favorite."

"Would you..." He kicked the gravel with the toe of his boot. "...like to go sometime?"

Whoa. Wait a minute. Was he asking me out on a date? I shifted my gaze back down to the dog as I tried to absorb Parker's words.

I got so wrapped up with the dog that I didn't see anyone approaching. It wasn't until I heard the brusque, "What are you two doing here?" that I looked up...

...and saw Wayland Beckett staring down at me.

CHAPTER TWENTY-TWO

I . . .I. . ." The rest of the words wouldn't come. Thank goodness, Parker took over.

"We're here to pick up the dog, Mr. Beckett. We're taking him to my place."

Whew. Parker to the rescue, again. That should alleviate any concerns on Beckett's part, hearing that the dog was going to Parker's place, not the clinic.

Or not.

"I don't want to see this mangy mutt anywhere near my property. You hear me? And if he does show up—"

Parker's expression tightened and I worried he might come out swinging. "Mr. Beckett, with all due respect, he will be taken to the clinic for medical care, which—as I'm sure you can see—is urgently required. And we will probably walk him in the yard, so it's very likely you *will* see him there. That will be unavoidable as we take care of him to try to undo the damage that has been done here."

"Then I will—"

"You will be lucky if we don't contact the county to file charges against you."

Whoa. Brave move, Parker.

"Charges? Against me?" Beckett looked flabbergasted by this notion.

"Yes." Parker crossed his arms at his chest and glared at the man with such intensity that I broke out in a sweat. "You own this property, right? And the dog lives here? In these conditions? This is a serious case of neglect."

You could've heard a pin drop.

"Why, this isn't my dog and everyone knows it," Beckett said after a few seconds of strained silence.

"We received a call that a dog residing on this property was neglected." Parker reached into the back of his truck and pulled out a leash, which he fastened to the faded collar the dog was wearing.

"Yes, actually. That's the point. He—"

"Neglect of an animal in Washington County can result in charges, fines, even jail time. Now, I can call animal control, if you prefer that we not take him with us today. Of course, the county will see a neglected dog, wasting away from lack of care. And they will be looking for someone to blame. But that's your choice, sir. Just let me know what you'd like us to do."

"Well, I—" Beckett paused and raked his fingers through his hair. "Just get that mutt off my property. I don't want him here digging around. He's destructive."

As far as I was concerned the dog could dig a hole so deep this whole property would be swallowed up in it. That would make me very happy in my current state of mind.

"Oh, I'll be happy to take him, Mr. Beckett. If that's what you think is best." Parker led the dog to the passenger side of the cab and opened the door. He lifted him inside, then gestured for me to climb aboard. Less than a minute later, we were all three loaded in and pulling out of the driveway.

I turned, mouth agape, to stare at him. "Parker!"

"What?" He kept his focus on oncoming traffic as he attempted to take a left turn onto the country road that had led us here.

"That was. . .amazing!"

He pulled out and then turned to face me. "That guy grates on my last nerve."

"Mine too, but what you did back there was just. . .over the top. Like, that's going to go down in history as one of the best dog rescues ever!"

"Mari, that dog walked straight up to us. There was no rescue necessary."

"Oh yes there was," I argued. "You totally saved his life. And, man!" I couldn't help but laugh. "Did you ever tell Beckett a thing or two along the way."

"Yeah, well, I could've said a lot more, but God put a clamp on my tongue, trust me. Ten thousand things went through my head that did not come out on my tongue." He flashed a coy smile, followed by the words, "You're welcome."

"You said just enough. And I'm so proud of you." I suddenly felt completely overwhelmed. And filled with gratitude. "You have no idea how grateful I am right now, Parker. Seriously."

The dog was grateful too. He nuzzled close to me and rested his head on my shoulder. I patted him and then reached into the fast food bag for the rest of the cheeseburger, which he wolfed down.

"Did you really mean what you said back there about taking him to your place?" I asked. "Because if you did, that would be an answer to prayer."

"Of course. If that's what we need to do, then that's what we'll do." He glanced my way. "I hope you know I'd do just about anything for you, Mari."

I believed those words too.

"Beckett's not going to be happy when he sees this dog in our yard, but I don't really care what he thinks right now."

"Me either," I said. "We'll add him to the Woof Gang."

"Woof Gang?"

"Our pack. That's what I'm going to call it. And I won't even try to keep them quiet."

He cleared his throat. "So, um. . .you never answered my question earlier."

"W–what question?"

"About Triple B's. Want to go sometime? On our lunch break?"

"Ah." *That* question. "Sure," I managed. "I swoon over Triple B's burgers."

"I'd pay money to watch you swoon."

Okay, was it my imagination, or was he flirting with me? Things suddenly felt awkward. Weirdly intriguing, but awkward. I'd never given a moment's thought to going on a date with Parker. Honestly? I'd been too distracted by Tyler. But in that moment—as I stared into those beautiful eyes—*yes, Grandma Peach, they're very blue*—I found the idea mildly appealing.

And, man. Now that I'd locked eyes with him, I couldn't seem to see anything else. Except that crooked smile. And that splattering of freckles across his nose. I'd never noticed those either.

Focus, Mari.

Maybe a change of subject would help.

"Why do you suppose Beckett hates dogs so much?" I asked. "Because he's a landlord who's had to deal with them destroying his properties or something?"

"Could be, but from the looks of that dump, he's not a great landlord. Otherwise the property would be in livable condition. I don't think we can blame that on the renters. It was very run-down. Like I said, I've seen drug dens that looked better than that."

"So, what you're saying is, he's not good to dogs, or people."

"It would seem that way." He turned on his signal to make a right at the stop sign ahead. "And Mari, not everyone likes dogs. It's hard for us to imagine, but some folks are like that. They just don't do dogs."

"They don't know what they're missing." I wrapped my arms around the pooch's neck and planted a little kiss on the top of his head. "Dogs are the most loving, forgiving animals on the planet. Twenty minutes from now this little guy won't even remember that his former owners left him in the dust. He'll be eating high-end dog food and running around your backyard, playing."

Parker cleared his throat. "After he has a bath."

"True. He's a little stinky."

"A little?"

"My point is, he deserves a great home," I said. "The best."

"We'll find him that home. I'm not sure how, but we will."

He made the turn onto the main road, and I remembered something I'd forgotten to tell him earlier. I hollered out, "Parker!" and he slammed on the brakes.

"Don't do that, Mari! You scared me."

"Oh, sorry! I just wanted to tell you to take a left at the next street. We need to stop someplace on our way back."

"Where?"

"Maggie Jamison's place. She lives less than a mile from here, and I want to drop off the paw print we had made after Jasper passed."

He glanced my way and shook his head. "No way. That's not a good idea. Haven't you heard? She's filing a lawsuit. And you heard Kristin. She actually thinks Maggie might be the one who vandalized the building."

"I don't believe for a minute she's the one who tore up the clinic. She's upset but not violent. And maybe if we show up in person to show our sympathies at her loss we'll get a chance to see how she really is."

"Oh, I suspect we'll see how she really is, all right."

"You never know."

I guided him to Maggie's address. When Parker turned his truck into the long drive, I couldn't help but gasp. Her property was breathtaking. Gorgeous pecan trees lined the drive leading up to the ranch-style house. Off in the distance I caught a glimpse of the barn—a large red one, in pristine condition. Just beyond that was the pasture, where a couple of horses stood inside the fence—a beautiful large quarter horse and another smaller one, grazing nearby.

"Man." Parker let out a whistle. "She's living the life out here. Can you imagine?"

I could, actually. This place was pretty divine. And wouldn't that barn make a nice shelter for my pups?

"Oh, Parker!" I let out another squeal and he hit the brakes once again.

"What?"

"We should ask Maggie to help us with the rescue. This place is perfect. Then you wouldn't have to take the animals to your place."

"Hold up. This woman—who might be responsible for the damage to our clinic—is now going to be working with us?"

"I can see how that might be problematic." I sighed. "But, you never know! She might fall in love with Blacky and decide she can't live without him. That would be a start."

"You're actually thinking about leaving this dog with her?"

"We can't make it look like we're here with the dog on purpose. But, yes." The more I thought about it, the better the idea sounded. My gaze shifted back to the property. It was just too good an idea to pass up.

He pulled close to the house, and we got out of the truck. I gently lifted Blacky down, holding tightly to his leash. As we made the walk to her front door, my courage began to wane. Maybe this wasn't my brightest move. I'd just turned back to tell Parker so when the door swung open and Maggie stepped out. Judging from the tightness in her expression, she was none-too-happy to see us. She shot a villainous look our way and muttered, "What are you two doing here?"

Weird. This was the second time in less than fifteen minutes we'd heard those very words.

CHAPTER TWENTY-THREE

I turned to face her, my courage waning. "Maggie, I wanted to come to—"

"Skip the speech. I know why you're here, and it's not going to work. You've heard about the lawsuit I'm going to file and you're here to talk me out of it. Just admit it."

"Okay." I didn't even try to hide the sigh that slid out. I kicked some loose dirt off the toe of my shoe, happy to have a reason to look down, not into her eyes. "Guilty, as charged. But, Maggie, you know that Kristin did everything she could to save Jasper." I lifted my gaze, hoping she would see my point.

Her jaw flinched, and for a minute she looked as if she might tear up. "There were other treatments she could have offered. And she wasn't available on the day he needed her the most."

"It was her day off. But she came in the minute she got the news that he was about ready to pass. I was there. I saw him when you brought him in. It was gut-wrenching for all of us. You have to know that. We never forget those days, Maggie."

Parker cleared his throat. "There was really nothing else any of us could have done. We offered oxygen, which was what he needed most in the moment. But, he was too far gone. I'm telling you, his lungs were severely compromised."

"We see this all the time as the body shuts down," I said. "Once things reach that point. . ." I shook my head. "There's no coming back from that, Maggie. You were asking for a miracle. Kristin—we—didn't have one."

Her eyes flooded with tears.

The pup at my feet started to whimper, and I reached down to pet him, hoping he would remain calm.

Maggie jutted a finger in the dog's direction. "Who is this?"

"His name is Blacky. We just picked him up from a house a couple of miles from here. The family moved off and left him behind. He's been on his own for over two weeks. It's kind of a miracle he's survived."

"What?" Her voice tightened even more. "What do you mean, on his own?"

"They left him there with nothing to eat, no one to look after him, no water. . .nothing. Someone down the street stopped by to feed him from time to time but like I said, he's a real miracle."

"Who would do such a thing?"

"Exactly what I said."

Parker took the dog from me and calmed him down. I watched out the corner of my eye, grateful for his gentle touch with the poor thing.

"He's a lab mixed with cattle dog," Maggie said. "I know that breed well. Had a cattle dog growing up. You can tell from the ears, the way they stand up like that. A lab's ears wouldn't do that, but a cattle dog's would."

"Right." She knew her breeds, for sure.

"He looks hungry."

"I just fed him his first meal in the truck. We stopped and picked up a cheeseburger on the way to the rescue."

Her eyes narrowed to slits. "Cheeseburgers aren't good for dogs. You know that."

Sounded like something Grandma Peach might've said.

"I know, but I've always heard from other dog rescuers to stop and buy one on the way to a rescue because they love them. It's a way to entice them and that's the point. Rescuing them can be tricky, and you need every tool in the book."

"I suppose." She glanced back down at the dog. "This is something you do? Rescue dogs?"

"Sort of. It's my dream. I want to start a 501c3."

"She's already started the rescue part," Parker chimed in. "She saved a dog from the sewer last week."

"Not the sewer," I explained. "From a drainage pipe off of 36."

Fine lines formed on Maggie's brow, and she reached down to pet Blacky. "Oh, I think I saw something about that in yesterday's paper. Didn't put it together that it was someone I actually knew."

"Yeah, that was me. I rescued him and took him home with me. We've been trying to find his family ever since, but so far, no go."

"Ah. I guess finding families for them isn't as easy as they make it seem on those TV shows."

"No." An awkward silence rose up, and I decided I'd better say something more. "Anyway, we really do have a reason for being here. We stopped by to drop off something. I wanted to deliver it in person." I reached into my purse and came out with the little box holding Jasper's paw print. I pressed it into her hand.

"What's this?"

"Open it and see."

She pried the little box open and gasped when she saw the print inside. "Oh!" Tears sprang to her eyes at once. "I didn't realize you guys did this."

"We wanted to honor him. I hope you don't mind."

"Of course not. It's..." She shook her head. "It's beautiful, thank you."

"You're welcome."

I did my best to change the subject—to talk about her gorgeous property, to talk about Blacky, to talk about the weather. But she seemed completely distracted by the paw print in her hand.

We finally reached the jumping-off point, and I knew we'd better get on the road. I cleared my throat and said, "Well, we should get going. We have to figure out a plan for this guy." I knelt next to Blacky.

"What do you mean?"

"We picked him up, but we still have to figure out what we're going to do with him."

"Is that why you're here, to ask me to take care of that dog for you?"

I sighed. "I'll admit, the idea crossed my mind when I saw this glorious property. I can just picture this little guy running and playing out here in all this space. He needs a safe place to stay until we can find him a home. Or send him on transport."

"Transport?"

"Yes, to Brooklyn."

"Brooklyn?" She looked startled by this notion.

"Yes, I'm pretty sure the shelter is sending a busload to Brooklyn later this month. They usually do. If we can't find him a home between now and then we'll put him on the bus."

"For Brooklyn?" The word came out with a squeak.

"Well, sure. People up north need dogs. He's a dog. It's a win-win. And I can't keep him at my place, so my friend Parker here is going to help out until we can find someone to take him. He's been so good to me." I offered him a warm smile, which he returned.

He had, hadn't he? In that moment, as I realized the depth of what he had done for me, my admiration for my good friend went through the roof.

Maggie looked back and forth between us, as if analyzing the situation, and then knelt down to look Blacky in the eye. "That's all well and good, and I really admire what you're doing, but. . ."

"But?"

"But Brooklyn is a big city. This is a country dog."

"We'll figure it out. No worries. But, Maggie?"

"Yes?" She looked up from the paw print. "Will you think about what we've said? Maybe let go of this lawsuit idea?"

Tears brimmed her lashes and she nodded. "I'll think about it."

"Thank you." I gazed intently into her eyes. "You know, we all loved Jasper. He was one of my favorite clients."

Parker cleared his throat. "Hey, we're not supposed to have favorites, remember? That's Vet Tech 101."

"So, sue me." I laughed when I realized what I'd said.

Thank goodness, so did Maggie.

"I always loved the way he got the leash twisted when I tried to get him to follow me into the boarding area," I said. "And the way he argued with me when I tried to put him in the kennel."

"He never did care much for the kennel," Maggie said. She gestured to her expansive property. "He was more of a free-range dog."

"I can see why."

"I liked the way he jumped up and down like a yo-yo whenever I'd offer him a treat," Parker added. "Oh, and remember that time when you brought him in after he ate some grapes?"

"You guys were so good to me that day." Maggie sighed. "You got me calmed down. And you pumped his stomach."

"Hey, grapes can be poisonous to dogs," I reminded her. "We wanted to save him."

"You did save him."

"We always wanted him healthy and well, just like we want all of our clients." I gave her a pensive look. "And Kristin's the same. I promise you, she's an amazing vet. I wish you could've seen her with Beau Jangles, the dog I rescued. She and Tyler worked so hard to stitch him up and get him healthy so he could have the best chance at a good life."

"And is he living a good life now?" she asked.

"Yes." I couldn't help but smile. "I'm supposed to be looking for a home for him, like I said, but. . ."

"You've fallen in love with him."

"I have."

She sighed. "It happens."

My eyes met hers for a look that sealed the deal as I responded, "I know." In that moment, I realized Maggie Jamison wouldn't go through with that lawsuit. She didn't have it in her. She was just grieving a deep loss, one that had caused her to lose the ability to think clearly.

And if there was one thing I understood right now, it was deep loss and the inability to think clearly.

I also knew better than to ask her to take Blacky right now. Maybe she just wasn't ready for something like that yet. I couldn't blame her.

We said our goodbyes and headed back to the truck. I'd just lifted Blacky into the passenger seat when Maggie came running up behind us.

"Hey."

I turned back to face her. "Hey."

"Tell you what. Let's just let him stay here for a little while and see how he does."

"You sure?"

She nodded. "I've got the space. And I've even got bags of food that Jasper. . ." She paused, and for a moment I thought we'd lost her. Just as quickly she snapped back to attention. "Anyway, I've got the room, I've got the food, and I've got the time. So, what do you say? Maybe he should just stick around for a couple of days and see how it goes?"

That sounded like the best plan in the world to me. Before I could stop myself, I threw my arms around the woman's neck and offered my most sincere thanks.

CHAPTER TWENTY-FOUR

Grandma invited me to her place for a baking marathon the day after rescuing Blacky. She told me to bring Beau Jangles, so I showed up at her tiny wood-framed house on Maple Drive just after work with a bag of fast food tacos in one hand and a leash in the other. I felt sure she would have already eaten, but no. That did not appear to be the case.

As I walked into her quaint old-school kitchen—which hadn't changed one iota in my entire life—I picked up on her angst. Grandma glared at the bag of tacos and clucked her tongue. "I cannot believe you are bringing that into my house. Have we not talked about this, Marigold?"

"Talked about what?" I set the bag on the table, then grimaced when I realized she had a full meal prepared for us—some sort of boiled chicken dish with cabbage and a side of brussels sprouts.

Yippee skippy.

The tacos definitely sounded better, but I wouldn't argue the point.

She reached to take my taco bag with two fingers, as if scared to touch it, then moved it to the opposite side of the table. "We'll just put this right over here. Do you have any idea how much partially hydrogenated soybean oil there is in fast food?"

"No ma'am."

"Your arteries will be begging for mercy. But I have just the thing to clean them out." She pointed to the meal she had prepared and I swallowed hard. Ugh.

I'd have to sneak the tacos later, but they would get eaten. No doubt about that. She hadn't shown me any proof that they contained partially hydrogenated…whatever it was.

I looked around the kitchen, wondering about the cat. Hopefully there wouldn't be any scuffles between our two animals today. When I didn't see him, I released my hold on Beau Jangle's leash. He sniffed the air, probably confused by the contrast between the chicken and the boiled cabbage.

"Is Hector around?" I asked.

"Are you wanting to see him?" She seemed to perk up at this notion.

"Absolutely not!" did not seem like a kind answer so I went with, "I was just hoping he and Beau Jangles wouldn't end up in a scuffle. They didn't get along so well that day you came into the clinic. It really shocked me because Beau's good with Aggie and the other cats at the clinic."

Her smile faded. "Well, your sweet baby is just on a learning curve, that's all. I'm sure they'll be fine."

"Hopefully." Still, I wasn't so sure.

She reached for a dishcloth and wiped down a speck on the counter. "Hector's in his bedroom, though. I'm hard-pressed to get him out of there, these days, what with it being so luxurious and all."

"The cat has his own bedroom now?" I slung my purse strap over the back of the kitchen chair. "And it's luxurious?"

"Actually, it's more of a playroom." She wrinkled her nose and appeared to be thinking. "I don't like to have him in the kitchen when I'm baking because he can't be trusted not to jump up on the counter."

"Right. That makes sense. But, he has a playroom?"

"Haven't I shown you what I've done with Trina's old bedroom?"

Whoa. "You changed her bedroom? Does she know?"

"Nope. Not telling her either. If she wants to know anything about it she's going to have to come home and see it for herself."

Grandma led the way into the room that had once been my aunt's childhood bedroom, and I gasped when she swung back the door. It really did look like an official playland for cats.

Multi-tiered cat scratch tower. Check.

Wall-mounted shelves and perches, some at weird angles. Check.

Gazebo with interactive play station. Check.

Sign on the door reading HECTOR'S CATIO. Check.

Weirdest room I'd ever seen in my life. Check, check, check.

"Wow, Grandma. You're taking this very seriously."

"Yes, well. . .Trina's never coming back, so why not?"

"What do you mean, she's never coming back? Why would you say that?"

"Because, she's not." With the wave of a hand, Grandma appeared to dismiss the idea. "Anyway, it's nothing to fuss over. So, she's found a new life, new people. So what? I've got Hector. And you."

I wasn't sure if I should be flattered or mortified that I fell in line behind the cat. Clearly, I wouldn't be getting my own catio anytime soon. For that matter, there wasn't even a bed to sleep in, should I choose to spend the night sometime.

Maybe I should offer to do that sometime, so that Grandma wouldn't feel so abandoned. Clearly, she was struggling with pangs of loneliness.

"Grandma, you don't really believe Trina's not coming back, do you? I mean, she's busy, but she hasn't forgotten us."

Was it my imagination or did I see tears in my grandmother's eyes? I reached to give her a hug.

"I just miss her, that's all." Grandma's words came out strained. Forced.

"Me too."

And I had the distinct feeling we weren't just talking about Trina.

"I'm right here, Grandma," I said. "And I'm not going anywhere."

"You'd better not, Marigold. Because if you leave me too. . ." She shook her head and then quickly dove into a conversation about the cat's new playroom.

I did my best to play along, but I could tell she was more upset than she was letting on and that really worried me. Grandma Peach wasn't usually one to show much emotion. Except for that emotional outburst at the cafeteria over Donna Sue Specklemeyer, but that was an anomaly.

On and on she went, sharing about all the work she'd done on Hector's new room, as if she thought I would be interested. Thank goodness my acting skills were intact. I smiled and nodded. . .a lot.

"He needs something to keep him occupied. When he's bored, well. . ." She sighed. "You'll notice there's a slipcover over my sofa. He scratched up the arms."

"No way. Let me see." She led the way into the living room and pulled back the floral cover from the sofa's arm, revealing deep cuts in the fabric. "Oh no."

"He's just bored, like I said."

No, he was rotten, but I wouldn't tell her that. If she wanted to go on believing that her demonic cat was just looking for something fun to do, oh well. She didn't need to be challenged tonight, not when she was already in such a fragile emotional state.

I tagged along behind her, making my way back to the kitchen. I found Beau Jangles under the table with the fast-food bag in his mouth.

"No! Beau!" I reached to grab it, but it was too late.

My tacos were gone. Vamoose.

I lifted the bag and opened it just to be sure. Yep. All gone.

"That dog's gonna have a bellyache," Grandma said.

I wadded up the bag and tossed it in the trash, then took a seat at the table.

Pass the chicken and cabbage, please.

As I reached for my fork, Beau curled up at my feet. I tried to sneak a brussels sprout under the table, but my grandmother was on to me.

"No ma'am." She shook her head. "That dog doesn't eat from my table."

"But the Bible says that even the dogs get the scraps of the master's table." And, as far as I was concerned, brussels sprouts fell into the scraps category.

"Not this master. Not when I'm baking. It's unsanitary."

"You've already started baking? I thought you were waiting until I got here." I gave Beau Jangles a warning look as he tried to jump up on my chair and he settled back down at my feet. I took a bite of the chicken cabbage-thing. It wasn't too bad. Not tacos, but not too bad.

"I couldn't wait until you got here, honey. Sorry. And besides. . ."

"I know, I know. I'm a terrible baker."

"I wouldn't put it that way."

"Oh, I would. Remember that time when I caught my Easy-Bake oven on fire? I think I was eight?"

"Nearly burned down your mama's kitchen, as I recall."

"And that other time when you swore you could teach me how to make the perfect pie crust? I ended up with something as hard as a rock."

"I'm still not sure how that happened."

"Oh, I am. I didn't get the baking gene. That's it, plain and simple."

"Neither did your Mama or Trina."

"Are you sure they weren't adopted?"

She glared at me.

"I can assure you, they were not. And neither were you."

"Whelp, I didn't get the baking anointing. Honestly? I don't know a mixer from a blender. And if I ever do get married, I'm gonna ask Mr. Right to put vending machines in my kitchen in place of a stove and refrigerator. That's the only way he'll ever get anything decent to eat."

"Marigold Evans. You're as bad as Donna Sue Specklemeyer."

"But I have better hair."

"True. At least yours is real."

"And I don't have a husband, so this whole conversation is just plain silly."

"Oh, but you *will* have, if you'll just listen to me." She gave me a little wink. "Now, you go right on and eat that food, sweet girl. I'm gonna get this pie in the oven, then I'll join you."

"Okay." I took another bite. The chicken dish was growing on me. "I hope you're baking a pie for us too."

"I might have a spare." She began to whistle a familiar hymn as she settled into her work.

"Good. Because I'll cry without pie. And yours is the best."

"Thanks, honey. Your grandpa used to say he could fly to the moon on my pie crust, it was so light."

"Well, he was right. You should enter a baking competition, Grandma."

"Oh, I did. In 1993 I entered my apple pie at the county fair and won first place." She gave me a little wink. "This ain't my first rodeo, kiddo."

"You're the best."

"Hardly. But I do use fresh ingredients and make my own home-made pie crust. No preservatives in this kitchen." Grandma walked over to the counter and reached into a bowl to pull out a mound of pie dough, which she plopped onto the counter. "How do you think I've lived so long, honey? No preservatives touch these lips. Only wholesome foods." She sprinkled flour on the dough and then took a little nibble of the pie crust.

Should I tell her that raw flour wasn't wholesome? Nope, I'd let it sit there.

"Hey, I'm all for preservatives," I interjected. "I figure they'll add years to my life. They'll preserve me." I laughed. "Get it?"

She didn't laugh. Oh well. I'd tried.

"You'll figure out the value of sensible eating when you're my age, I suppose," she said. "After they've plucked out your gall bladder and roto-rootered your intestines in one of those colonoscopy-thingies."

Didn't that sound lovely.

I finished up my dinner then made my way to the barstool to watch her chop up the apples and sprinkle them with cinnamon and sugar. Yum.

Unlike Grandma, I consider a balanced diet to be a cupcake in each hand. So, watching her work her magic in the kitchen with all these sweet treats was kind of like going to an amusement park without the price of the ticket.

I reached for a bite of apple and popped it in my mouth. She slapped my hand. "Hey, now, I've already measured those."

"Oh, oops. Sorry! Who are we baking for today, Grandma?"

"I thought it might be nice to make a pie for that wonderful doctor at your clinic."

"Oh, Tyler! Great idea." Boy, it would really impress him to show up with a homemade apple pie from my grandmother.

"He was so sweet, to offer to take in that big black dog for you." She gave me a solid stare. "You know, Marigold, I'd have to say he's a keeper."

"The dog?"

"No, the doctor."

Ah. I could see where this was going. "I think you're talking about Parker, Grandma. He's a vet tech, not a doctor. And he didn't end up with the dog in the end. Maggie Jamison took him."

"She's a good lady. I've known her since she and your mother were friends during their growing-up days."

"Maggie grew up with Mama?" This was news to me.

"Mm-hmm. They were very close at one time. Sixth grade, I think. Now, let's go back to talking about that handsome vet with the blue eyes. I think you two are a match made in heaven. And I dare say he might be willing to buy you a vending machine to put in your kitchen if you ask him. He seems very amiable."

Oh boy.

"Or maybe, just maybe, you could learn a little something from me about how to keep a man well fed."

No doubt about that.

She dumped the bowl of apples into the pie crust and stirred them around with a fork, then added a bit more cinnamon and sugar mixture to the top before adding the top crust. "Point is, he deserves a pie for offering to take in that big dog, the one in the picture you sent last night. Even if he didn't end up with him. His willingness shall be rewarded."

"Yes." I gestured to the lovely pie in front of me. "And amen."

"Just promise me you won't give any of it to that terrible man who works behind you."

"Beckett? It's funny you should mention him. I just saw him last night when we picked up the dog."

"You saw Beckett with a dog?" She seemed startled by this possibility. "I thought he hated most living creatures."

"The dog was actually at one of Beckett's rental properties. Did you realize he owns properties?"

"Oh yes." She rolled her eyes as she reached to open the oven door. "Money pits, if you ask me. Dumps."

"That's what I said!"

"He rented one of them out to a family in our church a few years back, then refused to take care of the place. They were without water for weeks. And their little girl was badly injured when she fell through the rotten deck out back. I'm telling you, he's not a good man, Mari."

She closed the oven door with the pie safely inside and then reached for a rag to wipe down the countertop.

"Wow. Well, the place we saw last night was awful too. Very run-down. Dilapidated. I couldn't believe anyone lived there."

"Yep. He owns several of those, and from what I understand, the city has had to get involved in a couple of cases on behalf of the renters. The folks I know who rented from him—and they were the cutest young couple with a little girl barely toddling around—they ended up breaking the lease because he refused to do right by them. And when they did...Whew!"

"What?"

"He took them to court for breach of contract. I don't know where he found an attorney willing to take such a crooked case, but he did. Another shady character, no doubt. He seems to be surrounded by those. I don't know where he finds them, honestly."

"Like things attract."

"True."

"So, what did the court decide?" I asked.

"They ruled against Beckett, which is what started the big brouhaha at the church. Most of the folks were sympathetic toward the family, but a few were old-time friends with Beckett. Cohorts in crime, I guess you'd call 'em. So we ended up with a church split, and all because of that horrible man. I swear, he's so cheap he wouldn't give a nickel to see Jesus ridin' a bicycle."

I had to laugh at that one.

"So, let me ask you one question, Grandma."

"What's that?"

"How did he come to be in a position of power in the church in the first place?"

"Oh, that." She stopped wiping down the counter and paused for a moment. "I have a better perspective on that than most, I guess, seeing as how I'm older than Moses."

"Grandma!"

"And it's not preservatives keeping me alive and kicking, just so we're clear. But my point is, I've been around awhile and I know the backstory on some of these folks. If you'd be interested in hearing any of it, I'm happy to share.

If I wanted to hear? Well, of course I did!

CHAPTER TWENTY-FIVE

T he Becketts were hard and fast members of the First Prez going back to the turn of the century," Grandma explained.

"Which century?" I asked.

She stared at me, probably trying to figure out if I was messing with her. I wasn't.

"Nineteenth to twentieth, of course. These folks were some of the original founders. So, when Beckett was born—probably in the late '40s—they'd already been around a good, long while. They ruled the roost, as it were."

"Oh, I see."

"Your mama raised you at Grace Fellowship—and I tolerated that notion after some serious prayer and fasting on my part—but I suppose other denominations face similar situations. It's a matter of control. Some folks have more power than others. They determine who the church hires and fires, and they control how the money is spent."

"And that's what happened with Beckett? He had that kind of power?'"

"It started with his daddy, who was responsible for firing the last pastor, back in the '70s. Then when old man Beckett died, Wayland just stepped into his spot, like some sort of puppeteer."

"Who gave him that kind of power?"

"His daddy." She paused. "Anyway, his knickers were always in a knot over something or another. It was a tough season for our church, I'll just leave it at that. Not one I'd like to repeat anytime soon."

"That's awful. The people of the church didn't get to make the decisions?"

"Oh, everything was voted on, you understand." She gave me a knowing look. "Like that matters."

"I see."

"Let's just say he was very persuasive and leave it at that. And it didn't help that he always had his fingers in every financial pie." She paused and startled to attention. "Oooh, pie! I just remember that I want to make a sweet potato pie for Myrtle Mae Caldwell."

"But this is apple pie month," I argued.

"Honey, my themes aren't some sort of hard and fast rule. I'll make whatever pie I choose."

My goodness, she was getting cheeky in her old age, wasn't she?

"Myrtle Mae is going in for a knee replacement tomorrow morning," Grandma explained. "So she's going to need fortitude. My sweet potato pie will give her the antioxidants she needs while she heals."

Along with a possible brown sugar coma, but I wouldn't say that.

"So, back to Beckett. . ." I really wanted to get to the bottom of this. The man had a backstory, and apparently the whole "wholesome CPA" schtick was just that. . .a schtick.

Or maybe I was just judging him too harshly.

"He's no good, I'm telling you. There's something about the man that makes the skin crawl. He's just not. . .genuine. I can't tell you how many times over the years I felt like praying down a little fire and brimstone over him. But I didn't."

"Is this your way of saying he's not who he says he is?" I asked.

"Right." She nodded. "He was our church treasurer for years. And I don't want to point fingers, but the church was really struggling in those days, which I found so odd. I mean, First Prez has a lot of wealthy members." Her nose wrinkled. "Well, we did back in those days. Many of them have died off now."

"I'm sorry, Gran."

"My point is, we should have been in good shape financially. I know that most of our members were very generous so I never could understand why we always fell short on the budget. We worked extra-hard to come up with fundraisers and such to stay on top of things, but those were some lean years, when he was in charge of the pocketbook."

"Oh, I remember. You guys did those fun holiday markets."

"Yes." She nodded. "And thank God for them. We managed to keep the church in the black instead of the red. But, according to our board members, it was close some months. We almost didn't have the money to pay Reverend Nelson a few times, but he stuck around anyway."

"Wait, Reverend Nelson almost didn't get paid?"

She nodded. "Yes, that's right. He's a good man, willing to keep on working, even if the paycheck doesn't show up. I sure admire him."

"Me too," I admitted. "I remember going to Christmas Eve services with you as a little girl, how he kept me awake during his sermons, even though we went at an ungodly hour."

"Eleven p.m. every Christmas Eve, like clockwork." She laughed. "I still go, if you want to join me."

That sounded like a good plan, actually. Maybe I would go with her this year. It might be just the thing. . .for both of us.

Grandma started mixing up the dough for Myrtle Mae's sweet potato pie, and I wondered if maybe she'd forgotten about the one she was supposed to be feeding me. I got up and started searching for it. A quick peek in the covered pie dish on the opposite side of the kitchen revealed a cooled apple pie. I grabbed it and reached for a knife.

"Cut me a piece too," Grandma said as she continued to work.

Should I mention that she hadn't eaten any of the chicken casserole yet?

Nope. I just cut two slices of pie and put them on plates, then settled back down on the barstool to watch her bake Myrtle Mae's pie.

"I always got the feeling Wayland had some sort of get-rich-quick scheme going on. He tried to get folks in the congregation to invest, but

Reverend Nelson put a stop to that. He's a tough cookie." She paused and snapped her fingers. "That's what I forgot."

"What?"

"Cookies. For Reverend Nelson. He loves my spice drops at this time of year. My goodness, but that man does go on about my spice drops."

Okay then.

"You're not cooking for Curtis Elban anymore?" I leaned my elbows on the counter and gave her an inquisitive look. "Because just last week you were baking him an apple pie."

"*That* is a subject best left alone." Her eyes narrowed to slits. "Anyway, Reverend Nelson is a good man who deserves some cookies, so maybe I'd better throw together a batch when I'm done with Myrtle's Mae's pie."

"Is the good reverend single, by any chance?" I asked.

She stopped her work and turned to face me, planting her fists on her hips. "Now, what kind of question is *that*?"

"Exactly the kind you would ask me," I countered. "And, hey. . .you're the one who taught me that turnabout is fair play." I took a bite of the pie and practically swooned. "Oh, yum."

Grandma walked back to the pantry to grab the ten-pound bag of granulated sugar. Then she wrestled a smaller bag of brown sugar into her arms as well.

"Reverend Nelson is a widow," Grandma said. "His wife was a good woman, albeit a little on the portly side. Now, I don't want to say she ate her way into an early grave, but the dear soul died with a tortilla in her hand and a platter of fajitas in front of her."

Okay I almost choked on my apple pie right then and there.

Grandma plopped the sugar onto the counter next to the bowl of dough. "Happened at Mario's."

"My favorite restaurant!"

"I know." She flashed me a knowing look. "But my point is, he loved her all the same—expanding waistline or not—and never had an unkind word to say about her. Or anyone else for that matter. Except Wayland Beckett."

"Oh? He didn't care for him?"

"That's putting it mildly. We were so surprised when things went south and Reverend Nelson gave Beckett the boot."

"Wait, what? Beckett was booted from your church?" This was a shocker, for sure. I'd grown up in Brenham, for pity's sake. How could I not know this stuff?

"Let's just say Reverend Nelson finally talked the board into removing Beckett from leadership. And trust me when I say he wasn't interested in staying unless he could be in charge, so he moved on."

"But, why?" This story held me spellbound, like a kid eyeing the cookie jar. "What did Beckett *do*, exactly?"

"Reverend Nelson wouldn't elaborate. But Myrtle Mae's husband Leroy was on the board at the time, and he came home trembling that night, according to Myrtle Mae. Had to take an antacid and go straight to bed."

"Are you sure it wasn't something he ate at the potluck?"

Okay, I had assumed the potluck part, but there was always a potluck going on at First Prez.

"Nope. Reverend Nelson shared with the board that Beckett couldn't be trusted and that was all Leroy would say. I suspect the good reverend will go to his grave with the details of his dealings with that awful man. But I trust my pastor. If he says Beckett's evil, he's evil. If he tells us to steer clear, we steer clear."

"It's just so strange. How is it possible Beckett has kept his business afloat all these years if he's so untrustworthy? I mean, there's a steady flow of cars coming and going from his office every day. That parking lot is full, Grandma."

"No one I know uses him."

"Really?"

"Really. I'm telling you, Mari, most of us who've been around awhile wouldn't give him access to our financial records. I'd be too nervous about what he'd do with that information. Or with our money. Like I said, he always had a scheme going."

"So, why the crowd at his office?"

"That's the question, now isn't it?" She gave me a knowing look. "Someone oughta figure that one out."

I paused to think it through. "Cassidy says October is a big tax month. Folks who file for an extension have to get their returns done by the 15th of October or pay penalties. So, we figured that's why he's got so many clients over there."

"Humph."

"Don't believe it?"

"Oh, I believe his parking lot's full. No doubt he's got people flocking to him for some reason. But I can assure you that people who need a legitimate CPA avoid him like fleas jumping off a freshly washed pup. He's just plain mean. Would you go to a butcher who's just plain mean?"

"Well, I don't go to a butcher, so. . ."

"Okay, a dry cleaner then. Would you go to a dry cleaner who was just plain mean?"

"We might need a different example, Grandma."

"Would you buy fajitas from a man who was just plain mean?"

"Yes." I nodded. "Yes, I would. I would buy fajitas from anyone, anywhere, anytime, no matter their temperament. Because that's the kind of girl I am. Fickle."

Grandma sighed just as the buzzer on the stove went off. She took several steps in that direction and pulled the door open. "You just remember what became of Reverend Nelson's wife, Mari."

I wouldn't forget anytime soon. But, honestly? Meeting my Maker with a tortilla in my hand and a platter of fajitas in front of me? Yeah. . . there were worse ways to go than that.

CHAPTER TWENTY-SIX

On Wednesday morning I dressed for work and headed out, as always. Beau Jangles did his morning business in the bushes outside of my front door and we took off toward the parking lot, ready to get this day started.

I headed straight for my SUV and unlocked the passenger side door to put Beau inside. As I settled him into his new car seat, a male voice sounded from behind me. I startled to attention and turned, then gasped as I saw Matt Foster standing so close he could reach out and touch me. My heart sailed to my throat and I took a giant step back, slamming into the car door.

Beau must've picked up on my fear because he barreled in Matt's direction, as if ready to attack. I held tight to his leash, but he bared his teeth and growled. Not his usual routine with people we met.

"We need to talk." Matt's words came out forced. Strained. Was it my imagination or was the guy shaking? That couldn't be good.

I slipped my hand in my pocket to feel for my phone. If I needed to, I could press the emergency button to summon the police. But, standing here in a public parking lot, surrounded by apartments on every side? Surely he wouldn't pull something in an open area like this. I prayed.

Still, I didn't trust him as far as I could throw him. And with the amount of adrenaline coursing through my veins right now, I felt like I could probably throw him pretty far. Into the next county, maybe.

Beau continued to do that low growl thing and I fought to steady my breath. My gaze shifted to the right and the left, hoping someone would appear.

Then, off in the distance, a neighbor entered the parking lot and walked toward his car. I shot him a wide-eyed look and he paused, as if wondering what to do. My penetrating gaze sent subliminal messages: Come. And. Help. Me.

Beau started barking in earnest now and lunged at Matt. I gripped the leash until my palms smarted.

Matt took a giant step backward and put his hands up. "Keep your mutt away from me."

"Then you're gonna have to stay away from me. Because I can promise you this. . .if you're here to cause trouble, he's going to react and there won't be anything I can do to stop him once he gets started. This dog is a rescue, and I don't know his background. Could end bad."

"I'm not here to hurt you." Matt took another small step back and raked his fingers through his messy hair. "I want you to talk to Isabel. Tell her to give me another chance."

There was a zero percent chance of that happening, but I let him keep talking, hoping he would stay calm. I shot another gaze in my neighbor's direction and he took a few steps toward me, obviously getting my vibe. Matt hadn't picked up on the fact that someone was joining us until the man was right next to him.

"Everything okay over here?" The older man looked like a fairly typical Texas Good Ole Boy, just what I needed right now. He had the muscles to take Matt down, should the need arise. And judging from the tightened look on his face, he'd taken down meaner guys than this.

"We're great," Matt said.

I gave the man another wide-eyed look, not wanting to say anything that might set Matt off.

My neighbor stood at attention, as if ready to come out swinging.

This did not deter Matt. He just kept chatting, like we were old friends.

Judging from the pleading look in his eyes, he was really here to ask a favor. Did he think I was that stupid? Or that gullible? Was I really supposed to tell my friend to give this lunatic another shot?

"I want you to tell her I'm getting better," Matt said. "I'm gonna go to AA. Get clean and sober. And then I'm gonna. . ." He raked his fingers through his hair. "It'll be different. Like, for real this time."

Note to self: Anytime they say "for real this time," turn and run in the opposite direction.

Fortunately, I didn't have to. Matt did the turning. He walked back to his truck and climbed in. And just like that, he left me alone with my neighbor.

Who introduced himself as Chuck and told me that if I ever needed anything to let him know.

I thanked him for coming to my rescue and did my best to give him the shortened version of the story. Then, still badly shaken, I climbed into my car and drove to work. As I pulled out of the parking lot, I saw Chuck approaching Matt's truck. Was he going to talk to him? Well, good. Maybe he'd warn him to stay far, far away from me.

I kept checking the rearview mirror all the way to work. I didn't want a repeat of what had happened the other day. But, he didn't follow me this time. Maybe Chuck was stalling him so that I could get away. Probably.

I pondered Matt's words all the way to the office. Maybe he really was going to AA. Maybe that would help with any addictions he might have. But, would it solve the anger problem? Would it keep him from gaslighting my friend? Was one intricately tied to the other?

I'd rather see her date the abominable snowman than go back with that guy.

By the time I turned onto the street behind the clinic, I was in a calmer state. Well, until I saw Beckett's office. Man, his parking lot was full. Kind of strange for so early in the morning. Did people really get up this early to do their taxes?

I took note of the Tax Masters sign and saw that it looked pretty dilapidated. Kind of like that broken-down house Beckett owned, the one where I'd picked up Blacky. Was everything in the man's life in a ruined state? Sure looked that way.

"What are you up to, Wayland Beckett?" I muttered under my breath. "What's going on over there?"

I'd always found it a bit odd that a man like Beckett ran an accounting firm from an older, renovated home. He didn't come across as the quaint, homey type. Then again, I'd never been inside. Maybe it was a fiasco, like his rental houses. And, now that I'd heard Grandma's story about the damage he had done at the church, I had to wonder why people used his services at all. And what kind of services, specifically, he offered.

I reflected back on what my Grandma Peach had said about his office: *"Do you actually know anyone who's been in there?"*

I didn't. But, I made it a point to keep an eye out, to see if I actually recognized any of the vehicles. Not that I knew everyone in Brenham, but I'd been around awhile. I knew people. None of these cars looked familiar, though.

I pulled into the clinic and smiled as I looked at the front of the building. In all the chaos of the recent couple weeks, I'd forgotten to check out the new glass. I knew that Tyler had paid extra for the safety glass feature. Maybe it would protect us, should the need arise.

I prayed the need would not arise.

As I walked inside, I toyed with the idea of not telling Isabel about my encounter with Matt. But a part of me thought she should know. So, I walked to the grooming area for a chat as soon as I arrived. I spilled the beans on all that had happened, and she looked mortified.

"I'm so sorry that happened, Marigold."

"He seemed pretty genuine," I said. "But. . ."

"Oh, he's always genuine. That's the problem." She lifted a tiny terrier to the grooming table and fastened a lead around his neck. "When he gets like this, he really means it. Until he doesn't."

"So, he's told you before that he would go to AA?"

"Maybe ten thousand times." She reached for an electric razor and started buzzing around the pup's head. The tiny pooch stood frozen in place.

"I see."

Isabel continued to work, her eyes on the dog, but her words directed at me. "And he always means it. But he never follows through. There's always some excuse. And then the cycle begins all over again. He starts drinking. Gets angry. Takes it out on me. And things escalate. It's a never-ending cycle."

"Sounds horrifying."

"It is. But I'm done now. I'm never going back to that."

"I don't blame you. Not at all. I wouldn't either."

She was getting pretty worked up, so I decided to give her some space. I had work to do, anyway.

I passed through the lobby but didn't see Cassidy in her usual place behind the reception desk. I peeked in Victoria's small office and found her there, hard at work on the computer.

"Oh, hey. There you are."

She looked up. "Hey. Sorry. Totally focused in here. Trying to get caught up."

"Victoria's stuff?"

"Yeah." She released a sigh.

"You okay?"

"I guess. I'm trying to work up the courage to talk to Tyler about applying for the office manager job."

"I'll pray that he gives it to you. You've certainly earned it, Cassidy."

"Thank you. I appreciate that. I'm starting to really like this little office." She gestured to the tiny room. "I'm already thinking of how I can make it my own."

"Buy a pea green sofa?" I suggested. "Put in a cherrywood table?"

Okay, that brought a smile to her face.

I headed to the lab and passed Tyler's office along the way. He came out with Kristin on his heels. He said a quick hello, then grabbed a chart from the reception counter and led her into Exam Room 1. Before he closed the door, I could've sworn I heard him say, "We have an applicant coming in at three. I think she might be just what we need."

Then he closed the door.

My heart rate went to double time, right then and there.

An applicant? For Victoria's job? Why hadn't he waited on Cassidy? She deserved a shot as much as anyone else. Maybe more.

Ugh. What kind of a boss was he, anyway? He should have at least given my friend a chance before calling in a stranger, someone who didn't even know the practice.

He opened the door and gestured for me to join them in the exam room, and I did my best to focus on the dog with the hernia. But I couldn't stop thinking about what Tyler had said. I needed to say something, and quick.

Only, I didn't have the courage. And it wasn't really my business, was it? Tyler owned his practice. He could hire—or fire—whomever he wanted.

Man. Sometimes it stunk, being the low man—er, woman—on the totem pole.

After our appointment with the hernia patient, I went straight to work in the lab and did my best to calm myself. I wanted to give him a piece of my mind, though. Ugh.

Around nine o'clock, Cassidy called for me on the intercom. "Marigold, you've got a visitor at the front desk."

"A visitor?" Strange. I wasn't expecting anyone. No doubt Grandma had stopped by with Hector for a follow-up.

I walked out to discover a woman standing at the reception desk, chatting with Cassidy. I didn't recognize her, but she looked right at me, as if we were old friends. Weird. She appeared to be well off—this, I gathered from the high-end clothing and the expensive Gucci bag she carried. And that hairstyle was top-of-the-line too. She didn't get that 'do at Curl Up & Dye, my favorite go-to hair salon for folks with a Jiffy Lube lifestyle and Dollar Store budget.

I took several steps in her direction, and her face lit into a smile as she extended her hand. "Marigold Evans?"

I extended my hand with a quick, "Yes, I'm Marigold." *Do I know you?*

"My name is Sabrina Murrell. I live in Houston. I saw the article in the paper about the dog you found. Actually, a friend from Brenham saw the article and forwarded it to me."

My heart immediately plummeted to my toes as I realized why she'd come. This woman was about to take my sweet Beau away from me.

CHAPTER TWENTY-SEVEN

Y ou've come for my Beau?" I asked.

"Yes, though that's not his real name, of course." She shuffled her bag to her other shoulder then reached inside to grab a compact to check her appearance. "Could I see him in person to know for sure that it's him? We always had a little routine, he and I. If it's really Ziggy, he'll do his usual thing."

"Ziggy?" No way. That didn't suit my Beau-Beau at all! Still, what could I do? I'd agreed to do that stupid newspaper interview. Now I had to pay the piper for my stupidity.

Why, Marigold? Why didn't you leave well enough alone? You had to have a few minutes of fame, and look what it's cost you!

She pulled out a tube of lipstick and swiped it across her lips, then stuck it back in her expensive bag, along with the compact.

I went to the back to fetch Beau Jangles, my heart in my throat. Along the way I passed Parker, who looked up from his work at the lab desk. "You okay? You look like you've seen a ghost."

"I think I have. The ghost of canine past."

"Huh?"

"A woman is here to claim Beau Jangles." As I spit out the words, tears began to flow. I couldn't seem to stop them.

Before I could compose myself, Parker rushed my way and wrapped me in his arms. I found myself leaning into him, tears plummeting as I poured out my heart about how much I loved that little dog. About how I'd made a huge mistake, agreeing to the interview. About how I wanted to run off—right here, right now—and not take him back in the lobby. Would that be unethical? Immoral? Maybe Beau and I could go to Nashville, go on tour with Aunt Trina. Yes, she would hide us away from that awful woman with the ruby lips and Gucci bag.

Okay, so my thoughts were a little irrational, but in my current state of mind they all came tumbling out as if they made perfect sense.

Parker let me carry on and didn't say a word, but when I finished, he tilted my chin and gazed into my eyes with such compassion that it actually felt like ointment over my situation. Crazy, how he always managed to do that.

"First of all, stay calm."

"I. . .I am."

"No, you're not. But, you can get there if you try. Take a deep breath. God will work this out, Mari. I know He will. Go get Beau and take him out there, but trust Him with the rest."

"O–okay." I sniffled and then reached for a paper towel to dry my eyes. Before I could grab one, Parker had pressed one into my hands.

Parker to the rescue.

I cleaned up my face then went to get Beau Jangles from the boarding area, where he'd been hanging out with the Great Dane, Huntress. The two of them were BFFs. They were the perfect Mutt & Jeff duo. I didn't blame Huntress for falling head over heels for my Beau. Everyone loved him. Absolutely everyone.

The tears threatened to come again, but I forced them back. Instead, I called my sweet boy and he came to me. With the usual spring in his step, he followed on my heels into the lobby.

The moment he saw Sabrina, he started jumping up and down.

No!

I didn't want him to celebrate. I wanted him to act oblivious. Or upset. Or. . .something. But, not happy.

The crazy pooch did the funniest little dance, then ran in circles around her, multiple times in a row.

"And, *there* we go!" She laughed and patted him on the head. "Always his crazy, hyper routine. We called it Ziggy's jig. Such a funny little thing, isn't he? And so light on his feet!"

I couldn't deny the obvious. This dog knew her. Well. And apparently he liked her enough to dance a little jig.

So much for running off to Nashville. This dog was headed to Houston. And knowing that broke my heart.

She knelt down and patted him on the head, but not with the level of intensity I would've expected from someone who'd been missing her best friend for weeks on end. Instead, it was more of a tolerant pat, like one would give after scolding an errant child. Weird.

"Ziggy was my mama's dog," she explained. "We've been looking for him everywhere!"

"Ah, I see."

"Mama passed away a few weeks back, and the dog got out on the day of the funeral. We had a houseful of people at her place after the service, and one of the kids left the door open. I didn't even realize he was gone until after our get-together with the family had ended. I figured he was hiding under the bed to get away from the crowd. That's often what he did when he got overwhelmed."

"He loves to hide under the covers when he's scared."

"Does he? I don't remember that part."

"Yep. That's his MO."

"Mama knew all of Ziggy's little quirks, but in those final months it all faded. If you still have any doubts that he belongs to us, I can show you all sorts of pictures of this dog with my mama over the past couple years as she was on her cancer journey." Sabrina paused. "My mom, not the dog. From what I could gather Zig-Zag here is in perfect health."

"Zig-Zag?"

"Yes, that's what she called him. Crazy, right?" Sabrina scrolled through her phone and found a picture of her mother with the dog. Sure enough. Same exact markings. Same goofy expression on his face. And what a sweet photo of him with his owner. That precious woman looked so frail, and yet so happy to be spending time with her pooch.

Oh, man. These people really *were* his people. And that realization made me feel sick inside. The dog I'd fallen in love with was about to head off to his real home. He would forget all about me.

"I believe you," I told her as I passed the phone back her way. "It's just that we had no way to trace an owner because he wasn't microchipped. And he didn't have a collar or tags or anything."

"That's my fault." She sighed and I could see the pain in her eyes. "I was so busy taking care of Mama in those final months that I didn't follow through on the promise I'd made to her to get him chipped like I should've."

Now that, I could understand. A lump rose in my throat, and I did my best to press it down. Those last few weeks with my mama. . .

No. I wouldn't let my emotions take me back there. But I suddenly had tremendous empathy for this woman, even if it meant having to say goodbye to the pup I'd fallen in love with.

"I live in Houston and would drive in whenever I could," she explained, oblivious to my internal ponderings. "But my attention was always on Mama, not the dog. And every time I came, she was a little worse off than the time before. I'll be honest. . ." She glanced down at Beau. "I pretty much just tolerated him. Is that awful?"

"Understandable under the circumstances. When you're grieving. . ." I paused and fought the temptation to tell her that I'd just lost my mama too. "When you're grieving, you pretty much forget that life is still going on around you. You just do the best you can."

"Exactly. I fed him and made sure he had what he needed, but I definitely wasn't very hands-on with him. Maybe that's why he took off, because he was feeling overlooked?"

"I doubt it. He's just frisky like that. But, man. . .he's had a lot of hands-on time since I found him, so his life has definitely changed."

"Oh?"

"Yep. He's the office mascot." I grinned as I watched him in action, greeting an incoming client who had arrived with a timid little terrier. "Actually, Dr. Tyler has an elderly cat named Aggie who's our official mascot, but Beau Jangles here is a close second. Everyone who comes through the place loves our Beau."

"I still can't get over that name." She laughed. "Beau Jangles. I mean, he's a dancer, all right, so it fits. But it's just so cute and funny. You're a great name-giver, Marigold."

"Thanks. We think it suits him."

"It really does. You've done really well with him. He looks great." She paused and appeared to be thinking. "I mean, he's a cute little thing—" The dog barked at her and ran in circles around her once again. "But I'm not really a dog person, so I don't have a clue what to do with one. I did what I could, for Mama's sake but I might have to lean on you for advice if I take him with me."

"If?"

She wrinkled her nose. "Mama would want that, but, like I said, I don't really do dogs. I have a cat named Felicity and she's a little—shall we say—finicky. I don't think she'll get along with a dog very well. But I'm willing to give it a try, just to make sure he doesn't end up out on the street again. Or in one of those shelters. That would be awful."

"Oh, he won't end up out on the street again, or in a shelter. I can assure you of that."

"Oh?"

"Let me ask you a question." My courage kicked in as I posed the question on my mind: "Do you have other family members who might want him, or—"

"I'm an only child. My daughter is grown and married, but they have a new baby and their hands are full." She cast a hopeful glance my way. "Do you know anyone who might want him? I mean, he's a gorgeous dog and I know for a fact he's pedigreed. I'm sure we've still got the papers somewhere."

"As a matter of fact. . ." I knelt down and wrapped my arms around Beau Jangles' neck. "I know the perfect person to adopt him. And the answer was as plain as the nose on my face all along. I fell in love with the little guy the night I rescued him from that drainage ditch."

"You rescued him from a drainage ditch?"

"A pipe, actually. I climbed inside of it to get to him. Nearly got arrested that night."

This, of course, led to a lengthy conversation about all that had transpired the night I'd rescued Beau Jangles. By the end of our conversation, Sabrina and I were both in agreement. This little dog was mine. All mine.

He'd found his home at last.

After she left, I practically skipped back to the lab to tell Parker the good news. I found him organizing supplies. He must've picked up on the joy in my expression because a broad smile lit his face.

"So, you're keeping him?" he asked.

As I nodded, I felt the sting of tears in my eyes. "Yes. I think I knew it in my heart all along that he was going to be mine. I'm a foster fail, Parker."

"I'm glad." He knelt down and the dog licked him on the cheek. "Kind of nice that it worked out that way, if you ask me. I would've missed him if he'd gone away."

"To Houston, no less. That's where the lady lives."

"Well, we can't have that, can we?" He boxed the pup's ears. "Nope, you're staying right here, an official mascot of the Lone Star Veterinary Clinic."

"Official mascot?" Dr. Kristin's voice sounded from the hallway. She walked into the exam room and looked back and forth between us. "Is Beau Jangles staying?"

"Yes! I'm adopting him," I explained. "I just got the go-ahead from the owner. Actually, the owner's daughter. Beau's real owner passed away a few weeks ago and he snuck out on the day of the funeral. They've been looking for him ever since."

Kristin gave me a compassionate look. "I think that's perfect, Mari. You lost your mama. Beau lost his human mama. You're meant for each other. Don't you love it when things work out like that?"

I did. In fact, I liked it so much that I burst into tears, right then and there.

CHAPTER TWENTY-EIGHT

In spite of the good news about Beau Jangles, I couldn't stop thinking about what I'd overheard earlier this morning. Was Tyler really going to interview someone else for Victoria's job instead of offering it to Cassidy?

A little before three I finally worked up the courage to approach him, to share my thoughts on the matter. Only, I was too late. The moment I walked into the lobby, the front door swung open and a gorgeous young woman entered the building. She looked like a fashion model—tall, slender, and very well put together. Her hair must've taken a while to style like that. Wow. And she definitely didn't get her clothes at our local super center. That cream-colored blouse hung loose and flowy, the perfect complement to the fitted jeans and high-heeled boots.

We. Were. Doomed.

She walked straight up to Cassidy at the reception desk and announced that she had an appointment with Tyler to apply for a job.

Poor Cassidy! Her eyes widened and her lips parted in frozen silence. The girl couldn't move. I didn't blame her. I watched it all from the reception counter, where I pretended to be tidying up our heartworm meds display.

This chick didn't really look like office manager material, to my way of thinking. Who hired someone that young to take on such a big task? What kind of experience could she possibly have? And she was pretty chatty, not something you usually saw in the office manager type. We needed someone serious, someone practical, someone who knew the ropes. We needed Cassidy, and I would fight tooth and nail for her.

If I could just work up the courage.

Cassidy called for Tyler over the intercom and he entered the lobby, then walked right up to this young woman and shook her hand. After that, he ushered her into his office. She tagged along behind him, all smiles, the heels on her boots *click, click, clicking* across our tile floor. Ugh.

"What do you think is happening in there?" Cassidy whispered to me.

"Why are we whispering?" I whispered back.

"I dunno. Just nervous, I guess."

"About Tyler giving your job away to a total stranger, you mean?" I shot her a knowing look.

"Is that why she's here?" Tears sprang to Cassidy's eyes. "That jerk! He knew I wanted that job." She began to pace the area behind the reception desk. "Why would he do that to me? And, without telling me? Who does that?"

"Apparently Tyler Durham." My gaze narrowed. "But don't worry, Cassidy. He and I are going to have a few words when this interview is over. I've already got it all planned out in my head."

"You do?" She looked deeply appreciative. That, and a little terrified.

"Yep. And I know for a fact the others will back me up. Isabel. Parker. Even Kristin. We were rooting for you to have that job."

"You were?"

"Yep. So, if he hires little Miss Washington County in there, we're gonna stage an intervention."

"I appreciate that, Mari, but that's just plain awkward."

"Nope, it's the right thing to do." And I was gearing up to do it, even now. He'd hire this new cover model over my dead body.

As I tried to formulate a plan, I caught a glimpse of someone else coming through the front door of the clinic. Cameron Saye. Well, terrific. Just when I thought the day couldn't get any better.

He approached, looking back and forth between Cassidy and me.

"Looks like I missed something important. What's going on, ladies?"

I wanted to say, "None of your business," but Cassidy beat me to the punch by telling him about the interview going on in Tyler's office.

"So, Ty is taking applications?" Cameron's gaze narrowed. "I thought he wasn't hiring anyone new right now."

"He's replacing our office manager, who has decided to become a full-time stay-at-home mom," I explained.

"Ah. Weird. He told me—" Cameron paused and shook his head. "Anyway, I think it stinks, Cassidy. Tell you what, if I ever get my practice up and running, you can come work for me."

"Really?" Her eyes widened.

Oh no you don't, Mister.

I glared at him, willing him to stop this nonsense before it went any further.

Cameron's presence distracted Cassidy from the goings-on in Tyler's office, but I still couldn't figure out what the guy was doing here. Why did he keep coming around? What did he want. . . really?

A few minutes later the door to Tyler's office opened and he stepped out with the pretty little miss beside him. The young woman shook his hand. Judging from the broad smile on her face, things had gone well.

Apparently a little too well, at least to my way of thinking.

"Thanks for coming in, Brianna," he said with a wave as she walked toward the door. "I think you're going to be a valuable addition to the team."

Oh. No. You. Didn't.

"I can't wait." She giggled and then patted a random Scottish terrier on the head before heading out of the front door.

Cameron's gaze followed our new employee, and I could practically read his errant thoughts.

Lovely.

I crossed my arms at my chest and glared at my boss. After all my months of swooning over him, he'd done this? No thanks, Tyler. The man I'd once cared about had given away my best friend's job. What could I possibly do to fix things now?

Parker entered the lobby at that very moment to call the Scottish terrier's owner back to an exam room. He took one look at my frozen position and eased in my direction.

"What did I miss?"

"He went and did it. He hired a new office manager."

I spoke the words under my breath, but Tyler must've heard me. He turned my way, worry lines creasing his forehead.

"No." He shook his head. "No, I didn't."

"You didn't?" These words came from Cassidy, who held tight to the terrier's file. "But—"

"Nope." Tyler looked back and forth between all of us. "Brianna was applying for the position of receptionist."

"Receptionist?" Cassidy and I both responded at once, the word coming out as more of a squeal.

"Well, yeah." Tyler looked directly at Cassidy. "We don't need an office manager because I've already got one, and she's perfect for the job. She's been doing the work all along and has proven she's got what it takes." He flashed a bright smile and then extended his hand in Cassidy's direction. "It's yours, Cassidy, if you want it, complete with a nice salary and the world's smallest, windowless office."

Her mouth flew open. "W–what? Are you serious?"

"I am. I knew, the minute you were interested, that you'd be perfect. It's the right thing to do. Victoria needs—and wants to be home with her baby. You need—and want—a position that will free you up to do what you love. And I need—and want—everyone to be in the place where they're the best possible fit. For you, that's office manager. If you'll agree to it, I mean."

"I agree! I agree!"

Parker called the terrier's name, and the dog's owner rose and led him into the exam room. I walked over to Cassidy and gave her a hug. Then, just for fun, I threw my arms around Tyler's neck too.

"Thank you," I said. "That means the world to her. I know it does."

"Of course. I want what's best for this practice. I hope you all know that."

Out of the corner of my eye I caught a glimpse of Cameron as he sidled up next to the reception counter. I gestured for Tyler to join me in the hallway, hoping to speak to him privately about the situation that appeared to be brewing between my best friend and his former nemesis.

"Tyler, why does Cameron keep coming around? Do you think he's just stringing Cassidy along to get what he's really after?"

"That's kind of his MO, but he's just a big flirt. I don't think he would really hurt her. But the ladies have always swooned over him. You wouldn't believe how many girls over the years asked me for his number. They thought, because he was my good friend, that I'd just hand it out."

"So, you were good friends at one point?"

"During our undergrad years we were in the A&M Corps of Cadets together." He shrugged. "I did my best to befriend him. He needed one, for sure. But we didn't have a lot in common. I'm so. . ."

Good? Kind? Wonderful?

"Boring. You know? Not into partying and that whole scene, which was definitely where he excelled. So, when the girls started coming around, asking for his number, I had a hard time giving it out."

"For his sake? Or theirs."

"Maybe both?" He sighed. "He's not a bad guy, Mari. He's not. He's just not. . ." Tyler's nose wrinkled. "Not a believer."

"Ah." I definitely understood that.

"And his choices, his lifestyle, they don't line up with the principles I've held to."

"Is that why you wouldn't give him a job?"

His eyes widened.

"Yeah, I overheard him through the door one day. He got a little loud."

"He's passionate." Tyler shrugged. "But here's the thing, Mari. Look around you. When you come to work every day you're surrounded by like-minded people who will pray for you if you need it, and help you if you need it."

"As I've learned, for sure."

"There's a reason for that. That's the kind of business I want to run. I'm not saying I would discriminate against someone based on their religion or anything like that. I'm just saying God happened to give me several staff members who have similar values with mine. Cameron does not."

"Is that why he didn't get the job?"

"I didn't give him the job because Kristin was the better candidate. That's it, plain and simple. If a position ever opened up for a third vet, I'd consider Cameron. But I'd have to have a chat with him first about flirting with all the ladies. He's always been like that, and it sends the wrong message. Results in broken hearts and weird expectations. I would hate that sort of dynamic around here. It's been so nice not to come in and deal with a bunch of soap opera drama. You know?"

Hmm. So, was he saying that he didn't want his employees to date one another? I'd never thought about that before.

"I'm happy with things the way they are." Tyler gave me a compassionate look. "And in case I haven't said it often enough, I'm more than thrilled with the job you're doing—not just here in the clinic but with the rescue dogs too."

"Thank you. That means a lot."

"I hope you know I'll do my best to take care of their physical needs, Mari. I have a heart for the lost too."

"I know you do. I've seen you volunteering at the shelter, giving of your time."

He sighed. "I feel really bad about that, by the way. They need my help tomorrow, and I can't go."

Oh! A chance to impress him. I squared my shoulders. "Tomorrow's my day off. Can I help?" I followed that offer up with a bright smile.

"I'm sure they would be glad to have you. But are you sure you want to go on your day off?"

"Sure, why not."

"I know they were hoping for a vet, but I'm sure they'll be thrilled to have a tech on board. And let's face it, Mari. You can do almost everything I can do, short of surgeries."

"Shh." I put my finger to my lips. "We're not supposed to let people know that."

He laughed. "That's my way of saying I think you're incredibly valuable. Don't ever forget it."

"I won't."

I gazed into his eyes, thinking I'd have that same jolt I'd experienced that afternoon in the truck with Parker.

Nope. Not even close.

The face I saw gazing back at me was a kind face. A friendly face. A compassionate face.

Just not the face for me.

CHAPTER TWENTY-NINE

The following morning, I headed into town with Beau Jangles at my side. Cassidy had agreed to watch him at the clinic while I drove to the shelter to volunteer in Tyler's place. I was nervous about what I'd agreed to do, but—for sure—knew that I couldn't take Beau with me. The risk was too great to bring a healthy dog into the shelter environment right now. With distemper being such a critical problem, I would never put Beau in harm's way. Nor would the shelter allow it.

So, off to the clinic I went, knowing my sweet boy would be right at home with my coworkers.

My coworkers.

I thought about Isabel and wondered how she was holding up. In all the chaos of yesterday afternoon, I'd forgotten to check in on her. Matt Foster was noticeably quiet. I prayed it would last but had a nagging suspicion he would turn back up, angrier than ever. Ugh. I hated that we had to live with that hanging over our heads.

Still, I knew that Parker was looking out for Isabel.

Parker.

The edges of my lips curled up in a smile. Thinking about him made me want to talk to Aunt Trina. Maybe it was time to confess that I'd finally noticed his blue eyes.

I used my car's Bluetooth speaker to call my aunt, and she answered after the second ring.

"Hey! I was just thinking about you."

"You were?" I laughed. "Well, great minds." I kept a watchful eye on the traffic around me.

"Yeah, believe it or not, I think I've worked out a plan to come home for Christmas."

"No way!" Tears sprang to my eyes at once. "Really?"

"Yep. But don't tell Mama Peach, at least not yet. I want it to be set in stone before she hears, just in case something goes wrong at the last minute."

"I pray nothing goes wrong. How long can you stay?" I eased my way into the lane to my right so that I could turn at the next corner.

"I'm thinking from the 23rd of December until January 2nd. How would that be?"

"Like heaven." I giggled. Then I happened to remember something important she needed to know. "But there is one little teensy-tiny problem."

"What's that?"

"Grandma turned your bedroom into a cat hotel."

"A what?"

"No joke, Trina. You'll have to see it to believe it. She's turned your bedroom into a catio for Hector."

"Do I even want to know what a catio is?"

I stopped at the red light and had a moment to explain. "Actually, in his case, it's a playroom. And I'm not sure I could do it justice in words. I'm going to have to take pictures and send them to you. It's pretty remarkable. Or, horrifying, depending on how you look at it. But, the point is, the cat got your space."

"Hector, the demon cat. . .has his own room?"

"Yeah, he needs it, actually. She's baking for so many different men right now that the cat would be in the way, so she wants to keep him preoccupied."

"Wait, she's baking for lots of men now? What does that even mean?"

"Whelp, I thought she had the hots for Mr. Elban, but it turns out he's just stringing her along because he's really got the hots for Donna Sue Specklemeyer. And we all know that Donna Sue's probably going to kill him with her fried chicken."

"He's dying?"

"Oh, not yet. But he will. Sooner or later." The light changed and I turned right.

"We all will, sooner or later."

"My point is, Grandma has moved on to the reverend now."

"Reverend Nelson?"

"Yep."

"Marigold, he's eighty-one years old, if he's a day."

"Well, apparently he can't get enough of her spice drops, whatever that means."

"Ick."

"Right?" I groaned.

"I think she's missing Daddy." Trina grew silent for a moment. "And I wonder—what with all of this feeding of other men—if she's trying to get some sort of redo."

"What do you mean?"

"Daddy had so many health problems. I think Mama always blamed herself. She honestly tried to help him get control of his diet, but he was so stubborn. The man loved his cheeseburgers and fries. You know? And did you ever see him without a Dr Pepper in his hand?"

"This apple doesn't fall far from that tree."

"Neither does this one." Trina laughed. "I'm up eight pounds now."

"That's more than Curtis's dog."

"Huh?"

"Never mind." I laughed so hard I nearly drove off the road. "So, you think Grandma blames herself for Grandpa's death?"

"Baking is her love language, and it's the way she ministers to others. I would never ask her to stop. But I suppose on some level she has to justify all of that sugar she's passing their way."

"She's always carrying on about how her ingredients are natural and whatnot," I responded. "Maybe that's just how she makes herself feel better about it all."

"Point being, that she is human. She wishes she could save everyone, but she can't. So, instead, she blesses them with her sweet treats to brighten their lives."

"I love that about her," I responded. "And I can totally relate to the wanting to save people part. Only, with me, it's dogs."

"Yes, and that's admirable."

"I think I probably want to save dogs because I wasn't able to save Mama. You know? Maybe I'm more like my grandparents than I realize— saving the helpless with a Dr Pepper in my hands."

"You're more like your mama, actually." Trina's voice trembled. "If Vanessa Evans was anything, she was a giver. And so are you. You're just like her, honey. So you go right on giving."

I felt a lump the size of Texas fill my throat. I tried to press it down, but it refused to budge. If I didn't change the subject, I was going to bust into tears and ruin this whole conversation.

"I still can't get over what you said about the catio, though," Trina said after a moment of silence. "I've been replaced by a cat."

"He's definitely living the high life," I explained. "Hector's got a cat tower, a cat bed, a bunch of toys, and even this weird, random play yard gazebo-ish thing. Kind of like a rabbit hutch, only bigger."

"A rabbit hutch?" She groaned. "Where's my bed?"

"No bed. And I wouldn't recommend sleeping in there, even if she'd left the bed. What with the random crooked perches on the wall. He might jump on your head while you're sleeping."

"Crooked perches?"

"Kind of hard to explain. Like shelves, only installed at weird angles. It's like a catwalk." I laughed at the pun. "He can walk up and down them."

"You're telling me that the demon cat can scale the walls of my bedroom?"

"Former bedroom."

"Right." She paused. "So, where do I stay if I do come home?"

"You can always stay at my place. I have a second bedroom."

"True. But she would kill me."

"I haven't checked Grandma's guest room, but I'm guessing it's still intact. If you don't mind decor from the 1980s."

"Don't mind a bit. In fact, I'd be disappointed if she changed it."

"Perfect!" I was giddy at this news. I could hardly wait to see Trina in person. In the meantime, I had a lot of tea to spill. "Trina, I have so much to tell you! I have this client—Maggie Jamison—she lives out on a ranch on the road to Round Top."

"I know Maggie Jamison."

"You do?" I tapped the brakes as the car in front of me came to a stop at the next light.

"Yes. She and your mom were good friends back in the day. I worked at the Sonic when I was a teen. They were both at Blinn College at the time. She would stop by every morning on her way into class and order the biggest Dr Pepper we sold, a Route 44."

"Oh wow."

"She was always a big tipper." Trina laughed. "But, what about her?"

"She's living on this big piece of land west of town, and I'm hoping I can talk her into letting some of the dogs stay there. She's already got one—a lab mix named Blacky. I think he's probably having the time of his life out there."

"How many dogs are we talking?"

"Oh, I've just got Blacky at the moment, but I'm working a hoarding case today, so who knows how many might come out of that."

"You're really doing this."

"I am."

"Honey, I'm proud of you. You can tell me all about it when I come. But what about funding? Do you need money?"

"Is this a trick question?" I laughed.

"You'll have to have resources to get started. And you'll need money to file a 501c3. I think that process takes a couple months."

"Yeah." I sighed. "But it's time."

"It is. And we can talk it through when I come. Even if I'm not there in person to help you with the rescue, maybe I can help in this way?"

Wow. I hadn't imagined she would be interested in funding the plan, but maybe she was. I eased forward in traffic once again.

"First I need to settle on a place. Some land. Maybe a barn to use for the shelter. A small house for me. It'll all come together as soon as I find the place. But in the meantime, I plan to talk to Maggie about using her place."

"Sounds like a great plan. But Mari, I'm serious about helping financially. Once you've got your nonprofit status, I can donate to help you with the purchase of some of that."

Tears sprang to my eyes.

"It's what your mama would've wanted," Trina said. "And you're gonna need money."

"Thank you. I won't turn you down if that's that you want to do."

"I do." She paused. "Hey, the next time you see Maggie, ask her if she remembers me. I used to annoy her to no end, always tagging along with your mama. I wonder if she remembers."

"I'm sure she does, Trina. You're kind of a celebrity around here."

"Oh boy. Well, don't roll out the red carpet when I come home, okay? I'd like to just disappear into the background for a few days."

"Like that could happen." I laughed. "Grandma Peach is gonna parade you through town. She'll probably get you your very own float in the Christmas parade."

"Oh, man. I almost forgot about the parade. Will I make it in time?"

"Just." I slowed down and turned onto Washington Street, nearing our office. Brenham's annual Stroll & Lighted Parade was one of our favorite annual events. I loved the farmers market and all the booths. Grandma loved selling her pies. And no doubt the whole town of Brenham would love that their favorite local celebrity was coming back to join in the festivities with them.

I drove past Beckett's place on my way in and paused when I saw the parking lot was, once again, full. So strange. Who had this many clients so early in the day? How many people could one CPA handle, anyway? Or, did he have a whole team? Yes, maybe that was it.

"Hey, I have to let you go, girlie." Trina's voice startled me back to attention. "I've got to get to the studio. But I'm so excited about coming home."

"Me too!"

"Don't tell you-know-who."

"I won't, I promise."

I eased my SUV into the clinic's parking lot and was surprised to see Maggie Jamison pulling into the spot next to me. She got out of the truck with Blacky at her side.

"Hey, is everything okay?" I asked.

"Yep. Just came in for his shots."

"But he just had the first round the other day. We gave them to him before leaving your house, remember?"

"Right, but he's due for his heartworm preventative. I already called yesterday afternoon and talked to Dr. Kristin."

"You did?"

"Mm-hmm." Maggie smiled. "And I insisted she take him on as her client. I have nothing against Dr. Tyler, of course, but thought it might be nice to let Kristin care for Midnight."

My heart swelled with joy at this proclamation.

"Wait. . .you've named him Midnight?"

"Yeah. I hope you don't mind, but that whole Blacky thing? It was too cliché."

"Agreed! I'm sure he'll answer to whatever name he gets used to."

"Oh, he already has."

We walked into the clinic together and she checked in with Brianna at the reception desk, then knelt to snuggle Midnight close.

"I just love this big old boy. Whatever breed he might be."

"Hey, maybe you could do his DNA," I suggested. "Then you would know for sure."

"Nah, I won't need that. Doesn't matter to me what breed he is. He's still perfect to me."

"So, does that mean. . ." I gave her an inquisitive look, already knowing her answer.

"Yeah, he's a foster fail." She flashed a mischievous look my way. "And for the record, I knew what you were up to all along."

"You. . .you did?"

"Yeah, of course. You come out to my place with a dog, under the guise of bringing me Jasper's paw print."

"Hey, I really brought you his paw print."

"I know, but. . ." She paused. "I saw right through that. I knew why you brought this guy." She gave him a kiss on the top of the head. "And I can't thank you enough."

What she did next startled me, and I wasn't easily startled.

Okay, yes I was.

Maggie Jamison threw her arms around my neck, wrapping me in a hug so tight I could hardly catch my breath.

CHAPTER THIRTY

Hey, I have an idea," I said when Maggie finally stopped hugging me. "Why don't you leave Midnight here to play with Beau and come with me to the shelter?"

"Why are we going to the shelter?"

"They need volunteers," I explained. "A hoarding case came in yesterday, and the animals need baths and shots and all sorts of veterinary care."

"And I'm going because. . ."

"I thought you might enjoy it," I said. "You're so good with animals. And they really need the help." I paused. "Unless you have big plans today."

"Nope. Coming here was my big plan."

I led her into Cassidy's new office and shared our plan. She thought it was terrific and was happy to watch Midnight.

"We'll take him in to see Kristin for you," Cassidy explained. "You don't worry about a thing. I only wish I could go with you guys. It sounds like so much fun."

Maggie didn't look convinced but agreed to come with me. In fact, she offered to drive. I climbed into the cab of her F-250 and we headed off to the county shelter, just a few miles away. As she drove, I did my best to make small talk, starting with the obvious.

"So, I hear you knew my mom."

"Your mom?" She gave me an inquisitive look.

"Vanessa Evans."

"Vanessa Evans was your mom?" She tapped the brakes and glanced my way. "How did I not put that together?"

"Maybe you never noticed my last name?"

"I should have realized. She always loved the name Marigold when we were young."

"Really?"

"Yes." Maggie smiled. "It was all those British novels she used to read. I think she thought Marigold sounded aristocratic."

"Oh my. I'm anything but."

"I still can't believe I didn't realize you were Vanessa's daughter. I'm so sorry I didn't catch on. I'm getting slow in my old age."

"Hardly. And you're not old."

"I was so sorry to hear about your mama's death." She glanced my way then shifted her gaze back to the road. "I was grieving my own loss at the time after losing Drew. I let time and space come between us. I hope you can forgive me for not being there for you."

"Please don't think a thing about it. Life happens."

"It does." She paused. "And so does death. I learned that the hard way, when Drew passed."

A comfortable silence grew up between us, and in that moment I felt a kindredness with her that I'd not felt before. If anyone could understand this road I was walking right now, Maggie Jamison could.

"I knew your mama from the time we were kids," she said after a few moments of quiet.

"And Trina too, from what she told me on the phone earlier."

"Trina." Maggie laughed. "She was always kind of a little brat. She used to follow us around, just to annoy us."

"So she said. But she told me you used to leave her really good tips when she worked at Sonic."

"I did. I've always been a big tipper."

"You've got a generous heart, Maggie, and it shows. That's how I knew you were the perfect one to take Blacky—er, Midnight." I gestured for her to change lanes so that she could make a left-hand turn at the next light.

"You set me up." She eased her way into the left turn lane.

"Kind of. But my intentions were pure."

"Sure they were." She laughed and then turned on her signal to make the turn. "Hey, whatever happened to your grandmother? I only knew her as Mama Peach."

"Oh, she's still around. Baking pies and sweet-talking the men."

"Oh my. She still bakes pies?"

"Religiously."

"She always was a religious woman." Maggie laughed. "She tried to get me through the doors of the Presbyterian church as a kid, but my mama wouldn't hear of it. We were Methodists, through and through."

"Sounds like Grandma Peach. She's probably still praying that you'll come around."

"No doubt." She eased the truck forward when the light changed and made the left-hand turn onto the road that would lead us to the shelter. "You know, she's the reason I love to cook."

"Really? I heard you were an amazing cook."

"You did? Who said that?"

"Grandma Peach. She said you make the best pot roast in town. Some sort of community potluck?"

"Yep. Back when I was a young bride Brenham used to have Picnic in the Park, an annual event. Potluck, as you said."

"So, it's true? You're a cook?"

"It's funny you should bring this up. If I had my druthers I'd parcel off most of the ranch—sell part of it and keep the rest for a little restaurant."

"Wow." This was quite a revelation.

"I'd keep the part with the gardens and start a restaurant near the front of the property. Something different. Everything fresh from my own garden."

"Maggie, that sounds wonderful."

"Doesn't it?" She sighed. "I think I'm at my best when I'm in the kitchen. I have this picture in my mind of a place where folks can come and eat a healthy meal, then walk the property, maybe see the goats and chickens. It would be..." Her words trailed off. "An experience. You know? Not just a meal, but an experience. Kind of a back-to-nature sort of thing. Back to the land, anyway."

"So, you would keep the goats and chickens if you sold off the rest of the place?"

"Yep. I'd build a little log cabin style restaurant with a place upstairs for me. And Midnight."

"Sounds dreamy."

"Yeah." She sighed. "It'll never happen, though. That property's not mine to sell. It belongs to my husband's family. Kind of a long story."

"Ah, I see."

I didn't exactly, but if she said it, it must be so.

"The ranch was my husband's dream, not mine." She pulled off her hat and raked her hands through that messy hair. "Now, I'm not saying I'd ever leave. You'd have to drag me off that land kicking and screaming. But my vision for it never exactly matched up with his."

"You would change things up?"

"If I had the option. But I don't. That piece of land has been in my husband's family for over a hundred years. When we married seventeen years ago, we actually signed a prenup, a life estate."

"What's that?"

"Basically, a legal document stating that if he passed away—which he has—I can stay here and live out my days. But I have no claim to the property."

"Oh, I see."

"Yes. My brother-in-law lives on the back of the property in the original home, the one they grew up in. It's a tiny little place, and he's settled there." She shrugged. "We don't really speak, so I can't tell you much more about him. He and Drew had a falling out years ago and things got testy. He didn't even come to Drew's funeral. Can you believe it?"

"No!" My mother's funeral was fresh in my mind, and I couldn't fathom Trina not showing up. How awful would that be? "So sad. And cruel."

"Yeah, definitely." She shrugged. "Life is too short for that. I hate division. I really do."

"Me too."

"So, that's my current situation. I'm there, but I don't actually own the property. In happier news, my brother-in-law is a bit of a pain, but he doesn't come around much. There's some saving grace in that, I suppose."

That made me even sadder, actually. In an ideal world, the two of them would come together and mourn Drew's loss, hand in hand.

But who was I to judge such things? I was barely able to navigate my way out of my own grief, let alone counsel someone else with theirs.

She changed the topic back to dogs, and before long I was in my comfort zone once again. I found myself telling her all my hopes and dreams, including my passion for dogs like Midnight, who simply needed a safe space. On and on I went, sharing my heart. I even told her about my passion for Dr Pepper. Apparently she shared that passion. We were Texans, after all.

We made easy conversation the rest of the way, arriving at the shelter at five minutes till ten, our expected arrival time. When we pulled into the parking lot I saw three of the county's impound trucks lined up against the side of the building.

Maggie slipped her truck into a nearby parking slot, and we got out and walked inside the front door of the building. I carried Tyler's medical bag in hand, ready to do whatever was required of me.

I'd been here dozens of times, of course. I'd volunteered years ago as a dog walker, and then again as a technician when I was in school. But since working at the clinic there hadn't been time. Until today.

I introduced myself to the woman at the front desk and within minutes we were led to a large room at the back of the building. We got to the large space at the back of the clinic where the rescue dogs were clustered in crates. My heart twisted at once when I saw how many we were dealing with. Goodness.

Maggie took one look at the line of crates and let out a cry. "Oh, this is awful!" She pinched her nose and shook her head. "Who would let them get in this condition?"

"It happens," I said. "But, brace yourself."

The vet in charge introduced herself. She looked to be in her early forties and, judging from her haggard appearance, hadn't slept much in recent days. I liked Daphne right away. She was practical, fast, and friendly. And über-grateful for the help.

"We got the dogs in last night and fed them," she said. "The owner had over thirty dogs on her property."

"Thirty?" Maggie pinched her eyes shut. "I'm trying to picture it but it's just not coming to me."

"Be glad you didn't see the property," Daphne said. "That image is seared into my brain forever now."

"No thanks." Maggie shook her head. "I'm happy to be here, but so glad I didn't go with you."

Daphne introduced us to the other volunteers, and we got right to work, examining the dogs, and then setting up a system for baths, flea and tick removal, and shots. I did my best not to get overwhelmed, but these poor creatures were mostly skin and bones. I wondered how many would survive here, at the shelter. Would they find the homes they needed or. . .

No, I wouldn't think about that. Right now I just had one job, to save as many as I could.

We continued to work for several minutes when I heard a rousing, "Hey, y'all" from behind me. I turned to discover someone rather unexpected had joined us. I nearly lost my grip on the leash I was holding as I stared up at that familiar handsome face.

"Cameron?"

He flashed a dazzling smile. "Yep. Hope you guys don't mind, but I got a call from Tyler. He said someone needed a vet?"

CHAPTER THIRTY-ONE

The next several hours were spent working side by side with Maggie and Cameron. I'd never been in this situation before, wedged between two people who—until recently—had been total strangers to me. Both of them, at least to my earlier way of thinking, suspects in the vandalism incident.

Not that I could possibly consider Maggie anymore. And even Cameron, whose arm was now healing, seemed a less likely candidate, now that I'd witnessed him in action, working with the shelter animals. At this very moment, he just seemed like an ordinary veterinarian. A good one, in fact.

Fortunately, we were all so preoccupied with the dogs that I didn't have time to ponder these issues for long. For sure, Cameron shocked me with his veterinary know-how. Turned out, the guy was genius material. He seemed to have a particular knack for diagnosing dogs, based on outward appearance. Not everyone had that gift. He could look at a pup and say, "This one's got parasites" or "This one's got an ear infection" even before a full exam. I'd heard of vets like this, but most were hands-on, doing a careful exam and then offering thoughts after-the-fact.

Daphne was thrilled to have him. To have all of us, in fact. She carried on and on, talking our ear off about the need for more medical care at the facility.

"I'll admit, the pay's not good," she said. "But I sure wish we had a second vet on hand. I can't tell you how many times animals have died on my watch simply because I had to sleep for a few hours."

"Don't you have techs to help?" Cameron asked.

"A couple, but they rotate shifts. I'm telling you, we're overbooked. And the pandemic really hit us hard. I don't know if you know this, but we actually had to shut down the facility for several months in 2020. A lot of our people never came back after that."

"What happened to the animals?" Maggie asked.

"They were farmed out to fosters or sent up north, but even the transport buses stopped for a few months. It was grueling. I can't tell you how many nights I spent curled up on the floor of a shelter kennel with a dying dog." She swiped at her nose with the back of her hand. "Don't even want to think about it now. I can't. I have to put it behind me. You do what you can. You know?"

I did. But, man. This gal had walked a hard road. A faithful road. She made what I wanted to do look like child's play. Maybe I'd judged the shelters too harshly. I hadn't walked a mile in Daphne's shoes. Maybe—just maybe— we were all on the very same team, trying to accomplish the same goals.

"I love these dogs and cats," Daphne said. "Sometimes too much. It's a detriment to my own health to give so much and still lose so many simply because we're overrun."

"Man." Cameron seemed to lose himself to his thoughts. "Not exactly the high-end practice we dream of in medical school."

"No." She emitted a wry laugh. "Not even close. But I can tell you, it's a thousand times more rewarding than making a huge paycheck. I'd be willing to bet I've saved over a thousand dogs in my ten years here. And that's a conservative number."

"Wow." He gave her an admiring look. "I'm sure that feels good."

"It would feel better if I could get a little sleep." She yawned and then laughed. "See there? I didn't even do that on purpose."

I didn't know whether to laugh or cry. The whole thing was like a kick in the gut.

In that moment, I realized I'd have to help Daphne. If I could get my 501c3 and find someplace to house the dogs, I could make a real difference here. I could help her find fosters. I could take some of the needy ones off of her hands. I could...

I could do a lot. And I *would* do a lot.

We lost Maggie for a little while as she headed off to the grooming area to bathe the dogs. She returned an hour and a half later, completely soaked, hair slicked back, but happy as a lark.

"Oh, my, that was fun." She laughed and brushed her hands against her jeans. "And I thought bathing Midnight was tough!"

"See any pups you can't live without?" I asked.

She gave me a knowing look. "How did you figure that out?"

"It happens."

"Well, there was this one little Corgi mix. Kind of reminded me of Jasper. But the one that really tore my heart out was a senior rat terrier. Ugly old gal. Kind of like me."

"You are neither old nor ugly," I said.

"But I am in need of a bath, so I have that in common with Gracie. That's her name, by the way. She was so good. She was super chill as we bathed her. I think she was just so happy to get those fleas and ticks off."

"You pulled ticks off of her?" Cameron gave her an admiring look.

"Sure. I'm a rancher. I've pulled many a tick off an animal over the years. No skin off my teeth."

Sometime after five, Parker and Tyler arrived. I was startled to see them, and even more surprised to learn it was so late. Had we really been here that long?

Still, a sense of relief washed over me as they came in and got to work beside us. By six o'clock I was exhausted. As in, flat-out exhausted and ready to drop. And I smelled as bad as most of the dogs I'd tended to.

Parker offered to take my place, insisting that I pull up a chair and rest for a bit. I was happy to oblige.

Tyler and Cameron worked side by side giving vaccinations and doing exams, cracking jokes and talking like two old friends. I found it all so strange.

"So, this is what you'll be getting into?" Maggie asked as she pulled up a chair next to mine. "When you start that nonprofit you were telling me about on the drive over?"

"Not exactly. If there's ever another hoarding case like this one, I won't be the one responding to it, they will. The county will do the intake then call on rescues to help them just like we're doing here. The ones that have room will take some of these pups off the county's hands and place them with fosters."

"I see."

"So, if I had Second Chance Ranch up and running, we'd take a few right now. Tonight. If I had a place, I mean. That way they wouldn't have to find room for all of them here at the shelter. They're overcrowded, as it is."

"Ah. You need help."

"I have Parker. He's willing to foster. Right, Parker?"

"Yep." He glanced up and nodded. "I've got a house with a yard and can take a couple, but that's about it."

"Sounds like what you need is more fosters and a dedicated space." Maggie seemed to lose herself to her thoughts.

"True. And things are going to get even crazier. Ever since that article came out in the paper, people have been calling the clinic with reports of dogs needing rescue. It's been a little crazy," I admitted. "I mean, I'm grateful for the article, because it brought attention to the problem. But I'm not quite ready for the rescue to get so much attention just yet. I think maybe I've got the cart ahead of the horse."

"Or the leash ahead of the dog." Maggie laughed. "Get it? Leash? Dog?"

"Got it." I couldn't help but laugh. "Anyway, I think that article has forced my hand. I'll have no choice but to file for a 501c3 now. My dream is going to become a reality, but only if I actually do the hard work." I paused to think through my plan of action but always seemed to get stuck right here—at the point where the paperwork began. "But then again, I have no idea how any of that is done. I should've been more prepared. Maybe I can find the paperwork online?"

"Actually, I've been looking into that for you," Parker said. "There are ways to fast-track a 501c3."

"Really?"

"Yes, there are companies that do that. And, after that article in the paper, I'd say you're gonna need it."

"You know. . ." Maggie paused and appeared to be thinking. "My attorney helps people set up 501c3s. He helped my husband with a boys' club ministry several years ago. I know he'd do it for you."

"The same attorney who was filing a lawsuit against me?" Tyler asked.

"Yeah, same one. Hey, I paid a retainer. Might as well use it. You know?"

We dove into a lengthy conversation about what that would look like, and before long she was fully onboard, not just to help me but to fund the legal part of it. I was so overwhelmed, I hardly knew what to think.

"So, it's all settled." Maggie flashed a crooked grin. "My attorney will handle the paperwork."

"And I'll foster. . .and help you with the rescues," Parker chimed in.

"And Lone Star will be your go-to vet," Tyler added.

"And I'll volunteer," Cameron said. He paused and appeared to be thinking. "Hey, could you use a van?"

"A van?" I asked.

"Yeah, my dad offered me his 2014 cargo van when he retired from his job as a plumber, but I didn't really have a use for it so it's sitting in my driveway taking up space. Drives great. I'll bet you could fit a lot of crates inside. Maybe even a mobile vet area with some equipment."

"A—are you serious, Cameron?"

"Sure. I might have connections for some of that equipment, by the way."

Okay then. I had help. And money. And a vehicle. And equipment. Now all I needed was property and my dream would truly be a reality.

Maggie must've picked up on my internal pondering.

"You know," she said. "While I'm alive and kicking, I can make use of my husband's property."

"What do you mean?"

"Maybe we could look at using my barn as some sort of temporary shelter? I don't think I could keep the dogs for long, but maybe a few days until you locate fosters or send them on transport?"

My heart was overwhelmed with gratitude and joy. "I'd love to come look at it, Maggie."

"Come anytime. For that matter, bring Beau and spend a night or two. I'll show you around the place and cook you a fabulous meal."

"Can I come?" Parker asked.

"Sure." She laughed. "You need food too?"

"Always."

"Me too." Cameron raised his hand.

Before long, she was agreeing to feed all of us, including Daphne, who really looked like she could use a good meal. And a good night's sleep.

"You're all welcome anytime, folks. I've got rooms to spare. Pick any one of 'em and I'll make you comfortable. It's been a lonely life out there on that massive piece of property. And I haven't had anyone to cook for since Drew passed." Her eyes glistened. "Sounds like I'd better warm up my oven."

"Please do," Cameron said, and then laughed.

"Bring your pets," she said. "Midnight is going to need a friend. Or two." She pointed at the dogs in the crates surrounding them. "Or twelve." The edges of her lips curled up in a delicious smile. "Speaking of which, I think I'd better go check back in on Gracie. She seemed mighty scared back there, all alone in that kennel."

"Mm-hmm." I laughed, in part because I could see the handwriting on the wall and in part because I totally and completely understood. That's how pups won us over, after all. They got their paws wrapped around our hearts and squeezed until we simply couldn't breathe without them.

Maggie rose and stretched. "After I check on Gracie I need to get back to the clinic to pick up Midnight. Then I think I'd better head home."

"I'll take Marigold," Parker said.

"Sure." Maggie rose and stretched. "I'm starving. Might have to drive through Triple B's on the way home and grab a burger. They're the best."

"Right?!" Parker looked my way. "We still need to go there, Mari."

"Oh?" Maggie looked back and forth between us. "You two haven't been?"

"We've been," I said. "Just not—"

"Together." Parker flashed me an impish smile.

"Well, you must remedy that. And I want to be the one to take care of it. Let me bless you." She reached into her purse and came out with a fifty-dollar bill, which she tried to press into my hands.

"Oh no!" I exclaimed as I pulled my hand back. "I couldn't possibly take that."

"Of course you can. Let's call it an investment. If I'm going to make monthly donations to your 501c3, I need to make sure you're in tip-top shape. And the only way to know for sure is to get some good Texas beef into your veins."

I laughed as she continued to press the money into my palm.

"Next time I see you two I want to hear how it went. And while you're there, go ahead and come up with your mission statement and a list of board members and all of that. I think my attorney will ask for it." She shrugged. "He owes me a few hours. I paid him in advance for, well. . ." She laughed. "Anyway, he owes me. And I'm sure it's going to be more than enough to cover any work related to setting this up."

I rose and gave her the biggest hug ever, then Parker walked her out to her car so she wouldn't have to go alone.

When he came back in, I heard someone's cell phone ringing. It took a minute to realize it was my own. I scrambled to get it out of my purse and glanced down at the screen, noticing Isabel's name. At once, my heart sailed to my throat.

What did Matt do this time?

I answered but before I could even say hello, she said, "He did it, Marigold. This time he *really* did it."

My heart hit my toes as fear swept over me. At once, I began to tremble.

"This time, Matt actually checked himself into a facility," Isabel said, her words flooding out in a steady stream. "He's in a program in Houston for the next six weeks. Can you believe it?"

CHAPTER THIRTY-TWO

I couldn't believe it. But it turned out to be true. Matt Foster had voluntarily signed himself into a facility in Harris County, near where his parents lived. For the first time in weeks, we could breathe easy. We still didn't know if Matt had played a role in vandalizing our facility, and at this point I was starting to wonder if we ever would. Maybe, while in rehab, he would develop a conscience and come back to us with the full story. For now, though, we all did our best to relax and enjoy the news that he was no longer in Brenham.

Isabel looked like a weight had been lifted off her shoulders. I'd never seen her this carefree. She spent the next several days completely enmeshed in her work, doing some of the finest grooms I'd ever seen. Truly, the girl had been set free.

Cassidy was super busy in her new role as office manager, so I didn't see as much of her. But getting to know Brianna, our new receptionist? That was the icing on the cake. Literally. Turned out the girl loved to bake. Every day, a different flavor of cupcake or cookie arrived in the lunch room for our enjoyment. If she was trying to bake her way into our hearts, it was working—one Snickerdoodle at a time. If I didn't watch myself, I'd put on ten pounds, just sampling the wares.

On the Monday after our big outing to the shelter, I checked in with Maggie. Turned out, she was having the time of her life with Midnight and her latest addition, Gracie. The senior pup still had some good years left in her, if such a thing could be judged from her boundless energy around the ranch. Maggie had other news for me too, which she shared with great fanfare when I called her Monday morning.

"So, I had this idea."

"Oh?" She had my undivided attention.

"Yes, you know how I told you that I love to bake?"

"Yep. So does our new receptionist, by the way. Have you met Brianna?"

"Can't remember, but hold that thought. She might factor into this. Your grandmother too, now that I think of it."

"Oh?"

"I've been baking. Hang on a second." She disappeared, then returned to the line. "Check your phone. I just sent you a picture."

I scrolled until I found the text box with the message from her. I opened the photo of the most adorable little dog cookies, shaped like bones.

"Are these for people, or. . ." I smiled as the realization hit me.

"For the dogs. An alternative to cheeseburgers," she explained. "Made with the finest beef in Washington County."

"Oh, Maggie, this is awesome. You did great!"

"Hey, I figured if you could sell them at the clinic maybe you could use the proceeds to help fund the rescue. And who knows, we might even be able to sell them in pet stores."

"This is amazing. I don't know how to thank you."

"No need," she said. "Just come visit me sometime. I've got this big property and it gets lonely out here. Bring Beau for a visit. Come hang out in my kitchen and visit with me while I bake."

"I will, Maggie, I promise."

As we ended the call, I couldn't help but think that my conversations with Maggie had gotten sweeter by the day. Maybe it was the fact that I was missing a mother figure in my life. Maybe it was her passion for the same things that I cared about. I wasn't sure. But, I did know that God had brought Maggie into my life and I was so incredibly grateful.

I was also grateful for someone else.

Parker.

He kept me captivated with his kindness and Southern charm. That, and the fact that he'd taken a foster into his home—an ornery black and white Jack Russell mix named Bandit. Turned out, the dog had earned his name. He was quite the little thief, according to Parker. The pooch ate his sunglasses, his favorite shoes, and a cell phone case.

Other than that, things were going great at Parker's place.

The biggest surprise of all? Cameron. He took in a big dog from the hoarding case—a gentle giant named Fred. Within days, Cameron stopped by to let us know that he couldn't live without Fred and would be adopting him right away.

"My work here is done!" were the only words I could come up with.

It wasn't, of course. There were a lot of dogs in my future, more than I could begin to fathom.

Brianna seemed interested in fostering and so did the attorney that Maggie put me in touch with. In fact, several people at the law firm latched onto the idea. Things were really starting to come together.

On Monday morning, after chatting with Maggie, I helped Tyler give Bandit his shots. He was a feisty little thing. I felt kind of bad for asking Parker to take him on, but if anyone could handle the pooch, he could.

After his shots and nail trim, I offered to take Bandit to the yard, hoping to get a fecal. We paced around the grass for a good fifteen minutes, but he refused to cooperate. He did, however, feel like jumping over the chain-link fence, which was exactly what he opted to do.

I'd seen a lot of fast dogs in my day but none this quick. Before I could say, "Bandit, no!" he was halfway across Beckett's back yard and headed straight for the back door.

I ran inside the clinic and called out for Parker, who came running. He took off after the dog—much as he had done with Huntress a while back—but this pooch gave him a run for his money. Bandit had found something along the edge of the house. He started digging right away.

Parker caught up with him, but the dog dodged him and headed back toward the fence. I watched all of this from our yard, hoping and praying Beckett would not come outside. I knew he must be pretty busy in there because his parking lot was full, as always. Weird, since we were well past October 15th now.

Still, it wasn't my place to question the man's business, especially not with the dog in my care tromping through his personal space.

And tromp Bandit did. He ran in crazy circles all over the yard. I called out to Parker, who put his fingers over his lips, as if asking me to be quiet.

Rude.

He knelt down along the edge of the house and seemed to be looking at something in the dirt. A few minutes later he came back to our side of the fence, holding his phone. Parker led the way inside the clinic and gestured for me to join him in the kennel area. There, he shared his suspicions.

"Bandit has a nose like nothing I've ever seen before. He can sniff out anything and everything. Dirty socks, leftover food, anything. You name it, he'll find it. But this time. . ."

He held up his phone and showed me a picture of something I couldn't quite make out.

"What is that, Parker?"

"Pretty sure it's drug paraphernalia. Some sort of crack pipe, I think?"

"No way."

"Yep. I didn't touch it. But I got pictures. I wanted to get Bandit back over here before he took off with it."

"Why would Beckett have something like that in his yard?"

"Why does he have a full parking lot? Why are there people we've never seen before coming and going? I'm guessing that accounting firm is nothing but a shell."

"A shell?"

"Yep, for what he's really up to over there. I think we've got a bona fide drug dealer in our backyard."

I gasped. "You don't understand. He was on the board at First Prez."

"Handling the finances, if I'm remembering what you told me."

"Right. And he owns rental properties."

"That are nothing but run-down shacks that look like drug dens. Get the picture?" His gaze narrowed. "He's one of those guys who's always looking for a way to bring in money. But when the church thing petered out—and I suspect he was shilling those people—then he needed something more. I'm guessing he found it in crack cocaine."

"Crack cocaine? I...I think I need to sit down, Cameron."

"What was the name of that officer you met the night you rescued Beau?"

"Dennison."

"You still have his number?"

"I do." And I located it right away. A few minutes later we had Dennison on the phone.

"Let me understand this," the officer said. "Your rescue dog found drug paraphernalia on Beckett's property? Are we talking about that cute little dog I helped rescue?"

"Different dog."

"You're really doing this, aren't you?" He chuckled. "You said you would, and you went and did it. You're rescuing dogs."

"Yep I'm starting a nonprofit and everything. So, from now on, when you hear me tell a story, you can assume it's all true."

Parker cleared his throat. "Point is, a new foster dog—one with some serious glitches, I should add—got loose and ended up on Beckett's property. He started digging along the edge of the fence, and when I caught up with him I saw what looked like a crack pipe."

"Could just be someone using in the vicinity. There's probably drug paraphernalia on your property too. We see them everywhere."

"Could be." Parker shrugged.

"He's got a crowd in front of his office day and night," I said. "I'm starting to think he's got people living in there."

"You think he's running some sort of cartel?" Dennison asked. "Transporting?"

That sounded like a viable option to me. In fact, the more I thought about it, the more it made sense. That would explain why we didn't know the people coming and going. They weren't locals. They were runners, carrying the drugs in and out.

"We'll get some officers over there. I'm guessing he's running drugs to and from the border. That would explain all of the cars and the strangers."

"Yes, just what I was thinking."

"Do me a favor and stay put where you are. And don't let the dogs out." He laughed. "Get it? Let the dogs out?"

"Got it," Parker said. "And, we won't."

We waited until we saw the patrol car pull up to Beckett's place and then all of us gathered at the window behind the lab to watch the goings-on. I had to strain to see the front of Beckett's building from where we now stood, but I could make out a little of his parking lot.

"Man, I want to go over there," I said.

"He told us to stay put, though."

"This is more exciting than a suspense thriller," Brianna said. "I'm so glad I got this job. Do you have any idea how boring my life was before I came to work here?"

I didn't, but I knew for a fact we were anything but. In fact, the crew at Lone Star Veterinary Clinic? We were downright adventurous. Or, as Grandma Peach was prone to say, we were fixin' to change the world for the better.

CHAPTER THIRTY-THREE

We watched with bated breath as the police overtook Beckett's tax office. I was astounded to see about a dozen people file out who were then cuffed and ushered to patrol cars.

"What in the world do you think they've been doing in there?" Cassidy asked.

"Oh my goodness." I stared at Parker. "Do you suppose. . ."

"They're definitely running drugs up from the border. And in exchange he's giving them a place to stay. That's my guess."

"Maybe?" I wasn't sure. But that possibility rang true. And it sounded like something a sleazeball like Beckett would do.

I was so happy to see Dennison return a short while later. He entered the clinic and met us at the reception desk.

"Sorry that took so long, folks. This story's about as twisted as my niece's boyfriend."

"How so?" Parker asked.

"Yes, what did you find out?" Tyler asked.

"We'll be unraveling it for some time, I suspect, and we've got a detective there now, getting more details. But, from what I could tell, Beckett's got a cartel, of sorts, going on over there. He's been giving dealers a place to stay in exchange for running drugs for him. There were a shocking number of people living in that little place."

"Wow, Parker, you were right." I gave him an admiring look. "You hit the nail on the head."

"So, all of those cars in the parking lot were really just dealers?" Parker asked.

"Oh, I'm sure some were customers," Dennison explained. "He still had a steady flow of clients, based on the files on his desk. He kept a real accounting office up front. Though, I think it's been a while since Beckett has renewed his license as an official CPA. I had one of my guys check his licensing and it's not current."

"Really?" This shocked me. "You're saying he's not a real CPA?"

"Anyone can check out their CPA online to find out if they're really who they say they are. Some of them pass their exam but don't keep the license current. That's the case here. But it's not the kind of thing most people bother to check out. They just see the initials CPA behind a name and trust that the person really is who—or what—they claim to be."

"So strange."

"It was a decent enough cover," Dennison said. "He just looked like a busy accountant."

"A very busy accountant," I added. But I've heard about CPAs going rogue. Don't they usually hit on elderly people? You know, they cheat older folks out of their retirement? Stuff like that?"

"Exactly. And all under the cover of being a legitimate public accountant. I think we're going to be unraveling this guy's tale for a long, long time. But, for sure, his sins are many."

A shiver went down my spine as I thought about this man's ties to my grandmother's church for so many years. No doubt he had used the church's funds to invest in some of his schemes. The very idea made my blood boil. My grandmother gave her hard-earned money to that church. How much of her giving had been used in such a way?

"So, do we assume Beckett was the one who broke into our place that night?" I asked.

"No need to assume," Dennison said. "Remember that white striped ski mask you guys saw in the video?"

Tyler nodded. "Sure do."

"We found it and a computer like the one that went missing from your place that night you were hit. We'll double-check, but I'm pretty sure it's yours."

"Oh wow." I could hardly believe it. "So, Beckett did it."

"More likely he had someone else do his dirty work for him," Dennison explained. "The man doesn't really get his own hands soiled."

"In other words, one of his henchmen did it." Parker shook his head. "Figures."

A shiver ran down my spine. It gave me the creeps to know we had an entire group of people living directly behind us, all of them up to no good.

And their official ringleader? A former leader at my grandmother's church. That made me so angry I wanted to spit nails. I could only imagine what Grandma Peach would say when she found out all of this.

"So, the man is running drugs."

"Among other things. That office is just a shell for all the things that were bringing in the real money, the drugs. Throw in some rental houses and other shady investments and I think it's pretty clear, this is a guy who had his fingers in a lot of pies, and most of them were poisonous."

"Sounds like the words *dirty dealings* would sum him up," Parker said.

Man, Grandma was right. She had this guy pegged all along. Still, the idea that a dealer lived so close was enough to give me the willies. "No wonder Huntress was so interested in digging her way under the fence that day," I said.

Dennison looked perplexed. "Who's Huntress?"

"A Great Dane. She went crazy when I took her out there. Almost destroyed the fence trying to get underneath."

"These dogs are really helpful with cases like this," Dennison said. "They have keen noses."

"Which must be one of the key reasons why Beckett was so angry that a vet clinic went in directly behind his place of business." Parker said. "That explains his paranoia, the anger, all of it."

"That, and he's just a really hateful man," Cassidy threw in.

"Right." I sighed. "Well, thank God for Bandit." I patted our little ornery foster on the top of the head then turned to face Parker. "That's some dog you've got there, wouldn't you say? I think you should probably keep him, Parker. He might come in handy."

"Because I have so many drug stings in my future?"

"You never know. If we start going into shady places to rescue dogs, we might. I'm just saying, that's a good dog. He's got a bloodhound's nose."

"Actually. . ." Dennison walked over and patted Bandit. "I'd love to take this little guy and train him."

"Really?" Parker and I spoke in unison.

"Yeah, I've been wanting a dog. I told you that. But sometimes it's just a matter of waiting until the right one comes along."

"And you think Bandit's the right one for you?" I asked.

"I always enjoyed playing cops and robbers. I'm the cop, he's the bandit. . ." Dennison laughed. "But I really meant what I said about training him. If he's really got a nose like that, then I think we could use him at the department. I'd like to look into it, anyway."

I wanted to burst into song, to do a little dance around the room. I wanted to sing at the top of my lungs, to proclaim to the world that a dog I'd rescued might, in turn, rescue others.

But I didn't. I just smiled and thanked Dennison, then explained the adoption process.

"I'm so glad I got to know you," he said. "Even if we did have to meet in the sewer."

"Not a sewer," I explained. "It was a—"

"Drainage pipe." Everyone spoke in unison.

I laughed. "I don't know why it's been so hard for me to admit I climbed into the sewer to rescue a dog. I guess I just don't want people to think less of me."

"Hey, that's what God did for us," Parker said. "No shame in that. If He can go to the low places to drag us out, we can do the same for His creatures."

"Well, amen," I said. My heart was overcome as I thought about the truth of those words.

And to think, this was only the beginning. Second Chance Ranch was just getting started. Where God would take us, I could not say. But I had a feeling we were headed into some amazing adventures, far beyond what I could ask or think.

And—as I gazed Parker's way—I had to admit one more thing. That fella with the gorgeous blue eyes? I was mighty glad he was coming along for the ride.

CHAPTER THIRTY-FOUR

On the first Friday in November, Parker and I finally went on a real date. He took me to Triple B's. I was a nervous wreck, like a silly schoolgirl headed out to her first homecoming dance.

He picked me up in his truck, apologizing in advance for the dog hair on the seat. His latest foster—a cairn terrier mix—was a real shedder.

Like I cared. I moved his dog's leash and bowl over to make room as I climbed in, and we were on our way to the restaurant.

"So, did you hear about Cameron?" Parker asked as he eased his truck out onto the highway.

"What about him?"

"They offered him a job at the shelter. . .and he took it."

I gasped. "Oh, Parker. This is perfect."

"It's funny, isn't it? I mean, how God always works everything out. I never would have believed that guy was worth his weight in salt, but now I . . ."

"He's a good guy."

"Who happens to look like a supermodel."

"Does he? I hadn't noticed."

"Sure you hadn't." He laughed. "But I'm not too worried about him. I mean you're here with me, after all."

"Which is just where I want to be." I reached over and took his hand and gave it a squeeze.

It felt so good that I left it there.

In fact, we were still holding hands a few minutes later at Triple B's when the waitress brought menus. So, we unlinked our hands and ordered double cheeseburgers, jumbo fries—his with melted cheese and bacon, mine without—and two extra-large sodas.

Then we shared our hearts—about everything, from my journey through grief after losing my mom to his passion for inner-city ministry. After the food arrived we dove right in, enjoying bite after bite. I might've just hit the jackpot with this guy. Finally, someone I could eat in front of without worrying about how I looked. He was way too busy enjoying his burger to judge the sloppy ketchup dribbling down my chin.

When we finally slowed our pace, Parker asked a pointed question. "Hey, did you do that assignment Maggie gave you?"

"Assignment?"

"She wanted you to write a mission statement for your organization for her attorney, right? Have you done that yet?"

"Nope." I shook my head. "Haven't had time. Between the job, the dog, and all of that chaos with Beckett, there hasn't been a hot minute to do anything."

"Let's do it right now." He pulled out his phone and opened the notes app.

"I don't even know what goes into a mission statement."

"A mission statement answers the 'why' question. Why do you want to save dogs?"

I felt the sting of tears in my eyes at once. It felt silly, crying over animals I didn't even know, but I couldn't help myself. Someone had to stand in the gap for them, after all.

"Parker, someone has to care. There's a need and the need is great. I want to rescue as many as I can—those with special needs, those who would fall through the cracks otherwise."

He turned on his audio recorder and pointed his phone in my direction. "Say that again."

"I want to rescue as many as I can. Those with special needs, those who might fall between the cracks. Like the seniors. And the amputees. And those born with abnormalities." I paused to think it through. "But not just those dogs. The ones that would be hard to place in a shelter because of fear issues. Or the ones that come across as aggressive but they're really not. They're just scared out of their wits because they've been living on the street for so long. Like Beau. That poor baby was living in a pipe. He was a matted mess. I had to go to the deepest places to find him, but he was so worth it. Look at him now."

"He's perfect."

"He is."

"Okay. But what about the people?" he asked.

"I can't rescue all of them." I took a sip of my soda then leaned back in my chair. "That's your job, Parker."

He laughed. "No, that's God's job. I meant, what sort of role do you want people to play in your organization? Why do you want to connect with people?"

"Oh, that's easy. I need fosters. Lots and lots of fosters, willing to take dogs into their homes and feed them, socialize them, teach them to play nicely with others. And I'm sure I'll need additional veterinary care, especially if I take on cases from other counties. I'll need to connect with vets in those areas so that we have access to spay and neuter services all over. I need people willing to transport, not just from state to state, but sometimes from county to county, even foster to foster. And I will need financial support. You know?"

"I do."

"I'll need a board of directors." I narrowed my gaze. "And I think I know exactly who to ask."

"Oh, right. . .Tyler." Parker grinned. "He'd be perfect."

"Not exactly who I was going for, but thanks for playing."

"I'll think about it. What else?"

"I can see fun outreach opportunities at local pet stores, where dogs are available for adoption. Oh, and cute little tags with the name of our rescue on it, in case any of the fosters run off. Then people will know who to call if the dogs get out."

"And?"

"And I see cross promotion with other rescue organizations. Some are small-dog focused. Some are breed specific. But mine are going to be Hill Country dogs, in every shape and size. But these other groups will be companion groups. Does that make sense?"

"Sure. You help them, they help you.'"

"Exactly."

On and on I went, sharing my heart. Then he shared his. Then we ate some more. And talked some more.

We had the best conversation ever. I ended the date with one very important question: "Parker, what are you doing after we leave here?"

"Hadn't thought about it. Why?"

"Would you like to come over to my place and hang out for a while? Maybe watch a movie? I think Beau Jangles is long overdue for some time with you."

"Sure. Do you have Dr Pepper?"

I laughed. "Is this a trick question?"

"Blue Bell?"

"Parker, please. I'm a Texan. Of course I have Blue Bell."

"Okay, just checking. I was going to stop at the grocery store on the way over and grab some homemade vanilla."

"Um, I think you mean cookies and cream."

"No, I meant vanilla."

"Are we having our first fight?"

He laughed. "If this is how we fight then let's do it every day. Okay?"

"You've got it." I offered him a little wink. "I think I'm gonna love fighting with you."

"Same."

He paid the bill and then pulled my chair out for me. What a gentleman. I reached for my purse and then stood. As we walked toward the door, I thought I heard a familiar giggle from the booth in the back of the room. I turned back and strained to see past the crowd of people, and finally caught a glimpse of someone I knew.

Make that *someones*.

"Hold that thought, Parker." I took off toward the back booth and barely got stopped before crashing into it—just as Grandma took a big bite out of her double cheeseburger.

Which she chased down with a swig of her jumbo-sized soda.

After eating a French fry.

"Grandma Peach!"

She almost lost her grip on her soda. I wasn't as worried about that as I was about the fella sitting across from her.

Reverend Nelson. Nibbling on a fried chicken wing.

Oh. My.

"Mari!" Grandma dabbed at her lips and then threw her napkin over her plate, as if to hide the evidence. "I had no idea you would be here."

"Clearly." I clucked my tongue. "Grandma Peach! I thought you didn't touch anything with preservatives or artificial ingredients. And what was all of that about not drinking soda? Didn't you say it was going to kill us all?"

"Well, I..." She pretended to cough. "We've all got to go sometime."

"Yes, that's true."

"So, I imbibe every now and again. Sue me."

"Grandma Peach. Really? Imbibe?" I doubled over with laughter and then finally got myself under control. "It's okay to admit you're normal, that you eat an occasional cheeseburger. That you drink a soda every now and again."

"Amen," Reverend Nelson said, and then shoveled a fry in his mouth.

She pulled the napkin off her plate and reached for her burger. After swallowing down another bite, my grandmother swiped at her mouth with the back of her napkin and said, "I'm not perfect."

"Who said you had to be?" Reverend Nelson reached for her hand.

They gazed into each others' eyes a good ten seconds. So awkward. Then Grandma turned her attention to me.

"Marigold, I've been working hard to take care of myself so that I'll be around to watch you and that handsome doctor get married and have a couple of kids." She reached for her soda and took a swig. "But if I keep eating like this, I won't be around much longer. No pressure, but the two of you had better hurry up."

I crossed my arms at my chest and gave her a knowing look. "Grandma?"

"Yes, honey?" A hint of a smile tipped up the edges of her lips and I could tell she was messing with me.

"He's a vet tech."

"Oh, I know." She gave me a little wink and then swiped a fry off the reverend's plate. "Just promise me you won't feed him fried chicken, honey. 'Cause you know that story never ends well."

I shifted my gaze to Reverend Nelson, who set his gnawed chicken wing down on his plate and reached for his soda.

"What's that you say?" He pointed to his ear. "Don't have my hearing aid on."

"The man's lying like a snake," Grandma countered. "He doesn't wear a hearing aid."

Reverend Nelson gave me a little wink and then reached for another chicken wing.

I decided to leave well enough alone. I turned to grab Parker's hand with a cheerful, "Ready to go?"

"Mm-hmm. Where'd you say we're headed, again?"

Silly man. He knew the answer, of course—to sit on my pea green sofa.

JANICE THOMPSON, who lives in the Houston area, writes novels, nonfiction, magazine articles, and musical comedies for the stage. The mother of four married daughters, she is quickly adding grandchildren to the family mix.